LAW & DISORDER

A Camilla MacPhee Mystery

Mary Jane Maffini

RendezVous
Crime

Cover art by Christopher Chucky, design by Emma Dolan

We acknowledge the support of the Canada Council for the Arts for our publishing program. We acknowledge the financial support of the Government of Canada through the Book Publishing Industry Development Program (BPIDP) for our publishing activities.

RendezVous Crime
an imprint of Napoleon & Company
Toronto, Ontario, Canada
www.napoleonandcompany.com

Printed in Canada

13 12 11 10 09   5 4 3 2 1

Library and Archives Canada Cataloguing in Publication

Maffini, Mary Jane
        Law and disorder / Mary Jane Maffini.

(A Camilla MacPhee mystery)
ISBN 978-1-894917-86-5

        I. Title. II. Series: Maffini, Mary Jane. Camilla MacPhee mystery.

PS8576.A3385L39 2009   C813'.54   C2009-904775-6

In memory of Lyn Hamilton, world traveller,
inspired mystery writer and wonderful friend

ONE

How do you keep a lawyer from drowning?
-Shoot him before he hits the water.

L ess than two short weeks after I'd shoved my thermal
socks to the back of the drawer, the temperature hit 32°
Celsius with a humidex reading of 40°. Welcome to June in
Canada's capital.

I blotted my forehead with one hand as I chugged up
the wide stone stairs to the Elgin Street courthouse. The
excellent air conditioning system in the building was only
a secondary factor in my decision to spend the morning in
court. It seemed like the right day to look into a murderer's
eyes as his seemingly endless trial drew to a close. I was
looking forward to the final arguments. Lloyd Brugel was
about to get what was coming to him: a guilty verdict. In
time, that would be reflected in an appropriate sentence:
twenty-five years without parole if not actual dangerous
offender status. But one step at a time. Conviction first.

Don't take my word about Brugel. Ask any of the kids
who found themselves hooked on crack cocaine at bargain
introductory prices or the fifteen-year-olds who were forced
into prostitution. Or pick one of the hundreds of broken
people who got in his way. I knew many of his victims
personally. I wished more of them were alive to see Brugel
go down. I tried to resist rubbing my hands in glee, but only
because that would have meant spilling my iced cappuccino.

In the course of the trial and the interminable months leading up to it, I'd repeatedly reminded myself of the principles of law that keep me going:

Innocent until proven guilty? That's the biggie.

Reasonable doubt? Also high on the list.

The right to representation? No argument.

In spite of all that, I believed Brugel was guilty from the second he was frog-marched out of Red Roxxxy's, the sleazy strip joint where he based his underground kingdom. I had done a little dance when I'd first heard the news. Hey, appropriate is not my middle name. I planned on doing a joyful jig when the sentence was read. I just hoped I wouldn't throw my back out.

In the foyer near courtroom 23, I narrowly avoided Sergeant Leonard Mombourquette slithering out of the elevator.

"Hey, Leonard, watch out for your—"

"Don't start with me, MacPhee," he said, narrowing his beady eyes. "I'm one month from retirement, and I'm facing a lot of paperwork."

Fair enough. Mombourquette had been my brother-in-law Conn McCracken's partner in Major Crimes for more years than I could count. Even though Conn now wasted his days on the golf course, I saw no harm in being civil to his former partner, this once. With his soft, greyish skin, twitchy nose and missing chin, Mombourquette might be the spitting image of a rodent, but, after all, he was *our* rodent. Practically a family pet. He not only continued to hang out with that same brother-in-law and my sister, but he seemed to have a thing going with my old buddy Elaine Ekstein, the well-known rogue social worker. All to say, opposites attract and there's no accounting for tastes and any more aphorisms anyone else would care to contribute.

I just hoped the decidedly NDP Elaine and the definitely Conservative Mombourquette never chose to talk politics. Kaboom.

Before we could enter, we idled by the metal detector outside the courtroom, and I made nice while the female police officer checked the contents of my handbag and we went through the detector one at a time. "So, Leonard, you here to see Brugel go down? Payoff time?"

"You betcha. Wouldn't miss it. Seeing that scumbag convicted will be the highlight of my year. Maybe even two years. Worth not retiring last winter just to savour it."

"For me too. I wish Laurie Roulay was still alive to see it."

Mombourquette shook his head. "That was a real shame about that girl. Thorsten sure took her apart on the stand."

I paused, thinking before I spoke. Laurie Roulay's suicide two weeks after her testimony had shaken me badly. After a moment, I managed to say, "It was brutal. There's no trick too low for our Rollie. I'm glad Laurie held together long enough to testify. Her testimony will help sink Brugel. I wish I'd realized how fragile she was."

He glowered. "Me too."

"But hey, Leonard, not even that scum-sucking bottom-dweller Thorsten could get Brugel off this time."

An assistant Crown attorney swung past us in the hallway, his black gown billowing. He snickered and called back over his shoulder, "Don't hold back, MacPhee. How do you really feel about Thorsten?"

"Jackass," I muttered.

Mombourquette pulled out a handkerchief and wiped the back of his neck. "Gonna be a scorcher. Enough to make you hope the trial drags on until July. I'd like it to be cool for my remaining days."

"Hard to believe it's your last twenty."

"One hundred and sixty hours, but who's counting."

"Excellent. Let's go watch the circus."

*   *   *

You would think, with a case of this magnitude, that courtroom 23 would be standing room only, but there were fewer than twenty people in the room, not counting judge, jury, plaintiffs, court staff, cops, and a solitary reporter. Even so, the early morning scents of aftershave and fruity shampoo were gradually being replaced by sweat and overheated footwear. The few people in the room were buzzing softly. Madam Justice Pierrette Lafontaine sat purse-lipped at the bench. I wondered idly what that would do to her signature red lipstick. My sisters tell me that's a dated look, but on Judge Lafontaine, it sent a powerful message: Don't mess with me or I'll drink your blood. She feared nothing. Especially not passing trends. Maybe that's why I always admired her.

The Crown attorney fidgeted like a kid awaiting Christmas morning. Would Santa bring him closing arguments that would lead to a conviction? And eventually a life sentence? Or would some small word or concern reduce the sentence to the lower end of the scale? Twenty-five with no parole would be good for the Crown attorney's career. It would help in moving up and out.

I glanced around for my friend P. J. Lynch, who covered the courts for the *Ottawa Citizen*, but there was no sign of his carrot top and gap-toothed grin.

In between eyeing the prisoner's dock with amusement,

the Crown appeared to be flirting with his blonde colleague. I assumed she was a new assistant Crown and I figured the ink wasn't dry on her yet. The rumour among those who cared was that she was so good, she would leave him in the dust. I certainly hoped so.

There were no legal aid lawyers for Brugel. He could afford to hire and fire the very best. Rollie was Brugel's third lawyer and perhaps his most expensive.

On the right side of the line of lawyers, a thin and jittery young man glanced behind him, his forehead furrowed in concern. He was wearing a navy suit that seemed to have been intended for a larger man. From my previous court visits, I recognized Jamie Kilpatrick. He loosened his white shirt collar with his fingers. I knew he was the one junior lawyer that Rollie had on his payroll. In this case, rumour had it that the indentured serf took care of all the work, while Rollie did whatever you do when you're a scum-sucking bottom dweller. Although right at that moment, the scum-sucker was nowhere to be seen. The hapless Jamie seemed even more nervous than usual.

Maybe Rollie was in the men's room, adjusting his handmade silk tie. He was as expensive as he was effective, and he did look very good in Harry Rosen suits. I took comfort in the thought that even he was not likely to win this time.

Brugel faced the bench and the jury behind bulletproof glass. The rest of us got a view of his shaved head gleaming, his neck as thick as a fire hydrant. He was one scary dude. He'd built a business running drugs and prostitutes, with extortion as a sideline, and yet, he'd never done a minute's federal time. He gave the impression he thought he was top dog in this court, and he'd probably be in charge behind bars too.

The Crown maintained that Brugel had ordered the crime, and an underling named Guérin had delivered. Guérin's own legal team had cleaned him up, cut his hair, somehow even covered the jailhouse tattoos on his neck, but he'd still oozed criminality. Some gifted dentist had done a cosmetic job on his teeth, no doubt using the proceeds of a couple of wasted young lives. But no cosmetic procedures could fix those hard, dead eyes. They were the kind of eyes you might expect on someone who had dumped a bound and injured competitor into a car and set it on fire. That fire had spread to the victim's home, killing his seven-year old daughter and leaving Laurie Roulay, his common-law wife, with scars from the third degree burns. That's what she got for trying to save her child. Guérin was a guy with fifty priors, who'd already served more than ten years in prison, not counting the misdeeds no one had ever pinned on him. He hadn't had much to hope for except a view of bars and razor wire, so he'd managed a deal of sorts in return for testifying against Brugel. It was a case of the puppet fingering the puppermaster, and the prosecution had gone for it in a big way. When the time came, Judge Lafontaine was likely to dish out the most stringent sentence against Brugel. Even that would be a disappointment for those who favoured drawing and quartering.

Of course, the defence was expected to keep things rolling.

Judge Lafontaine had now narrowed her eyes. I knew Lafontaine had a long fuse, but when it hit the end: look out. Rollie Thorsten had definitely tried to ignite that fuse during Brugel's trial. Next, Lafontaine would flare her nostrils. I'd enjoyed it when Rollie had tested the judge's tolerance. Privately, I'd been rooting for a contempt of court charge against him, but I never got lucky.

There was a rustle by the door in the back. Mombourquette and I turned as the door opened and a court officer rushed forward up the left aisle. A murmur swept the room. I didn't know this officer, but like everyone else that morning, he was sweating.

At last, flared nostrils from the judge.

A whispered consultation.

The judge spoke to the court clerk.

The clerk said, "All rise. This court is now recessed until this afternoon at two."

The judge always gets the last word. She said, "Mr. Kilpatrick, you may join me in my chambers."

*   *   *

As we trickled from the courtroom into the third floor foyer, we were passed by P. J. Lynch, my redheaded reporter friend. P. J. was running late, swimming against the tide and elbowing his way to the front of the courtroom.

He turned and mouthed, "Hey, Tiger. What the hell happened?"

I just grinned. P. J. brings it out in me, although as a rule I trust him as far as I could throw my Acura. Never mind, I like his giant freckles and the gap between his teeth as well as the carrot top. "Don't ask me. You're the reporter. But now that I see you, I believe you still owe me twenty dollars."

Mombourquette merely sneered. Reporters have that effect on him. Come to think of it, so do lawyers. We flowed toward the elevator, although I was tempted to watch and see if P. J. would get out of line and try to ask the judge a question. A contempt of court charge might be interesting, but, after all, most of the time P. J. is my friend, so I called after him. "Remember the rules."

"Well, that was a letdown," I said to Mombourquette. "I was hoping to see Brugel get hammered by the Crown."

"Me too. But there's always this afternoon. By the way, Elaine tells me you're selling the house on Third Avenue," Mombourquette said, casually, as we ambled along, in no hurry to get back outside to the hot mist. That's the problem with having your friend date a cop, there's even less privacy than usual.

"I'm thinking about it. I never felt right living there. I don't feel entitled to the money either."

"You take life too seriously. Think about it. You work for ten years, you get injured, you get beat up, you get half-drowned, you get evicted, then someone leaves you a house and some money. You can't just accept that and chill out?"

"Guess not."

"No wonder your sisters always get their backs up."

"My sisters' backs are not my problem. I'm considering a plan to make things right with that house."

"Going to get Justice for Victims going again? Did I forget to mention your office got blown up?"

I shrugged. "I don't think I'm going back to that. There's a lot more assistance for victims now than there used to be. There's victims' support in the Crown's Office, in the police department, and some high profile groups offer it too. It was just me and Alvin at JFV anyway. I think we'll both be glad to move on."

As Alvin Ferguson has always been the world's worst assistant, the modern office equivalent to wearing a millstone around your neck while being taunted by an albatross, I felt the need to add emphatically, "In separate directions, it goes without saying."

Perhaps the emphasis came from the fact that Alvin had been camped in my house since his most recent housing problems. This was hard for many people to understand, but suffice to say that I am a MacPhee from Sydney, Nova Scotia, and Alvin is a Ferguson from Sydney, Nova Scotia, and, as long as my father is alive, I will have to honour the Cape Breton tradition of helping one's compatriots.

Mombourquette had moved on conversationally. "You're what, forty? You could go back into practice. Maybe even legal aid."

I thought he was going to choke from laughing. When he pulled himself together, he said, "Hey, why not join one of the big criminal defence firms? You could end up representing guys like Brugel."

"True enough. Or I could just stick pins in my eyes. In the unlikely event that I go back to legal aid work, I'll let you know, Leonard. In the meantime, try not to worry your fuzzy little ears about me."

"Speaking of Alvin, that place of yours might have been easier to sell before your crazy assistant redecorated."

I shrugged. What could I say? Alvin has an artistic talent that has to be experienced to be believed and a spirit that can't be crushed. I'd been in Italy. He'd been watching the fort. The house was just in the wrong place at the wrong time. And after all, it wasn't like I even liked or wanted it. On the other hand, I couldn't let Mombourquette take a free shot at Alvin.

"I kind of like the Italian theme," I lied.

Mombourquette rolled his eyes and kept pressing my buttons. "Pull the other one," he said before changing the subject yet again. "What about Ray Deveau in Sydney? Anything happening?"

"Does the entire population of Ottawa have to be

informed about every detail in my life?" I snapped.

I had reason to snap. My sisters were bullying me to remarry. Edwina, Donalda and Alexa kept harping that ten years was long enough to be widowed. Everyone in my family found Sgt. Ray Deveau of the Cape Breton Regional Police irresistible. I found him irresistible too, maybe even more than irresistible. Calm, gentle, supportive, cute, widowed as well. He'd been a good husband, and he was still a fine father. Maybe they were right. I kept mentioning that there are 1,641 kilometres of Trans-Canada Highway between Ray and me. I guess I was the only one who thought that was any kind of an impediment.

"You'll be the first to know if anything changes in my relationship status, Leonard. But you know what, that would make us cousins of a sort."

He flinched.

I grinned. Wolfishly, I hoped.

Mombourquette averted his eyes. "Something's happening."

Kristen Wentzell, a cop I knew by name and reputation, was approaching us. With her blonde hair and piercing blue eyes, she could have had any of the more commanding female roles in a Wagner opera. She ignored me. "Did you hear the news, Lennie?"

"Hear what?" Mombourquette said. His whiskers twitched. He did not tilt his neck to look up at Wentzell, who was easily six foot two. She took up a lot of space. The Kevlar vest didn't flatter her, but it did add to her imposing demeanour. For a split second I wanted one for myself.

"You call yourself a detective? We just got the word about Thorsten. Do you know where he showed up?" Wentzell was enjoying herself. Cats and canaries came to mind.

I said, "The bottom of your kid's aquarium?"

"Close," she said, giving me a booming laugh in return.

If there's one thing Mombourquette hates, it's other people's banter. "Spit it out, Wentzell."

Wentzell's grin slipped. She glanced at Mombourquette, possibly thinking about snapping him in two.

I nodded encouragement. "Can't wait to hear it."

I thought I heard Mombourquette mutter, "Broad really pisses me off."

I said, "In our lifetime, Constable Wentzell. Detective Mombourquette has places to go, people to see, possibly even things to do."

She deflated slightly. I am such a killjoy. "Word is they found him swimming in the Rideau."

"Rollie Thorsten? The consummate defence hack? What was he doing in the river instead of in court?" I bleated, falling into the trap.

Wentzell shook her head. Her blue eyes were shining.

Mombourquette said, "What of it?"

"On the bottom," Wentzell said, obviously disappointed that she couldn't drag the story out any further.

I said, "On the bottom?"

"You got it."

"You mean drowned?"

She grinned happily. "Just preliminary information, of course."

Mombourquette said, "Dead's good enough."

I gave him a dirty look and turned back to Wentzell. "Are you sure?"

"Looks like it." By this time, her grin was practically tickling her ears.

Mombourquette brightened. "Best news I've heard in months."

Wentzell's voice had carried, and a murmur was sweeping the area. Shocked as they were by the idea of Thorsten's death, people around us chuckled nervously. The news was spreading like a brush fire through the crowded hallways.

"Too bad I'm on duty or I'd go celebrate," Wentzell said.

"What is the matter with you?" I said. "You just told me the man's dead."

"Where's your sense of occasion?" Wentzell said.

Speaking of sense of occasion, at that moment P. J. Lynch, who obviously smelled story, elbowed his way toward us, red hair tousled, determination across his face. People stepped out of his way. At this stage of his career, P. J. needs a big story, something that will catapult him out of the day to day stuff. If Rollie Thorsten had really been found dead at the bottom of the Rideau River, that could be quite a boost for him.

I guess P. J. had never seen Wentzell before, because he stopped and stared. In a cartoon, he would have fallen flat on his freckled face, and giant red cartoon hearts would have circled his head. In real life, he just stood there, apparently stunned. P. J.'s probably five eleven, but Wentzell managed to look down on him.

"You should close that mouth of yours before you start to drool," Mombourquette said helpfully.

Wentzell smirked, folded her arms, and looked away.

It takes more than that to keep P. J. down. In fact, he can't be kept down. I wouldn't waste my time trying. He deftly moved in front of Wentzell and stuck out his hand. "P. J. Lynch. I'm from the *Citizen*."

"You'll have to wait for the press briefing," she said.

"Hey, not everything's about work," P. J. said. "I just thought that I heard you saying something about—"

"No comment."

Wentzell swaggered off down the hallway, substantial blue backside swaying. P. J. waited only a second before he followed as if in a trance.

"He's absolutely smitten," I said to Mombourquette. "I guess there's something to be said for combining business and pleasure."

"Truly pathetic," Mombourquette said.

"For sure, she'll chew him up and spit him out. She is one tough cookie."

Mombourquette's nose twitched. "That might be fun to watch."

As Wentzell elbowed her way through a group, one bystander turned away, avoiding her neatly. There was something familiar about him. I spotted a pair of hazel eyes and a stray lock of soft sandy hair falling over them. Sure enough, there it was: a crooked little-boy smile as the hazel eyes met mine. My all-time favourite client and the most talented burglar Ottawa had ever seen, Bunny Mayhew, the only man in the world who could ever look fetching in a flame-orange jumpsuit with the words Regional Detention Centre written on it.

Damn. Why was he at the courthouse? It would be a shame if Bunny were pulled back into the criminal life he'd worked so hard to escape in the past few years.

I leaned closer to Mombourquette, something I usually avoid. "Did you just see Bunny Mayhew? What would he be doing here?"

"Time, I hope," Mombourquette said. He's a lot less sentimental than I am. They may deal with the heavy hitters, but there's no warm and fuzzy spot for burglars among the guys in Major Crimes.

"Maybe he's a witness in something," I said. "That might explain it. He told me he was going straight."

Mombourquette snorted, "And you believed him? You've really lost your edge, MacPhee."

I had believed Bunny. And maybe that was dimwitted of me. Of course, I wanted it to be true, for his sake as well as for his wife and young daughter. Sure he may have been a thief with a weakness for Canadian art, but to do him credit, Bunny never allegedly stole a single item from a person I could imagine liking. In my opinion, Bunny Mayhew represented the best the Canadian criminal classes had to offer.

Plus, I owed him a lot. Even so, I didn't want to find myself back in court defending him or even angling to get him a decent legal aid lawyer.

Seconds later, Bunny appeared at my side. He grabbed my arm. Mombourquette gave him the rattiest look in his repertoire. "Bugger off."

Bunny recoiled. "But I need to talk to Camilla."

"Here's the thing, I'm talking to her, and you're buggering off."

Bunny turned to me. "Is that police brutality?"

"Probably. Give me a call at the office, Bunny. You have my number."

Bunny stepped back. "Really? I didn't think you had an office any more. Did you rent a new space?"

"Never mind, call me at my cell number. It hasn't changed. It doesn't matter if it's an office or not."

"I already called your cellphone. This is urgent."

I stared back at the boyish face, the sandy hair, the pleading eyes. "Fine," I said, "what is it, Bunny?"

Mombourquette looked as though he might go up in flames, leaving the rest of us to inhale the stench of burnt fur. Deep down I knew part of the reason was that Elaine, Mombourquette's main squeeze, had once been Bunny's social worker. She'd known him since he first hit Juvie. She liked Bunny even more than I did. Maybe more than she liked Mombourquette.

All to say, Mombourquette was immune to Bunny. "That's it, Mayhew. I don't like lowlifes interfering in my conversations."

I said, "Get a grip, Leonard. What's the matter with you? Wait for me outside, Bunny."

To tell the truth, it was astonishing to see Bunny melt into the throng of people. One minute there, then as if he'd never been. It's a talent really. I imagined it must have come in handy in his former line of work. I didn't think much more about it. Mombourquette and I went back to cheerfully speculating about exactly what might have sent Rollie Thorsten to the bottom of the Rideau.

TWO

Why should you swerve to avoid hitting a lawyer on a bicycle?
-Because that bicycle just might be yours.

After the excitement of the courthouse, I clomped off down Elgin Street, pondering life as I went. For one thing, why were Bunny Mayhew, P. J. Lynch and Leonard Mombourquette so present in my life when the one guy I really cared about wasn't? Ray Deveau didn't have Bunny's movie star looks, or P. J.'s quick wit and drive, or even Mombourquette's furry familiarity. He was an unflappable cop with a solid sense of humour, a good father, a companion, a shoulder to cry on and a friend. Best of all, unlike the rest of the world, he liked me just fine the way I was. And I liked him a lot more than anyone I could think of. Of course, he was inconveniently located in Sydney, bound by family and a twenty-year career with the Cape Breton Regional Police. That was the bothersome part. If I'd seen a garbage can, I would have kicked it in frustration just thinking about that.

But quite apart from the state of my personal life, the day had been just plain bad. The distressing part of having Rollie Thorsten die in his dramatic way was that it would derail the Brugel trial yet again. It was good news for bad guys. So good, in fact, that I stopped to wonder if Lloyd Brugel might not have had something to do with it. Stranger things have happened after all. Laurie Roulay's death was a result of Brugel's actions even if it had been by her own hand. As I said, there's never a garbage can when you really need to kick one. If my sisters had been in town, they would have told me to stop feeling sorry for myself and get a job. Luckily they were far far away on a three-week cruise.

There was no sign of Bunny anywhere. But with all this stuff on my mind, I didn't give him another thought.

* * *

At two in the afternoon, I was back in Court, curious to see what the judge would make of all this. The jury was in place, the prisoner in his bulletproof box. Brugel turned to face the jury and even in profile, his usual alpha dog sneer was evident. I could only see the back of the Crown's head, but his shoulders were slumped.

As everyone rose and I caught a glimpse of Madame Justice Lafontaine's face, I knew I wouldn't like the news. Or she might have just bitten into a bad clam.

The judge said, "As a result of the death of Mr. Brugel's counsel, Mr. Thorsten, and the withdrawal from the case of Mr. Thorsten's junior, Mr. Kilpatrick, the Court has no choice but to recess to allow Mr. Brugel time to find new legal representation in this case."

Brugel smirked.

The judge fixed him with a warning look. She is known for having little time for alpha dogs and their packs. She does, however, adhere to the rules.

The judge swept from the room, robe flowing. As the door closed behind her, we began to trudge out of courtroom 23. Mombourquette hadn't been there to witness this part. It would have ruined his day.

After all those months of doing the work while Rollie

took the credit, young Jamie Kilpatrick had a chance to be in charge. This could have been the case that made his name, no matter what the outcome. So why the hell had he withdrawn?

*   *   *

"What difference does it make?" Alvin Ferguson, my ever-present former office assistant said after I'd stomped around the house for ten minutes, swearing. I'd topped off the stomping with a major rant. Alvin watched from the kitchen door, resplendent in the Cape Breton tartan apron that someone had given me years ago. He must have found that at the bottom of my kitchen drawer. As there is almost nothing in the house left unpainted, he has turned his hand to collecting and testing heritage recipes. Luckily he wasn't testing any of them in this weather.

I said, "It makes a big difference."

"This Brugel is still on trial anyway. They've got him, right?"

"They have him now. But if he keeps on finding ways to stall, the world can change, and they may not have him forever."

"What's that supposed to mean?"

"He's fired lawyers before." I leaned against the crumbling faux stone wall that Alvin had thoughtfully painted as part of his Tuscan decorating theme. The walls were somewhat at odds with the sleek stainless appliances in the modern kitchen, but congruity has never been Alvin's strength.

"He has?"

"Sure. Why do you think this case has been dragging on for so long?"

"I really don't know. Can you fire your lawyer?"

"Happens all the time."

"But why does that hold up the case?"

"Because you are entitled to representation."

"Yeah but…"

"And you are also entitled to be represented by someone you believe has your best interests at heart."

"You think that's a good thing?" Alvin magically produced a glass of ice tea. "There's mint in this. Give it a try."

"Some accused misuse this right. They fire perfectly competent counsel, just to stall."

"But what does it get them?"

"It gets them a delay. In Brugel's case, it has gotten him two delays before this latest setback."

"Why would anybody want a delay? Don't they want to get the whole thing over with?"

"Not if they know they're guilty and they're pretty sure they're going to be convicted and be stuck behind bars for a damn long time. There are two solid reasons for delaying, Alvin. The first one is that if the person has been in custody during the trial, they might get two for one credit for that time served."

"What does that mean anyway?"

"Two days taken off his sentence for every one served."

"Really? Do you think that's—"

"It's the way it is in our system, Alvin. Although the current government is trying to change that. And the other point is, and this is much more important, the longer the trial drags on, the harder it will be for the Crown to control or even locate key witnesses."

"What do you mean, control? You mean the Crown tries to control witnesses? That's just plain wrong."

"I mean they encourage them to stick to their stories.

And remember them. They get them to show up. They get them to stay clean and sober if they can."

"Oh, that's all right. I guess."

"And they don't want them recanting their testimony either. It goes without saying."

"They do that?"

"Sure. Often, in criminal cases, some of the witnesses are going to be criminals too. Or they're going to be connected with the accused in some way—relatives, neighbours. But the most important thing is to keep them from leaving town or worse, disappearing."

Alvin's eyes bugged out. "Disappearing?"

"Sure. Some of them will just drift away. A couple will get arrested here or somewhere else. Some might be discredited. Others will die from disease or even lifestyle. And a few will take off in the hope that they won't have to testify."

"Why?"

"Lots of reasons, Alvin. But the main one is that they're scared. A guy like Brugel needs time to make the kind of threats that can drive a witness away. The longer he waits, the more time his associates have to intimidate key witnesses. Or worse."

"You don't think they'd actually kill anyone, would they?"

I rolled my eyes. "Alvin! We're discussing Lloyd Brugel. He's on trial for murder. This is the first time they've actually had a chance at getting a conviction. And as far as killing someone, remember Laurie Roulay—she died because of the incredible stress she faced from this. She had threats from people. She knew they were watching her. It was bad enough that she'd lost her husband and one of her children, but she knew they could still get into her apartment. She knew they watched the schools where her remaining children went. She got notes too. That's the kind of thing the notes hinted at."

"That must have been a nightmare."

I nodded. "No one should have to go through anything like that. Even behind bars, Brugel is very dangerous."

"But didn't this Rollie Thorsten have a chance of getting him off?"

"Rollie's strategies were working well. Even so, I have to ask myself if Rollie wasn't worth more dead than alive, in terms of delaying Brugel's trial that little bit more."

*   *   *

The blanket of humidity actually seemed to lift when the thunderstorm broke at around ten that evening. Lightning lit up the sky, rain slashed down in sheets, thunder boomed. I counted, one two three seconds. Not so very far away. It finally occurred to me that some of the booms were coming from the front door.

Gussie, the purely temporary dog in my household, lay snoring on the sofa. He managed to continue sleeping through thunderstorm and banging.

When I whipped open the door, preparing to snarl, Bunny Mayhew stood there, shivering. Tonight the golden burglar boy had lost his lustre. His sandy hair was dark and stringy.

He glanced over his shoulder, then turned those puppy dog eyes on me. "Aren't you going to let me in, Camilla? It's horrible out here."

I stood back. "I thought you were going to wait for me outside the courthouse. How did you find out where I live?"

A look of hurt flickered across his movie star features.

Even rivulets of rain and hair hanging in damp strands can't take anything away from our Bunny. "I'm a burglar, not an idiot."

"In that case, there's no keeping you out, I suppose." I gestured for him to follow me.

"It's a terrible thing," he said, as he stood and shook in the hallway. "I don't know what to do. Or what to think. It's like a nightmare."

I rubbed my temple. "I'm beginning to get the nightmare part."

"What do you mean?"

"Forget that. Just tell me what exactly the terrible thing is, and we can all get on with our lives."

"That's why I'm here."

"You're dripping wet and you're shivering. Let me get you a cup of tea." I always end up feeling sorry for Bunny, even though it took me a while to let him come in out of the pouring rain. "While I'm getting it, just tell me what the problem is. Succinctly."

Alvin took that moment to stick his beaky nose around the corner. "What's going on? Oh, hello, Bunny. Do you need a towel?"

"Hey, Alvin." Bunny's smile, the one that Elaine refers to as "the beatific burglar", spread across his face.

Damn. I hoped they wouldn't get into a long chinwag. Between Bunny and Alvin, the world could grind to a halt.

Alvin was already halfway up the stairs.. There was no point in hanging around waiting for him to come down. He could get distracted in an infinite number of ways. I headed toward the kitchen. Bunny followed, dripping water in small well-formed puddles.

"What is the terrible situation you need to talk about,

Bunny?" I said as I reached for the kettle.

From the covered bird cage in the corner, Lester, or possibly Pierre, gave a disgruntled chirp.

"You know, the thing with Rollie Thorsten."

Alvin called down the stairs, "Do you mind if I bring one of *your* towels, Camilla? They're nice and they're clean."

As if it mattered what I said. I plugged in the kettle and kept cool. "Whatever."

Bunny said, "He always seems very nice."

I stopped and turned around. "Have a seat, Bunny. And don't let yourself be fooled by Alvin. Stay on topic. What about the thing with Rollie Thorsten?"

Bunny settled damply at the smart little bistro set by the side wall of the kitchen, in front of an exuberant faux grapevine which curled around a couple of Corinthian columns. He was looking perplexed.

"He's a bit young for you, though. And I'm not sure about the ponytail and the earrings. I would have thought you'd be more likely to go out with some kind of NDP speech writer or—"

"Earth to Bunny, Alvin is my office assistant."

"But this is your home and it's ten at night and he's here."

"He has accommodation issues. So Rollie Thorsten? What about him? Are you looking for details about his death? Because I don't have any."

Bunny's voice went up an octave. "Of course, his death. What else would I… What's that on your ceiling?"

"Grapes," I said. "Doesn't everyone have a grapevine painted on their ceiling? Don't get sidetracked. What exactly about Rollie's death brings you out to my house on a rainy evening, Bunny? Forget the murals."

While I waited for Bunny to figure out my meaning, I

got the tea from the cupboard. I decided on an extra bag for pain and anguish.

Bunny said, "It's like the others. Don't you think?"

"You lost me there. What is like what others?"

"I meant Rollie's death. It's weird."

"People drown, Bunny. I heard he'd been drinking, and he wasn't wearing a flotation device, and a high percentage of people who do drown fit into those categories too." I didn't bother to articulate my notion that Brugel might have orchestrated Rollie's demise. Bunny was agitated enough as it was.

"These crumbling stone walls," Bunny said, reaching out to run a hand along my kitchen wall. "Are they...?"

"Real?" I finished. "No. Alvin painted them while I was in Italy. Back to topic." The kettle shrieked and I warmed the tea pot with the boiling water, drained it, and made the tea.

"It was a surprise for her," Alvin said, appearing at the door with my favourite oversize bath towel. He handed it to Bunny and said, "I turned it into a villa."

"Wow."

Alvin lowered his eyes modestly and blushed. "Those wine bottles in the wine cellar there aren't real either. Every inch of this main level has an Italian theme. Do you like the murals?"

Bunny turned his beautiful eyes on me. "Were you surprised?"

"What do you think?"

Silence. Finally Bunny said, "I think you probably were."

"Right. The coliseum on the dining room wall really threw me. So now that pressing decorating discussion is out of the way, Bunny, what exactly is your point about Rollie Thorsten?"

Bunny opened his mouth.

I added, "In twenty-five words or less."

"Boy, that's harsh, Camilla. The guy's dead."

"Oh, cry me a river. He was playing hardball trying to get Lloyd Brugel unleashed on society. It was a heinous crime, yet he took witnesses apart on the stands. One of them killed herself. He can't be dead enough for me."

Bunny said, "I'm never exactly sure what heinous means."

Naturally, Alvin joined in the conversation. "You may have noticed that Camilla is not the most sentimental person in the universe. Or the most grateful I might add," he sniffed. "I have turned my hand to cooking. I think that is a form of artistry in itself. Not that she appreciates any of it."

Bunny turned to stare at him. It could have been the nine visible earrings, or the ponytail or even the beaky nose, but most likely it was the strange turn the conversation had taken. Whatever, it got Bunny off track.

I said, "Butt out, Alvin. This is business."

Alvin said, beaky nose high. "Go ahead, Bunny."

I said, "And make an effort not to drive me crazy."

Bunny stood wrapped in my best bath sheet, shivering.

I tried for control again. "Bunny, go to the living room. Sit on the sofa. Move the dog out of the way. The cat too. Now. Alvin, since you're the office assistant, you can pour the tea when it's ready. Bunny takes his with three creams and three sugars."

Alvin, hovered between the door and the living room. "Cream in tea? But that's not—"

I shot him a warning glance. "Just this once: no arguments. Milk first in mine."

Bunny said as he blotted himself off. "I got these notes."

Alvin stopped and turned.

"Notes?" we said together.

Bunny flicked his glance from me to Alvin and back. "Yes. What?"

"What kind of notes?" I wasn't sure why "notes" would have an ominous ring, but I felt a little throbbing in my temple. Why hadn't I gone into dentistry instead of law?

"They were like jokes."

"Jokes," Alvin said.

"Yes." Bunny's teeth chattered.

I said, "What kind of jokes? You mean cartoons?"

"No, I mean jokes. Lawyer jokes."

I said, "I hate goddam lawyer jokes. What about client jokes? Or accused jokes?"

Alvin said, "We got them too."

I said, "We did?"

"I showed them to you, but maybe I didn't mention that they came in the mail. I don't always bore you with every detail."

"Apparently not. So, now, Bunny, can you tell me what's so important about these jokes?"

"Well, they died."

"Who died?"

"People," Bunny snuffled. "And now Rollie."

"And the jokes are connected how?"

"I don't know. But they are."

Like many dealings with Bunny, this situation seemed baffling. I sighed and said gently, "Who do you think is sending these so-called jokes? Why would you have anything to do with lawyer jokes?"

"I have no idea, Camilla. I mean, it's not like I'm that easy to find. No one knows where I live."

I could feel the faint stirrings of a familiar headache. "Have you been hiding?"

"Well, sure. That's my point. I got plenty of reason to hide. I want to keep my family away from, um, former colleagues and all that. I told you I was going straight, now that Tonya and I have Destiny to think about. It's not that easy, but mostly I'm a stay-at-home dad. But I got a part-time job in a framing shop and everything. I'm doing my best to keep out of trouble."

"That's wonderful news, Bunny. I knew you had what it takes to go straight."

"It takes a family, I guess. Problem is I moved to Barr-haven, and now I'm getting the jokes in my new place."

"Change of address cards?" Alvin chimed in.

"No way. I try never to have an address."

Alvin said, "You don't have an address? Why not?"

"Bad idea for a couple of reasons."

The cops would be one of those reasons. Bad companions probably another.

Bunny said, "I use a mail drop. I don't get that much mail anyway. Tonya picks it up. I'm not taking a chance."

"So the jokes are forwarded to your mail drop. But you know, Bunny, that really doesn't seem too—"

Bunny twisted in agitation. "No! That's not it. They're in my mailbox."

Alvin said, "Maybe everyone's getting them. Because—"

Another interruption from Bunny. "I asked all my neighbours, and no one else was getting unsigned jokes in the mail."

I tried to be the voice of sanity. "So, let's see if I understand. You get these jokes and then someone dies?"

"Yeah. It sounds really dumb."

"People die every day. I read the obits, but I don't feel responsible for them," I said sensibly.

"But it's like I'm the messenger."

I said, "You mean the Bunny of Death?"

Bunny's chiseled jaw dropped. "What?"

"She's just kidding," Alvin said. "She enjoys incongruity."

"Yeah, you know," I said, "Angel of Death. Bunny of Death."

Bunny jumped to his feet and started to pace. "That's horrible, Camilla. Gives me shivers. And it's not funny. The Bunny of Death? I have a hard enough time sleeping nights as it is."

"I'm sorry. I didn't mean to upset you. I thought it was funny. I was making the point that you aren't causing people to die. Hold that thought, Bunny. Alvin, get in there and pour the tea."

If Bunny noticed the "hold-the-thought" instruction, he didn't follow it. "But I'm connected somehow. When one of these lawyer jokes comes, I'm going to hear about someone dying the next day."

Alvin said, "Lord thundering Jesus."

Bunny said, "It's making me crazy."

Crazy for sure and also unbelievable. "Exactly how many jokes have you received, Bunny?"

"Three. Rollie was the third."

Alvin ruined the moment. "Three?"

Bunny nodded.

I said, "And…?"

"And then the day after each one, someone died."

"Well, like who, Bunny?"

"Like Roxanne Terrio."

"Roxanne Terrio? I remember that. Didn't she die in a bicycle accident in Gatineau Park last month? That's what

I read in the paper. Anyway, Roxanne Terrio wasn't sleazy. Wasn't she a real estate lawyer? She didn't have the kind of clientele that Rollie had."

Bunny said, "Maybe she wasn't sleazy. But I got a joke the day before she died."

I decided to take control. "Coincidence."

"Then there was that judge, like federal court or something. Judge Cardarelle. I didn't know him."

"But he was a judge, not a lawyer. Change in pattern, Bunny. I think you're—"

Bunny shot back, "Didn't he have to be a lawyer first?"

"Point to Bunny," Alvin said.

"Not so fast. I don't even remember how he died. Oh hang on, yes, it was some kind of allergy. Anaphylactic shock. Just a tragic set of circumstances."

Bunny said, "Maybe. But I got a note."

"What precisely do you mean you got a note?" I asked.

"Well, the day after a joke comes, I get a note. Every time. With the dead person's name on it. How else would I know that their deaths were connected to the jokes?"

Alvin gazed at Bunny in amazement. I can't even imagine what kind of stunned expression I had on my face.

Alvin stopped staring at Bunny and started gawking at me. "I told you there was something weird about those freaking jokes that came in the mail, Camilla."

I would have sat down at that point, but Alvin had the chair and Bunny, the dog and the cat filled the sofa. "I thought those jokes were aimed at me," I said.

Bunny said, "Why would they be aimed at you?"

"Because I'm a lawyer. And they're lawyer jokes. And lots of people hate lawyers. We're easy to hate—until you need us."

"But you're not dead."

"I realize that. But maybe I'm the Camilla of Death."

Bunny frowned. "Sometimes you're just creepy, Camilla."

"Tell me about it," Alvin said, shaking his head. "But that's weird if we got the same jokes on the same day."

That reminded me. "Was this why you were trying to talk to me today in the courthouse, Bunny?"

"I wanted to tell you about all this, about the notes with the names on them. I was upset because I got another joke yesterday, and I thought someone else would die. They did."

Alvin said, "What did it say?"

Bunny glanced over, looking hopeful. "It was that old one about how do you stop a lawyer from drowning."

Alvin chuckled, "You shoot him, right?"

"It wasn't remotely funny the first thousand times I heard it, Alvin, and nothing's changed. Get out of the chair and pour the tea before it gets cold."

Alvin said to Bunny, "We got that one too."

Bunny said, "And today, I got a piece of paper with the name Rollie Thorsten on it."

I reached for the phone. "Who are you calling, Camilla?" Alvin and Bunny said in stereo.

"Confidential source. Just take care of the tea, Alvin. Bunny's shivering."

Mombourquette picked up at home on the fourth ring. "Sorry, I'm not Elaine," I said.

"That's good, because then there would be two of you," he said. "And I'd have to choose the other one. By any chance, do you own a watch?"

"I know it's late, but I need to find out what killed Rollie Thorsten."

"Why? You got an office pool going? With what's-his-name, the world's most dangerous assistant?"

"Yeah, that's it. Can you help me out here? I'm really hoping Thorsten wasn't shot first so he wouldn't have drowned."

"What? Are you...?"

"Just check that out, will you, Leonard and get back to me."

After I hung up, I turned to Bunny. He was sunk in a melancholy slump. Gussie the temporary dog had his head in Bunny's lap. Alvin had at long last produced the tea in his grandmother's tea set and added a plate of homemade shortbread to the tray. Bunny picked up his flowered cup and saucer with one hand and absentmindedly stroked Gussie with the other.

Alvin said, "Those shortbread cookies are the traditional recipe, except that I've added—"

I said, "Watch out, Bunny, Gussie's trying to get into your pocket. He likes to chew paper. I hope you don't have any valuable documents in there. Car registration, anything like that. I speak from sad experience."

"He chewed your car registration?"

Alvin interrupted. "It was an accident. You really should learn to let things go, Camilla."

Have I mentioned that Gussie started out as the Ferguson family's dog? But no point in harping. "So, Bunny, you didn't keep any of these so-called jokes?"

"Well, why would I? Did you keep yours?" Bunny's voice rose into a squeak. Alvin blurted, "It's not my fault. Gussie eats every piece of paper around here the minute it hits the floor."

Gussie gave a soft belch to reinforce Alvin's point. I didn't bother to inquire about why pieces of paper would be on the floor. "Be quiet, Alvin. Okay, Bunny, at what point did you start to realize there was something going on?"

Bunny shrugged. "After the second one, I guess. I thought it was kind of funny that each of those names arrived the day after a joke, but before that person's death became public. I mean when these people died, it made the papers."

I nodded. Bunny was right. People talked about it. People wrote about it. Cyclists had written furious letters to the editor after Roxanne Terrio's death. People had waxed eloquent about the dangers of nut allergies after Judge Cardarelle's demise. Everyone would be buzzing over Rollie's bizarre end.

"So, you don't still have any of the jokes?"

"Nah. Tonya is crazy clean. She hates any kind of paper around. She threw them out probably even faster than your dog could eat them. But when I got Rollie Thorsten's name today and I knew from the news that he was defending in Brugel's trial, I had to get over there to warn him if he was still alive. I heard there was a suspicious death today, but they didn't give the name on the news. I knew it would be Rollie Thorsten, because that's the name I got. I was too late."

"We didn't get that name," Alvin said. "I know because I open the mail and I would have—"

"Hold that thought, Alvin. So, Bunny, why did you come to me?"

"I thought maybe I could talk to you and explain about the jokes and the names and figure out what to do. I called your cell, and someone said you were in court today."

"That was me," Alvin said. "She forgot her phone at home."

"Then that Sgt. Mombourquette gave me the brush off. Do you think he's good enough for Elaine? She's really special and she deserves—"

32

"Bunny!"

"Sorry, so I came here tonight hoping you wouldn't think I was nuts."

"Not exactly nuts," I said.

"Maybe peculiar," Alvin said.

Bunny pouted. "You made fun of me. The Bunny of Death? Like I'm going to forget that anytime soon?"

"I think I said I was sorry."

"You didn't."

"Well, I am saying it now." Bunny has always been a sensitive flower. He said nothing, just kept stroking Gussie. Alvin seemed to have joined the conspiracy of silence.

"Fine," I said. "Alvin? Anything to add?"

"How was I to know that those names were connected to the jokes?"

My voice rose. "You mean to tell me we did get them?"

Bunny said, "What can we do about it?"

"In the end, I think you'll find that a lot of people probably got those jokes, and they're not really connected to us."

Bunny pulled his towel closer. "I sure hope you're right."

THREE

What do you call an honest lawyer?
-A statistical improbability

Saturday morning, I was annoyed bright and early by more knocking at the door. I whipped it open expecting to see Bunny there with yet another nutty bit of information.

A small, crisp woman with expensive blonde highlights gripped my hand and shook it. I was so startled that I hardly noticed that she'd actually stepped right into the house. Maybe I was taken aback because her teeth seemed to twinkle, and her skin glowed like she was some kind of magic lantern.

"Jacki Jewell," she said with a wide smile that left stars in my eyes. "You must be Camilla. It's wonderful to finally meet you."

I said, "I'm not sure I…" Oh, hang on. I knew the name Jacki Jewell. That toothy grin was plastered all over For Sale signs in The Glebe, Sandy Hill and New Edinburgh. But what the hell was she doing in my front hall?

Closing the door behind her, I discovered. "Your sister sent me," she said.

Of course. I should have known.

I said. "Which one?" Each of them is capable of meddling in my life in ways I never imagine until the meddling is in full swing and then it's often hard to find a defensive position.

"Edwina," she said cheerfully.

"Oh, well. She's out of town. They're all on a three-week

Mediterranean cruise along with my father. Not back until the first of July."

I didn't bother to add that I'd been reveling in a spell of peace and quiet without their daily badgering about my failure to measure up on so many fronts: quality of housekeeping, career path, marital status and driving skills being the main ones. Of course, I'd been dashing back and forth to Nepean to check on their houses every few days, but that was a small price to pay for peace and quiet.

Her expression stayed positive, but I sensed a bit of strain at the corners of her lipsticky smile.

"Yes, I know," she said. "But…"

"So whatever it is, I want you to know it wasn't my idea." I smiled grimly, expecting she'd take the hint.

"That's fine," she said, sticking to her guns. "Doesn't matter at all. There's no finders' fee for my services. I hear you're interested in selling this house."

"Well, I guess I've been thinking about it. A bit. I haven't really decided yet because…" I trailed off.

Of course, I'd been thinking about selling the house. That was putting it mildly. I'd inherited the property, car and a pile of financial assets. The house was pretty and convenient, but I had good reasons to feel guilty living in it. The neighbours were less than lovable and Alvin's decorating didn't help. To add to it, the house had been fully furnished, and now my own belongings and whatever had survived from my office were squeezed in too.

"Well, good, that's why I'm here."

"Doesn't work for me. I'm not ready yet. I have stacks of material from my previous office, and it's taken quite a while to get that sorted out. In fact, I'm working on that this weekend."

She reached out and patted my shoulder, something I've never really tolerated well. I barely resisted the urge to swat her hand, partly because I've been working on being a nicer person, but mainly because I didn't want a barrage of long-distance calls from my collective sisters admonishing me for my bad manners. Jacki Jewell must have read my mind because she withdrew her hand and kept it out of swatting distance.

She didn't lose her glow though, nor did her linen wilt. I had to hand it to her. "I can help with that. It's a specialty really. You'll be so glad when it's over."

"Thanks for your interest, but as I just clearly said, I'm not ready yet and—"

She opened her mouth.

I held up my hand. "And I don't do well under pressure."

Alvin's voice piped up behind me, speaking directly to Jacki Jewell. "It's so true. You'd want to watch out for that."

"Of course," Jacki Jewell's smile lit up again, "you won't get any pressure from me. That's why I have such satisfied clients." I think she believed that.

Alvin approached her, admiration on his face, his hand outstretched to shake hers. "Alvin Ferguson."

Gussie the dog took that opportunity to fart softly on the sofa.

I said, "In the interests of saving time, let me state categorically that I'm not ready to sell the house."

Alvin piped up, "But Camilla, just the other day you said—"

"Naturally," Jacki Jewell said, "you have to act when you're ready and not a moment before. If I could just look around a bit, that would help."

"Help what?"

"Exactly. At some point you will want to sell, and I can give you a few tiny bits of advice that will make that process easier, even if," she paused here for full effect, "you go with another broker."

And I will, I promised myself.

"What kind of advice?" Alvin said.

She turned her blinding smile on him. "Staging a home can make the difference between a quick sale and the price you want and a protracted and miserable selling period."

"Staging," Alvin breathed. "I've heard about that. You mean someone would come in here and make things look like a model home? That would be great, wouldn't it, Camilla? People do that for a living. I think I'd be good at that, myself. I'm an artist. I did these." He pointed proudly to the nearest Tuscan murals.

"Oh," she said glancing around and losing a bit of her bright colour, "did you? My."

My, indeed.

"Let me get you some lemonade, Ms Jewell," Alvin said, fluttering from the room like a lovesick moth. "I'd like to hear more about this."

As he disappeared from view, she leaned toward me and said, "First, I'd recommend getting rid of the murals. Contemporary buyers want neutrals, harmony and simplicity."

"Do they? Well contemporary buyers are just going to have to suck it up if they want this house. The murals stay."

"Oh, certainly, just as long as you realize that it will limit the number of people who come through."

"It will limit it to none, because if you recall, less than a minute ago, I said that I was not ready to sell."

"Well, of course, you did. And I agree, but we're just

blue-sky thinking about the future. Anything I could do to help make the transition easier for you and..."

"Alvin," I said.

Gussie yawned. The little calico cat got up and stretched.

"Your dog is quite, um…"

"Flatulent? Yes indeed, although I should point out that he's not actually my dog although he is lying on my sofa. He belongs to Alvin's brother, but for complicated reasons he's been here for a while."

"He seems to get along with your cat," she said, a tiny frown line appearing between her eyebrows.

"Again, odd as it may seem, that is not my cat. She belongs to a friend, Mrs. Violet Parnell, who is actually in the Perley Rideau Hospital recovering from a broken hip."

"Do I hear tweeting?"

"Lester and Pierre. Peach-faced lovebirds. Also visiting."

"That's a relief. Pets make it much harder to sell a place. So if these cute creatures could move on, things would go much more smoothly."

Gussie had been in residence for more than four years, and Mrs. Parnell's cat, for various reasons, had always more or less stayed at my place. The birds were just hanging around until Mrs. P. was discharged from hospital.

"Move on? That won't be happening."

"Well, fine, of course, it is your home. Keep in mind that a lot of buyers are afraid of dogs and others are allergic to cats. Birds make people nervous, but I'm sure we can work around that."

Was she deranged? "I don't actually have to work around anything, because I've decided I'll be happy in this house forever."

"Certainly, take your time and think it over. Do you

mind if I look upstairs?"

"Yes," I said, "I do mind. I'm not selling this house, and you can tell my sisters that from me. Now I'm extremely busy today, and you'll just have to excuse me."

"Absolutely," she said, not moving.

I opened the front door, letting in a blast of hot humid air. I smiled and said, "Goodbye, Ms Jewell."

To do her credit, she turned that right on its head. She glanced at her watch and raised her eyebrows. "I really have to go, but I'll just leave this information package for you. I'm here to help. I can certainly facilitate your paper purge."

"You don't seem to understand—my files are highly confidential."

"Confidentiality is one of our specialties. I'll call you."

As she minced toward her black Mercedes SUV, I lifted my middle finger. "Call this," I muttered.

Alvin scowled at me. "She seemed very professional. Knows what she's talking about. I bet she can sell anything."

"Well, she's not selling this house, Alvin. And I think we've seen the last of her."

I took advantage of having the front door open to snatch the mail, which must have been still sitting there from the day before, the office assistant once again asleep at the wheel. The mail contained the usual slim bundle of pizza delivery ads, fitness centre come-ons and bills, which were no longer a big problem for me.

This time there was also a single white unstamped, unaddressed number ten envelope. Sealed. I opened it.

Alvin always hovers when I get the mail. He likes to be in charge of all that exiting stuff. "I must have forgotten to bring the mail in yesterday. I've been busy with my cooking project. There are thousands of recipes for oatcakes." He frowned as I stared at the note.

I lowered my voice. "It says Rollie Thorsten."

"I honestly thought it was your brother-in-law, Stan, sending those jokes."

It would be just like Stan to try to creep me out by sending unfunny yet unsettling jokes in plain envelopes. This was the man who'd inserted whoopee cushions, fake dog turds and ice cubes with insects into every MacPhee family gathering that I could remember. I thought back to the stick-on cigarette burns on my sister's custom upholstery, the piles of plastic vomit under the coffee table. And those were just the highlights. This envelope business was all very Stanlike. But Stan was on the Mediterranean cruise with my sisters and the other two brothers-in-law and my father.

Maybe he had an accomplice. But Stan was as cheap as he was cheerful. His money went on Buicks and joke novelties. I couldn't see him paying anyone to do this. To the best of my knowledge, he had no cronies outside the family. My sister Edwina kept him on a short leash.

"Trust me, Stan isn't killing people, Alvin. He didn't even stay mad at me when I wrecked his Buick. Remember?"

"Who could be doing it?"

"I don't know, Alvin. Some pathetic soul with an axe to grind. I still don't believe it really has anything to do with me."

"If you say so," Alvin said.

He likes to have the last word.

* * *

"How crazy is that?" I said to the light of my life, Ray Deveau, doing my best to fill up the thirteen hundred minute block of telephone time we manage to talk every month. It's a necessary part of our long distance relationship. "Not that there's anything funny about the joke business."

"Maybe, just a…"

"Okay, but you live in Cape Breton. Here in Ottawa, we're more serious. All that Parliamentary protocol and everything."

"Not while you have Alvin with you, you're not serious."

"That's true. Remind me to send him back to Sydney, and the Ferguson family dog too."

"Returning to the jokes," Ray said quickly. "So you're saying you got these same notes too, and Alvin threw them away?"

"He showed them to me because they were lawyer jokes and he wanted to annoy me. But he didn't say where they came from and he didn't say anything at all about the names. I don't think he noticed them. They just went straight into the recycle bin unless, of course, Gussie ate them. Alvin figured I wouldn't be insulted by them, and that's no fun, and he couldn't figure out why anyone would send them, so, toss! No discussion."

"And Bobby did the same thing?"

"Bunny. Well, no. He doesn't get mail, I guess, just flyers, and he would look at anything with his name on it suspiciously. You know, the 'how did someone find my address?' kind of suspicion. He thought getting these things in a plain envelope was weird."

I couldn't see Ray over the phone and he couldn't see me. This was a good thing because it meant I could lie around in old T-shirts and baggy shorts and keep my hair pulled back in a shaggy ponytail. I didn't have to have a pedicure every month, as my sisters advised. It was the one good thing about having a significant other one thousand, six hundred and forty-one kilometres away. He could imagine me any way he wanted and vice versa.

Sometimes we were right about each other. At that exact moment, I knew he was scrunching up his face.

"And this 'Bunny' doesn't have them."

"His wife is crazy clean. They're gone."

"You sure they're gone? You should get the local boys to go over and search his house."

"Are you kidding? I can't do that to Bunny. Okay, he's been a burglar most of his adult life and probably when he was a child too, now that I think of it. But he can't have the cops traipsing all over his house. What if they found something incriminating?"

After a significant pause, Ray finally spoke again. "You know something? I have to put the cat out now. How about I bang my head on the sidewalk a few times while I'm outside?"

"See that's the problem, Ray. You're a cop. It colours the way you look at the world. I'm a lawyer. Bunny was my legal aid client for years. I'm attached to him. I can't traumatize him. Also, you don't have a cat."

A strange noise drifted over the line.

"Are you laughing? Ray? Cut that out. Oh, gotta go. It looks like Leonard Mombourquette's calling on the other line. I've been leaving messages for him all night. It'll be about the dead lawyer."

"Call me back right away. We have to work out the details about the girls."

"The girls?"

"Brittany and Ashley. Don't turn everything into a game, Camilla."

Details about the girls? The very mention of Ray's teenage

daughters was enough to make me edgy. Possibly because they both hate me.

"Sure thing." I didn't want Mombourquette to hang up.

"Don't forget."

"Yup."

I picked up Mombourquette's call. "What's happening, Leonard?" I'd been trying to reach him at home and on his cell and later at my friend Elaine Ekstein's place because he still hadn't called me back.

"If I tell you, will you stop calling?" he said. I thought I could hear Elaine squawking in the background.

I said, "Any luck?"

"It looks like your man Rollie was shot with a small calibre weapon. No ballistics results yet. This is not public knowledge, so if you tell anyone else, I'm coming after you."

"A small calibre weapon. Of course, that doesn't mean much. I don't actually know anybody with a gun."

"Oh, come on. You were a legal aid lawyer long enough. Everyone you dealt with had a gun. Hey, now your boyfriend even has one."

"Don't creep me out. I have trouble with the cop thing. So was there anything else?"

"It's not enough that the guy was shot and tossed off a boat? You wanted him garroted too?"

"Was he garroted?"

"No. We actually don't get a lot of garroting around here. But two out of three ain't bad."

"Aren't you playful tonight, Leonard? Was he bound?"

"What, you think there's a sexual component to this?"

"Ew. With Rollie Thorsten? That just makes my skin crawl. So if he was found in the middle of the Rideau, he must have been taken there on a boat. I was just wondering who he might get close to who might have a boat and might also have a gun. My point is just that it would be easy to narrow that down. Guys with guns and boats."

"Try to be a bit more politically correct, Camilla. Maybe women with guns and boats. Now, you want to tell me how come you asked about the fact that he was shot?"

"Do I have to?"

"Let's see. I'm Major Crimes, there's a killing with information known only to the killer, the police and the staff at the morgue. Hmm. So, in short, yes, you have to tell me."

"Fine, but you won't like it."

"Try me."

"I got a lawyer joke in the mail."

"Do I have to come over there and question you?"

"It's true. You know that old one, 'How do you keep a lawyer from drowning? Shoot him before he hits the water.'"

"You got this joke, and that caused you to think that someone might have shot Rollie Thorsten?"

"I was hoping these jokes were irrelevant."

"These jokes?"

"I've had a few of them. Anyway, it turns out the next day a name comes in an envelope. Alvin has been just throwing the names away or Gussie's been eating them. He didn't make the connection between the names and the jokes. But this is the third time it's happened. After we get each joke, someone connected with the legal community dies."

"Huh? So somebody's killing lawyers and sending jokes? Or sending jokes and then killing lawyers?"

"Yeah. Don't get upset."

"Are you kidding? I love the idea. Hey, listen to this, Elaine." A squeal in the background drifted over the line.

"Elaine does too."

The dial tone seemed to mock me as well.

I could tell I'd have a bit of work convincing Mombourquette that, just this once, I wasn't pulling his leg.

* * *

"Camilla?"

"Oh sorry, Ray, I got distracted. I had to walk Gussie, and you know how he sniffs every tree. I meant to call you back and I would have."

"Yeah well, it's one o'clock here now, and tomorrow's a working day, so I thought I'd speed up the process."

I chose not to remind Ray that I'd been worrying about how to keep the cops from going through Bunny's house once they found out he was involved, which they would. That would tick him off more. Of course, I knew that I couldn't hold them off and that bothered me. Nearly a million people in the Ottawa area, and somehow someone had picked Bunny and me to share the sick joke with. And why was that anyway?

"Camilla? Are you there?"

"What? Sure I am. I was just waiting for you."

"Okay then, here goes. It's about the girls."

"Oh, right," I said with feigned enthusiasm. "Ashley and Brittany."

"Yes," he said. Did I detect a little tone there?

They were the second reason I liked talking on the phone with him, rather than living with him. We each had our baggage. My dead husband, Paul, and Ray's memories of his late wife. In time we'd be able to have a great relationship. The presence of two teenage girls who viewed me as taking over their mother's place currently presented a bit of a hurdle. Even if they were both attending university in Halifax, a five-hour drive from dear old Dad.

"What about them?"

"You know they've been keen on Dragon Boat races since we had those events here in Sydney the last couple of summers."

"Right, and that's terrific. Happy to contribute," I said. This was going to be easy. Sponsoring the little beasts while they rowed for a good cause. Why not?

"You sound enthusiastic," he said, that teasing note creeping into his voice. I loved that voice, made my knees weak.

"I am," I said, "in a weak-kneed way, I am."

"Well, that's great. They'll be arriving in Ottawa this week."

"Did you say Ottawa?"

"I'm glad you're not too weak-kneed to be listening."

"They're coming to Ottawa?"

"Quit teasing. You know how much I appreciate this."

"Remind me why again?"

"The Ottawa Dragon Boat Race Festival is next week. I thought it had all been arranged, Camilla. We discussed it, and I talked to Alvin about it too the other day, and he said it was great. Don't you remember?"

In fact, I didn't. "It's just late, like you said, and I'm groggy. That's terrific. The Dragon Boat Races are a lot of fun. Are you coming with the girls? Because that would be really excellent."

"I have a work commitment that I can't get out of. Believe me, I've tried, but it's a course, and I'm locked into it. No choice."

"Oh."

"I'll be sorry to miss out on the race and, now that I

think about it, I wouldn't mind seeing you either."

I said, "It's wonderful. They're coming with a team, right?"

Ray was quiet for a second. Words like wonderful do not come naturally to me, especially in connection to visitors, aside from Ray, himself. Maybe I had overdone it again.

"Right," he said at last. "But there'll only be the two of them and they'll be busy. They're a real pair of water rats. They love this racing thing. And they don't mind sharing a room. Think how much worse it could be."

Despite the time of night and my state of mind, I managed not to say that I couldn't think of how it could be any worse.

FOUR

What is a lawyer's ideal weight?
-Five pounds, including the urn.

Morning comes early in the middle of June. When the first light of dawn scratched at my eyeballs somewhere around four thirty, I sat up in bed and started making notes.

By the time I climbed out of my bed, I had a plan. A long shower and my favourite green apple shampoo helped me to feel alive at least. I shook my hair dry and slipped into a pair of light cotton capris and a sleeveless top to set out with Gussie through the sleeping neighbourhood. I banged on Alvin's closed bedroom door as we stumbled by. Spare him the sympathy. He had it coming.

Twenty minutes later, Alvin gazed blearily at me across the kitchen. He squinted and turned back to sip his Cape Breton-style morning tea. "It's too early for you to be so grouchy, Camilla. And it's not fair of you to wake me up."

"Time to come clean, Alvin."

He glanced at me warily.

I pulled up the second stainless steel and leather chair. "I had a long talk with Ray last night. By any chance is there some small detail you might have forgotten to mention?"

Alvin had taken on the look of a mouse in his mousehole while the cat sat outside tapping its claws on the floor. In this relationship, I so rarely get to be the cat.

"Like what?" he said, sipping the bracing black tea.

We both knew perfectly well that there were many many

things Alvin could have forgotten to mention out of self-preservation, playfulness, or other Alvinesque reasons.

"Oh say, like Ashley and Brittany? Ray's daughters."

"What about them?" he said.

"Well, apparently they're arriving this week for the Dragon Boat Races. And they are staying here, in this house. Sleeping arrangements have been all worked out. Isn't that great? Everyone knows about it. Except me, of course."

Alvin swallowed. "Didn't I talk to you about all that?"

"I don't think you did, Alvin."

"I meant to. I had a chat with Ray one night when he was looking for you. I don't know where you could have been at the time."

"Walking the Ferguson family dog, I imagine. That is the extent of my social life lately."

"Whatever."

"And what all did you work out with Ray? Be precise."

"That they'd stay here, of course. What else would you plan to do with them? They're practically family. That's what I said to Ray. And he told me when they were coming and all that."

"That must have been when you filled me in on the details."

"Okay, okay. So I forgot. Lord thundering Jesus, Camilla, you always go on about everything. I have a whole lot on my mind lately. Now that you've shut down Justice for Victims, I have to find another job, and if you sell this house, I have to get another place to live. I'm working really hard to build my cooking skills and that's taking a lot of time and psychic energy."

"Spare me, Alvin."

"Everything is not about you, Camilla," he sniffed.

I have learned not to be distracted into losing my temper.

"But this is about me. Don't you think I might want to know when they're arriving, for instance?"

"I suppose."

"So did you write down the arrangements?"

"I knew I'd remember them."

"Fair enough. And do you remember them?"

I tapped my fingers on the table during the longish pause. Eventually, Alvin said, "Not exactly."

"Oh, great. Well, they're going to be here sometime, so you'd better figure out what needs to be done and how you're going to do it. Consider it a matter of life and death. I'd like a plan after I get back from my first meeting."

Alvin said, "But you don't have meetings any more."

* * *

I met P. J. Lynch for breakfast at the Second Cup near the Courthouse. I was already waiting with an iced latte and a blueberry muffin when he blew in the open door. His carroty hair was a bit rumpled, as were his yellow T-shirt and his cargo shorts. Maybe he'd slept in that shirt. Or maybe not, as he cultivates a wrinkled style. Particularly on a Saturday.

He stood in line until he snagged a double espresso and three chocolate biscotti.

"Any word?" I asked when he sat down.

"About what?" he said when he had inhaled his breakfast, setting some kind of chocolate biscotti eating record.

P. J. was a reporter who put his nose for news above all else, including confidences from his friends. I definitely didn't want to tell him about the lawyer joke that had preceded Rollie Thorsten's demise or the note with Thorsten's name on it.

I said, "I don't know. Anything."

"Could you be a bit more vague, please?"

"Hey, you're the reporter, P. J. You tell me."

"I gather you didn't read my piece in the *Citizen* this morning."

"It's early, P. J. And I didn't get much sleep. Oh, come on, don't get sulky. Do you want me to run to Mags and Fags and buy a *Citizen*? I'll do it if that means I don't have to look at your protruding lower lip."

"Funny. It was just about the weirdness of Rollie Thorsten dying right when Brugel's trial is coming to an end."

I feigned a total lack of interest. "Oh yeah?" I yawned to further the point.

"Am I boring you? I thought it was great human interest."

"Hmm. Did you hear anything about how Rollie managed to drown himself?"

"No reports available yet, but there's something funny going down. The cops aren't saying diddly."

"Really? Didn't you get anything out of Officer Wentzell?"

P. J. shot me a dirty look. "Don't mock me."

I said, "She just seems like such a nice girl. I don't know why they wouldn't release the cause of death. He was supposed to have drowned, but I heard a rumour that he was shot." I didn't let on that a joke was the source of the rumour and that Mombourquette had confirmed it.

"I heard that too." P. J. actually quivered. And he was lying. I can always tell.

"Maybe the cops are being cautious about information so the relatives don't get upset."

P. J. snorted. "Be serious. The path lab and the coroner might be discreet, but all the cops I know hated Rollie. They probably have a flock of plastic flamingos outside the station today."

I thought of Mombourquette and his visceral reaction to Brugel and his lawyer. "I suppose they all did hate him."

"Sure. He used to shred them on the witness stand. I know one guy had to take stress leave afterwards."

I shrugged. "They're trained to cope with that kind of treatment on the stand. They just say what they observed. They're not being accused of anything."

Unlike Laurie Roulay. She'd been accused of lying and of being in part responsible for the death of her daughter and that of the child's father. Specious for sure, and the judge rapped Rollie's knuckles for it, but the damage was done.

P. J. said, "Rollie had special talent."

"So they all hated him."

He narrowed his eyes, watched me with more suspicion than usual. "Do you know something about his death?"

"Me? What could I know?"

"My spider senses are tingling."

"Really? Have you thought about getting a job in a comic book?"

"Funny. But if you did know something, you'd tell me. Right?"

"Sure. And you'd tell me too, right? You want another espresso?"

"Nope. I'm heading out to dig up dirt. You better not be holding back, Tiger."

"Me? Dirt? I never touch the stuff. But I'd appreciate you keeping me in the loop."

He tilted his head. "Why's that?"

"Because I hated Rollie at least as much as any cop, and I'd salivate over the details."

* * *

The second item on my plan was a trip to Rollie Thorsten's office. The space was pretty much what you might expect: a straightforward legal office in a nicely converted old house on Somerset just west of O'Connor. It was a Saturday, but I figured the day after his death, someone might be there trying to figure what to do next. It was still before ten in the morning when I pushed the unlocked door open. The receptionist's desk was empty. No big surprise.

The furnishings were fairly new and typical, heavy on the sand and taupe. Good quality. The sense of dinginess and sleaze was all in my mind, I knew.

I heard a small sound from around the corner, and I stepped further into the office. I knocked on a wall and said, "Hello."

Jamie Kilpatrick, the fresh-faced junior lawyer who had been in court when Rollie failed to show up, jumped. He followed that by dropping the sheaf of papers in his hand.

"Let me help you with that," I said pleasantly.

I guess he wasn't reassured by my presence because he was practically trembling. "No, just leave them. Who are you? How did you get in?"

As this was not the time for sarcasm, I resisted. "The door was open. I was expecting a receptionist, actually."

"It's Saturday." What was that in his voice? Irritation? Or just plain fear?

He couldn't have been more than twenty-six, and if I read his body language correctly, he was a man who would leap backwards through the double-glazed window at the sound of a nearby hiccup.

"My name is Camilla MacPhee," I said, soothingly. "And I'd like to talk to you for a minute."

He said, "I'm not taking any new cases just now. And as

you can see, I'm really quite busy."

"Won't be more than a minute. First of all, my condolences on Rollie's death."

"What? Oh. Yeah. Thanks. But really, I hardly knew him. I'd just joined the office last year and..."

I smiled understandingly. "I understand. Not to trash the recently diseased, but I imagine you'd just discovered that Rollie was sleazy, difficult and inclined to take advantage of the staff."

He loosened his collar. "I wouldn't exactly..."

I added, "And now he's dead."

He sat down and nodded. For a moment he seemed like a little boy, lost and most likely in big trouble over it.

I said, "Murdered too, which just makes it even worse."

He glanced over at me. "What do you want?"

"Just to talk. I'm trying to understand what's going on. Did you see the lawyer joke that Rollie received before his death?"

"What do you mean? A joke? Rollie's death was horrible. Why are you talking about jokes?"

"I heard a rumour that he got one in the mail and then got a piece of paper with his name on it on the day he died."

"Look, I don't know what you want from me, but I don't have time for this kind of sick nonsense."

"Fine, but then, of course, I'm also interested in why you backed out of the Brugel case."

He stared at me, took his time. "It was really in fairness to the client."

"It sure was. I'd say it was Christmas in June, with a hint of Easter Bunny for Brugel."

He flushed. I think they call that shade puce. He sputtered. "I don't have enough experience to conduct this case. Rollie had all the background."

"Give me credit for a brain. First of all, Rollie was so lazy, he probably didn't wipe his own butt. You were the one required to do all the digging. You did the work, and probably knew the case cold. So let's not bullshit about that."

He straightened up and tried to save his dignity, although his lingering blush undercut that somewhat. "This is a private office. I believe I asked you to leave."

"Sure thing. But I imagine the court will find it interesting to learn that you've been threatened by Brugel and that's why you're backing out."

Amazingly, he went from puce to the colour of his dropped papers. I wouldn't have been surprised to see him crumple onto the floor on top of them. But I had to give him credit for trying to brazen it out. "I don't know what you're talking about. No one's threatened me, unless that's what you're trying to do."

"Nice save," I said, with admiration.

"As I said, no one's threatened me."

"No one suggested that it might be better for your girlfriend if you backed out?"

"I don't have a girlfriend. There's the door."

"Did your car have slashed tires?"

"I bike to work. No money for a car yet."

"Fair enough. Getting strange phone calls? Breathing on the line, nothing else? Finding your door open when you left it locked? Things mixed up on your desk?"

"Not that it's any of your business, but no."

Liar liar pants on fire. "Really?"

"I'm going to call the police now."

There are guys who can utter a threat and your life flashes before your eyes. Jamie Kilpatrick wasn't one of them. He couldn't have scared a toddler if he was dressed as the devil on Hallowe'en. I wondered how he'd ever make a go of it in criminal law. Not a good job for a guy who can't bluff.

"Go right ahead. I have lots of contacts there. They'll be interested to know why the Brugel trial is delayed yet again. Some of those cops have a real hate on for Brugel. If they thought you had dropped the case in order to help him get a delay, they could start hassling you. Big time."

He shrugged. "Let them."

That told me something. Jamie Kilpatrick was not afraid of the cops hassling him about withdrawing. He wasn't afraid of me, although lots of other people seemed to be. But he was afraid of something. What? Lloyd Brugel was on the top of my list of possibilities.

"Okay," I said, "did he kidnap your cat?"

"What? Are you crazy? What cat?"

"That's probably a good thing with Brugel's people threatening you. Your dog then?"

"No dog. No pets. No threats."

"You need some new lines, Jamie. I understand the part where you're afraid of something. And there's some reason for it. You should really tell me, for your own good."

He leaned over and picked up the phone. He pressed nine. Then one.

I raised my hands in submission. "Fine. Sorry I got you all steamed up."

He lowered the receiver, slowly, but didn't hang up. I glanced at his shelf as I backed from the room. A framed photo of a graduation day. A solemn Jamie with a beaming couple who looked to be in their eighties. The photo had been taken in front of a small post-war bungalow. A vast spreading maple shadowed the tiny house. Parents? Not likely. Grandparents then. I stared at the photo, then met his eyes.

I knew, and he knew I knew.

"Elderly," I said. "Vulnerable. Sitting ducks."

He whispered, "Get out."

I said, "I am not your enemy. Keep that in mind."

I left him alone.

I knew that if his grandparents had been threatened, he would never reveal that. Knowing Brugel as I did, I would have kept my mouth shut too.

*   *   *

My day was evaporating between pouncing on people, checking out my sisters' houses and watering their finicky houseplants, and phoning home to make sure Alvin was busy getting the boxes of office files out of the third bedroom to prepare it for Ashley and Brittany.

But there was one thing that I really needed to do. I pulled up into the parking lot of the Rideau Perley Veteran's Health Centre and walked across the lot to the building, past a group of residents in wheelchairs parked by the entrance, and through the automatic doors.

The commissionaire nodded.

"I'm visiting Mrs. Violet Parnell," I said. "She's in the convalescent unit."

The commissionaire at the desk said, "Oh yes. Violet. Along here. Then the first corridor on the left."

I knew the way, but I nodded my thanks. The corridor might have been ten miles long. Or it might have been that I was dragging my feet. Usually I am in a rush to see my friend, but usually I am not quite so worried about her. Of course, the Perley was spotless and pleasant, but there was no doubt in my mind that the people who came in here by and large weren't getting out again. Mrs. Parnell had been betrayed by her hip after a tumble in the shower the week before. I couldn't help worrying about my fearless old ally ending her days in a place with IVs and strangers in uniforms. It didn't bear thinking about. Guilt and fear were duking it out for top emotion as I trudged along the hallway.

Her door was open because you kiss privacy goodbye in a hospital. My heart constricted. I could almost hear it snap. The bed was made with military precision, but there was no sign of Mrs. P.

I leaned on the wall in shock. I knew people often die after broken hips. Maybe some of them even want to. But for Mrs. P. to pass away without me and Alvin with her, that would be unbearable. I found it hard to breathe, and my hands were shaking as I turned to hunt for a nurse. I found one at the nursing station, concentrating on a clipboard. She was round-faced and pleasant and looked happy in her pink scrubs. "Violet?" she said.

I nodded, mute for once, my heart thundering.

"Oh sure. She's down in the Pub. She said that the sun was over the yardarm, and one of the aides helped her into a wheelchair. I saw her fly by not long after. Are you all right? You're awfully pale. We don't need anyone bringing the flu in here, you know."

I grinned like a fool.

Her smile vanished. "Nothing funny about that. There are a lot of fragile people in this wing."

"I'm not sick," I said. "Just happy that Mrs. P. is all right."

She nodded and went back to her paperwork. I hightailed it down the hall. The song in my heart had spread to my feet.

The Pub was on the first floor, near the main entrance. It

smelled and looked pretty much like any other pub, which I thought was a good sign. Spilled beer is a great equalizer. Sounded like any other pub too, judging by the sports blaring from the large wall-mounted television and the laughter from the bar. I found Mrs. P. holding court. A pair of gents I took to be into their eighties were following her story intently. The story seemed to involve fighter planes, if her gestures were anything to go by.

"Ms MacPhee!" she said. "How splendid to see you!"

"You look great," I said. "I thought…"

"Old war horses," she chuckled. "We just have to pick ourselves up and get on with the battle."

Her colleagues nodded. No arguments there.

"And speaking of war horses, Ms MacPhee, have you had an occasion to meet the Colonel and the Major?"

Both men got to their feet, somewhat unsteadily, but fast enough. The Colonel leaned on a walker. The Major got by with a cane.

The Colonel nodded gravely. "Pleasure," he said.

The Major held out his hand. "Any friend of Violet's a friend of mine."

Mrs. Parnell's eyes were shining. It may have been the impact of the new friendships. May have been the Harvey's Bristol Cream. Hard to say.

"Get you another, Violet, while I'm up?" the Colonel said. "And how about you, young lady?"

Mrs. P. said, "Wouldn't say no."

"It's a bit early for me," I said.

The Major shot the Colonel a glance. "On me, this time, I believe."

"You've had your turn," the Colonel said, pulling rank.

"That didn't really count."

"Things are going well. Nice enough crowd around here. But I gather you have your share of troubles. A friend can tell."

I didn't want to tell her how worried I'd been about her. "Got a little shock, I suppose. One of Brugel's defence lawyers died yesterday."

She nodded. "Sorry to hear it. But you weren't fond of this fellow."

"I hated him and so did everyone else, and the worst part is the trial will probably be delayed."

"Is that so bad? Isn't that scoundrel locked up?"

"He is. But it slows the legal process and it increases that chance that something could go wrong. And it looks like he was murdered."

"Sorry to hear it might delay the trial."

"Me too. But at any rate, I'm glad to see you today."

"Every cloud has its silver lining and all that, Ms Mac-Phee."

"Are you all right here?" I blurted out. "Are you missing your apartment?"

"Not at all," she said. "I know that Lester and Pierre are safe with you for the time being."

"Hmm." Among the things I wasn't planning to mention was the now familiar sight of the little calico cat, whose new hobby was regarding Lester and Pierre with unwavering interest.

"The big obstacle is my music, of course. They won't let you boom Shostakovich here."

"But you live for your music."

"Never mind. I was able to order this online and problem solved," she said, pointing to a tiny iPod Shuffle on a string around her neck. "I've been able to download most of my standbys easily enough. Fortuituously, I'd already started the project before I took that tumble. I have a docking station with speakers, although I've been told to keep the noise down."

"Didn't that cost you a fortune? You already own all this music."

"Easy enough to upload them to my computer and then on to the iPod."

I stared at the tiny device. Mrs. Parnell is an early-adopter. I am a late, and if I can manage it, a never-adopter. She's always light years ahead of me on technology. I think it goes back to the days of her mysterious jobs in the federal public service. Whatever, this talent of hers has been extraordinarily helpful to me many times.

"Converting the rest will keep me occupied and out of trouble for the next while."

"Can I do anything to help?"

"Certainly. You can bring a batch of my CDs any time you get a chance to pick them up from my apartment. Young Ferguson brought a box the last time. You could take those back and bring replacements. That would be very handy. Would you mind?"

"I'll be glad to help."

The Colonel and the Major were now hobbling back. Each one had a Harvey's in a free hand and an expression of fierce competition in his eyes.

When they arrived and settled in, I asked, "What do you think of lawyer jokes?"

"Damned funny," said the Colonel.

"Deserve everything they get. Bunch of crooks," added the Major.

Mrs. Parnell fixed them each with a withering glance. "Ms MacPhee is a lawyer. And she is definitely no joke.

Why do you ask, Ms MacPhee?"

"Someone is sending me jokes in the mail. Today, one of the lawyers on the trial I was attending died yesterday in the same way as the joke. It's kind of creepy. I wondered how people felt about that sort of thing."

"Depends," the Colonel said, "on whether you've ever been on the wrong side of a lawyer. Haven't been myself, but I can imagine what it's like. Had a few colleagues who found out the hard way, come divorce time."

"All you have to do is listen to the news," the Major added, shaking his cane in my direction. "Makes you mad enough to horsewhip some of these people. They get away with everything. Subvert the course of justice if you ask me."

The Colonel nodded. "That trial we've been hearing so much about. Tell me we shouldn't bring back hanging. And the fellow who defended him? Should be strung up too."

I said, "Well, he's dead, if that's any consolation."

The Major thought for a few seconds and said, "I think it might be."

"Cause for celebration if you ask me," the Colonel added.

Mrs. Parnell raised her glass. "I'll drink to that. Sure you won't join us, Ms MacPhee?"

"Another time. I just dropped in to see how you were doing. I'm missing your company."

"I'm settling in well," Mrs. P. said. "Plenty of esprit in this old corps, as you can observe."

"I'll head back to your room and get the CD box. I'll bring replacements as soon as I can."

"Pub hours are two to three, daily," Mrs. Parnell said.

"I'll keep that in mind."

She'd already resumed her story before I reached the door. The Colonel and the Major went back to being riveted.

FIVE

Why did the lawyer cross the road?
-To sue the chicken on the other side.

Back at the ranch, Alvin was making progress. Most of the progress involved lugging banker's boxes full of files from the third bedroom to the basement. The rest involved shredding documents. I smiled approval. "No need to waste money on the gym," I said encouragingly.

"Very funny," he said, or something like it. His voice was kind of muffled.

"Don't let me disturb you. I'll be making a list of the people who hated Rollie Thorsten. That's work too, you know."

By the time Alvin got the last box down the two flights of stairs, I had twenty-eight names on the list. Mine was among them. Fair's fair. So was Mombourquette's. Others worked in the justice system in some capacity. Some of the people who would have had the best reasons to hate Thorsten were dead. People like Laurie Roulay. I put her name down anyway. To my knowledge, except for two children who survived her, she hadn't had any relatives who cared much about her one way or the other. Certainly she'd had no one to turn to when Rollie Thorsten laid her soul bare in court. I'd looked after her funeral arrangements myself. I'd been happy for once to have had that pile of ill-gotten gains that weighs so heavily on me. The children had wept. Even the CAS workers had cried. Alvin had actually sobbed, although he'd only met Laurie once. I may have shed a tear myself, and I distinctly remember Mombourquette's nose being pinker than usual. But that was it for Laurie, a girl with tattoos, a girl who had kicked crack cocaine to make a new life as a mother, a girl who had once lived on the streets, but who had the guts to testify against Brugel.

Of course, Brugel was on a different list: that one contained people who might benefit from Rollie Thorsten's bizarre lawyer-joke death, a list of one. I couldn't really think of anyone else.

"There have to be more," I said pensively to Alvin as he staggered up from the basement.

I thought he muttered something about trading places.

I still wasn't that happy with the one-name list by the time Alvin announced that the bedroom was empty of Justice for Victims crapola. His words. I headed up to check it out. Now that it was empty, I could see how it wouldn't really do the trick. It had no bed for starters, also no dresser, although I supposed that visitors could store things in the desk drawers once Alvin emptied them. He didn't react all that well to the suggestion, not that I cared.

"Two words, Alvin: Free and Rent. And a few more words: for the past year and a half. So let's take stock. Did you remember when they're arriving exactly?"

"I know it will come back to me."

"Let's hope. And what will they sleep on when they get here? Of course, I could have been thinking about this all along if I had known they were—"

"Who are you kidding?" Alvin said. "You wouldn't have behaved any differently if you had known."

I hated to admit he had a point.

He scrunched up his face. Sometimes that means he's thinking. I hoped this wasn't one of those times. "They have inflatable beds on sale at Canadian Tire this week," he mused.

Inflatable beds? I wondered what could go wrong with those. And also if that would be one more item for the girls to curl their lips at.

"They're really comfortable," Alvin said. "Trust me. My sister Frances Ann got one for guests, and it's great."

I didn't really trust Alvin, but Frances Ann was very sensible. "Good. That's one problem solved."

"Two," Alvin said.

"Two problems?"

"Two beds. I don't imagine they want to sleep together. Bad enough they're stuck in one room."

"Of course, two beds."

"I'll get two singles. And sheets," Alvin said. "We'll need two sets of sheets, pillows and extra towels and face cloths if they're here for a while. We're not really set up for guests. We might even need lightweight blankets."

"Blankets?" I said. "It's a million degrees lately. We're in the middle of a heat wave. Oh, never mind. Get whatever they'll need."

"A mirror, I imagine, as well."

"There's one in the bathroom."

"Not everyone's like you, Camilla. Some people care what they look like. I think Ashley and Brittany definitely fall into that category."

"Fine. Just take care of it quickly."

"Bedspreads," he said.

"All right."

"Pillow shams too, I suppose."

I narrowed my eyes. Was he yanking my chain? No. He appeared to be completely serious.

"I just wish I could paint the room," he said, looking around. "It's the one space I never got to decorate because all those boxes were blocking the walls. If you ask me, it's a bit dreary."

Dreary was good, in my opinion. "Too bad there's no time. You'll be run off your feet getting all this stuff."

"It's really beyond the call of duty, Camilla," Alvin said. But I noticed his eyes were shining. A shopping spree was right up his alley. I could always distance myself from the results.

"Do you need money?"

He held his head high. "I have savings. I'll pay whatever it is. You can reimburse me."

I was proud of myself for not mentioning that the only reason he had savings was because he hadn't been paying rent. Of course, we both knew I'd never asked him to pay any rent, and he had in fact offered. We were both living free when you thought about it.

Alvin left humming. "I need to get a bit more equipment for my cooking projects too. Just leave it all to me."

Well, I certainly intended to. I went back to staring at my sheet of paper. I had the feeling I was forgetting someone important.

*   *   *

"I have sources," P. J. said, lowering his voice in case any of the Saturday evening crowd of noisy people in D'Arcy McGee's pub might care what he had to say. Wishful thinking on his part. "This will blow the top of your head off."

I said, "Don't dramatize. And at the same time, please resist the urge to bullshit. Just tell me what you learned about Rollie."

"You are no fun, Tiger. Do you realize that? I can't believe we're having breakfast and dinner together on the same day."

"I am even less than no fun."

P. J. lifted his Alexander Keith's India Pale Ale and sipped, all the time looking at me so I'd know how unfun I was.

I have never minded being a drag. I picked up my hamburger and dug in. First of all, you get hungry after a walk from the Glebe to Sparks Street. And secondly, you never want to let P. J. know you're eager to hear what he's holding back on. I finished a bite and carefully checked out the sweet potato fries to see which little beauty I might start with.

The fry paused on the way to my mouth when P. J. remarked, "It wasn't an easy way to go. Shot and then drowned." I could sense his barely contained excitement.

"Shot and drowned? No, I don't imagine it was."

"My source said he was shot first."

"I had heard that he'd been shot and dropped in the water. I didn't realize he really had drowned. My own source left that out." This was a bit too close to that old joke for me. Damn Mombourquette for not mentioning it. Of course, he may not have known.

P. J. said, "It gets worse. Turns out he was shot in the knees. It would have disabled him, but not killed him."

"In the knees?" What the hell? Mombourquette sure hadn't mentioned that. I'd assumed Rollie had received the fatal shot in one of the usual places: head or heart. My dinner had lost its appeal. I pushed my plate away.

P. J. had ordered the fish and chips, and apparently his appetite was unaffected by the details of Rollie Thorsten's fate.

After a while, I said, "Are you saying Rollie would have

been conscious when he went into the water?"

P. J. chewed slowly for a while before saying, "That's what my source thinks. You know I can't reveal my—"

I snapped. "I'm not asking for the name of your sources, although anyone with half a brain could figure out it's that girl in the path lab. The one who has the hots for you."

"Really? How did you...?"

"Let me see. She works in the pathology department. She drools when she sees you. Tough one."

"Anyway, calling her 'that girl' isn't too politically correct, Tiger. Especially from such a knee-jerk left winger as yourself."

"There's nothing wrong with girls, P. J. Try to remember that for future reference. Now, just to finish up. Maybe Rollie was knocked out first and then shot and drowned."

P. J. shook his carrot top vigorously. "I think my source would have mentioned that."

I felt a buzzing around my ears. "So, then he knew what was going to happen to him."

"He must have."

"And he wouldn't have been able to move his legs properly when he went into the water."

"Yeah." P. J. actually put down his fork this time.

I said, "Someone really wanted Rollie to go out the hard way."

"That's it."

"They wanted him to know what would happen and probably why it was going to happen."

"Could have been up to three minutes, my source figured until he lost consciousness and drowned. That would be pretty rough."

"I can't even imagine who would do that to another person.

Even Rollie. He was just sleazy and opportunistic, not evil. I think that Brugel is behind this. He's the only person I can think of who is capable of it. And he stood to gain from Rollie's death."

"He's locked up solid in the RDC."

"And you think he couldn't make something like this happen?"

"I hear you," P. J. said, although I noticed he'd picked up his fork again.

I didn't.

*　　*　　*

When I arrived home, Alvin was in full swing, standing on a shiny new ladder in the third bedroom. Two boxes containing blow-up beds and several overstuffed plastic shopping bags were parked in the hallway. I managed to navigate my way into the room.

"Oh," I said. "I see you found time to paint after all. I thought we said that we weren't—"

"It needed brightening," he said.

"Well, it's certainly bright now. You know, I never would have considered Chinese red myself."

He shrugged and wiped a bit of paint from his nose. "They are here for the dragon boat races, Camilla."

"Hard to argue with that," I said.

"Too bad it's going to take four coats to cover this boring sand colour on the walls. I'll be here all night."

"My sympathies," I murmured as I shut the door.

*　　*　　*

I fell asleep mentally working my way through Rollie's better-known cases and the people he'd come up against. My list was by the side of the bed in case more names came to mind. At three in the morning, my eyes popped open, something that happened all too often. Gussie grunted reproachfully and Mrs. Parnell's cat stretched and turned her back to me to make a point. The point being that the night is for sleeping, not for gasping, twisting and sitting up in bed for the second night in a row. But sleep had been chased from my head by a face.

Annalisa Fillmore's face.

Of course.

It would be hard to imagine anyone who could have hated Rollie Thorsten more than Annalisa Fillmore. Why had it taken me so long to remember her? Annalisa's black eyes had flashed in my dream, but even after I snapped awake, I could still see her. The lingering image was that of a tall, svelte figure in a Sunny Choi suit speaking passionately into a microphone and decrying the state of sentencing in Canada. My sister Edwina once mentioned that Annalisa Fillmore only wore Stuart Weitzman shoes which set her back three hundred dollars plus. Her handbags would be worth more than my last car. I remembered Annalisa's face contorted with rage as she confronted Rollie on the courthouse steps. Rollie, dropping his customary unconcern for his fellow humans, had actually jumped back like a startled hamster. Some people had laughed at his panic. But I wondered at the time if Rollie hadn't hurtled out of her reach, would Annalisa Fillmore have pushed him down the wide courthouse stairs?

Even so, it was a serious mental leap from rage after a court case to shooting someone and pushing them from a boat into the middle of the Rideau to drown.

At four, I was still awake.

At five thirty, Gussie and I were back from our walk. I gave Alvin a break, but by six, I figured what the hell, P. J. might as well get up and confront the day too.

"What time is it?"

"Doesn't matter. We need to talk about Annalisa Fillmore."

"Who the bleep is Annalisa Fillmore, and why can't she wait until… My god, does my clock say six oh three?"

"Try and follow the script, P. J. Annalisa Fillmore is the founder of Mothers for Fair Sentencing. You see her at conferences. You hear her issuing juicy sound bites on the news after trials."

"Okay. And I care about this at six oh three because?"

"Because Annalisa Fillmore's fifteen-year-old daughter was killed by her joyriding boyfriend. The boyfriend got off with a non-custodial sentence. Although I think maybe he had to write an essay on road safety too."

"Sheesh."

"Exactly. It was before they enacted the street racing laws. Annalisa must have had an impact on those too. She lobbied like a house on fire. The kid wouldn't get away with it now, and trust me, he was a grubby little creep and as guilty as sin."

"Don't the courts decide that?"

"The court did decide that, but he didn't have a record, his parents were every bit as wealthy, well-connected and respectable as Annalisa Fillmore herself, and the boy's lawyer talked a good story. Brilliant even."

"Now it's six oh four, and I'm thinking this interesting information could have waited until eight thirty, nine o'clock, no problem."

"So guess who the boyfriend's lawyer was."

It sounded like P. J. was yawning. After a while, he said, "I can't guess my own name at this time of day."

"Give it a shot."

"Oh. You mean—really?"

"You got it. Our boy Rollie. She hated him. White-hot lava hated."

"I don't know if lava is white, but allow me to remark that you hated him too. Everyone who knew him probably detested him."

"Oh sure, no argument here. I'm actually on my own list of suspects. But we both know that I didn't kill him. I'm pretty sure you didn't either, although you will do almost anything for an exclusive. But this woman's emotions went way beyond our minor loathing. I worked with her from time to time on Justice for Victims matters, and she was deadly serious."

"You said you worked with her, so did you get along all right?"

"I believe in the rights of the accused to a fair and unbiased trial, no matter what I think of that particular individual or the crime. That seemed to be an issue for her, and we had words more than once."

"You had words with someone, Tiger? That's hard to believe."

"Hilarious, P. J. Did I mention she owned a boat? Some kind of yachtlike thing that you can actually sleep on. She was out on that boat the night her daughter died. I don't think she'd have trouble getting her manicured mitts on a gun either. She's loaded. Trust me. No one hated Rollie more than Annalisa did. I think she would have been capable of this. I think she would have thought it was funny. You awake now? Get cracking. You want that story? Let me tell you about a weird situation."

I got the impression P. J. wasn't yawning as I filled him in on what I thought he should know about the lawyer jokes. He said, "Okay, this is all very strange and hard to follow at six in the morning, but last night you convinced me that it was Brugel. I spent quite a bit of time on that idea. How do I know this isn't another of your tangents?"

"Not a tangent, P. J. I liked the idea that Brugel might have done it to delay his trial. He's vicious enough to have been amused by the jokes, but now I realize that Annalisa Fillmore is a much more likely suspect. So can you use the legendary sources to find out what she was doing the night that Rollie died?"

"Why kill him? Why not the boy who caused her daughter's death? You have to admit, it is a stretch."

"Gotcha. She didn't have to kill him, although she probably would have loved to. You see, he killed himself."

"Suicide?"

"Car crash. High speed chase with the police six months after his trial. I think Annalisa was enraged that he'd escaped her before she could personally do him some harm. I wondered at the time if that had sent her over the edge. So how about it, big boy? Got your interest yet?"

"I'm on it, Tiger."

*   *   *

Even though Jacki Jewell had left a chirpy telephone message indicating that she was planning to come by, I was still having a hell of a good day. By ten, I'd been through the remaining boxes of stuff that had come from Justice for Victims and had been occupying the corner of my own bedroom. I'd sifted out enough material for shredding to eliminate at least one filing cabinet. I was pretty sure that Annalisa Fillmore had bumped off Rollie Thorsten, and that would mean that I could stop being worried about this weird and wacky lawyer joke situation. I knew that P. J. would dig around until he got some answers. Just in case, I'd left a message for Leonard Mombourquette suggesting he might think about her as a perfect suspect. I may have been whistling. The doorbell rang and I hustled to answer it.

Jacki was standing on the front steps. This time she was wearing a pale blue seersucker suit that was businesslike, but also flattering. Despite the heat and humidity, it was still fresh and unwrinkled. I am always suspicious of people who can pull that off.

"May I come in?" she said, slipping past me before I could respond.

I realized that I'd been blocking the door. Not that it did any good. "Are you alone?" she said.

"Why?"

"It's just that your...young man seems to get a bit agitated when I suggest that the house would do better without all the...you know."

"What?" Of course, I knew perfectly well what. You don't need to be a Nobel Prize candidate to figure out that Alvin's decorating might be a hurdle for the discerning buyer.

She smiled.

I smiled back. Two can play that game. "He's upstairs decorating. Why don't you head on up and negotiate that with him?"

I thought she paled, just slightly. "Decorating?"

"Yes, we're having a few teenaged visitors here for the next while. I'm not sure how long they're staying, but they will certainly add life to this dreary old place."

She blinked.

For a fleeting moment, I felt all warm and fuzzy toward Ashley and Brittany. It didn't last long, but it was fun while it did.

I hooked up Gussie to his leash and said, "I'm heading out now. Good luck."

*   *   *

I was still a bit uncomfortable in my old apartment building. I kept expecting someone to call the police, even though we'd settled that awkward situation a while back. But I had my reasons, so I stomped down the hall to 1608. Under normal circumstances Shostakovich's Symphony No. Six or something equally booming would be clearly audible in the hallway. But with Mrs. P. in the hospital, it was quiet. I unlocked the door and stepped inside. I felt a wave of sadness. Would Mrs. Parnell ever be coming back to this apartment where we'd had so many good times? And for how long if she did? What lay ahead for my brave and splendid friend?

I shook myself and got down to replacing the first batch of CDs and picking up another boxful. It was a small errand and the least I could do for her. I tried not to mope about the empty black leather chair, the pristine modern room, the silent stereo system and the strange echo that the uninhabited apartment seemed to have developed. Still, moping wouldn't do anyone any good. We'd had a lot of fun in this room. How many times had I stood in here and asked Mrs. Parnell for advice or help? She'd never refused me and she'd always made the difference. That reminded me to pick up her best laser printer and a ream of paper before I headed out to the Perley.

Once I got there, I found Mrs. P. looking a bit frailer than the day before, perhaps because she was in the hospital bed and not surrounded by admirers.

"Ms MacPhee, what a nice surprise. You brought the CDs. That's splendid. I confess to being a bit bored. And boring."

"You're never boring, Mrs. P."

"Not like the days when we had such great adventures. Now I have nothing but time on my hands. I suppose I'm just missing my routines, although young Ferguson popped by earlier and cheered me up. Said you have him decorating for visitors."

I decided not to get sidetracked by that. Mrs. P. is inclined to support Alvin unconditionally.

"I need your computer-search expertise. Is there any chance you can give me a hand?"

Her eyes lit up. "A project? I'd be delighted. Spill the beans."

"I didn't like to talk about this in front of your friends yesterday, but there's some weird stuff going on. There's more than just that joke I mentioned. You remember Bunny Mayhew?"

"Our dyslexic art-loving burglar? Who could forget him? A delightful lad." She chortled merrily. I wished I could laugh half as heartily. I filled her in on Bunny's visit and his theory about the jokes being tied to the deaths. "So there are three possible victims, if Bunny's right, not that I'm convinced about two of them. There's no question that Rollie Thorsten was murdered. However, a woman called Roxanne Terrio, a real estate lawyer, died in an apparent biking accident and a Federal Court judge called Cardarelle expired from anaphylactic shock, if I remember correctly. I'd like to see what you can turn up about these people and their deaths, before I put my foot in anything."

"Young Ferguson mentioned this bizarre phenomenon on his visit. He said that you had also been receiving these cryptic attempts at humour. And you say your burglar chappie has been as well."

"Yes. Bunny's terrified. And while I remember the jokes and I did get Rollie's name, I'm not a hundred per cent sure that I received the first two names. The evidence seems to have disappeared, possibly eaten by Gussie."

"Are you at all worried, Ms MacPhee?"

"Rollie's death is definitely linked to the joke we received the other day. I'm not sure about the other two possible victims although Bunny's convinced. As we are both receiving these so-called jokes, it's obvious we're linked in the joker's mind. I don't know why. But this person must be unhinged, and given the horrible way Rollie died, I think we'd better find out soon."

"That is a concern. I am at your service, Ms MacPhee. Tell me how I can assist. I would welcome anything that would alleviate the tedium of the convalescent's bed."

"I realize you're supposed to rest up and recover from that hip fracture. But since you're stuck here with the computer on, could you check out the names I mentioned, snoop around, find next of kin, any articles written, obits, that sort of thing? Watch for any of the same names cropping up in each of their cases. I'm particularly interested in any connection with a woman named Annalisa Fillmore."

"Ah. The redoubtable Ms Fillmore. A splendid figure, rather in the grand style of Joan of Arc. I've seen her interviewed on television on a number of occasions. She certainly can liven up any newscast."

"Joan of Arc? I guess. Hadn't thought of her like that."

"Perhaps I am merely being fanciful."

"And the other one is Lloyd Brugel."

"This Brugel is a foul creature."

"Sure is, but he has quite an operation working for him. I'd rather our jokemaster turned out to be Brugel, but at the moment I'm pretty convinced it's Annalisa."

"It would give me great pleasure to dig around and see what I can turn up for you. And it will make the time pass more quickly."

"I brought your printer. I wasn't sure if you could have a printer here. But you have to promise that you won't get too—"

"Please don't worry about me, Ms MacPhee. I'm an old war horse happy to be back in battle, or on parade perhaps. And speaking of old war horses, the sun's over the yardarm. Would you like a Harvey's Bristol Cream to celebrate?"

"Bit early for me. I'm happy to take you down to the pub though."

"Strike while the iron is hot and all that. Mustn't let this unsettle you, Ms MacPhee."

"It isn't just the jokes unsettling me. I'm a bit distracted that Ray's girls are going to spend an unspecified amount of time in Ottawa. In my house. Without Ray."

"Forgive me if I'm overstepping, Ms MacPhee, but didn't you say you wanted to improve the relationship with those young women? Because of Sergeant Deveau?"

"I may have said something along those lines, but I certainly didn't think they'd come and stay with me. Remember the things they did to keep Ray and me apart?"

She reached over and patted my shoulder. "Learn to

pick your battles."

"I suppose you're right. as usual." I helped her into the wheelchair and we made very good time shooting through the hallways, into the elevator, then on to the pub where the Colonel and the Major awaited, eagerly.

I left the Perley, secure in the knowledge that Mrs. Parnell would soon be busily uncovering whatever extra material she could about the possible victims and the two most likely suspects. Somehow, and I never liked to inquire too deeply, she can get beyond the more conventional searches and even circumvent the odd inconvenient legal restriction. I would be very surprised if she didn't have her first results ready and printed shortly after the pub closed.

SIX

How many lawyers does it take to change a light bulb?
-Depends. How many can you afford?

I figured Jacki Jewell would be gone by the time I got back. I was right. There was no sign of her glossy black Mercedes SUV. However, I arrived home at the same moment as a Blueline cab pulled up in front of my house.

There was a flurry of excitement, then two vaguely familiar faces appeared. Two slender, tanned and beautiful young women emerged from the cab, wearing airy floral sundresses and twinkly flipflops. They both had the kind of glossy long hair that appears in shampoo ads. The subtle highlights on the brunette's hadn't come cheap, I was guessing. The other girl's formerly sandy shade had morphed to blonde. The blonde had hazel eyes. The brunette's were wide and green. My jaw dropped in a clichéd fashion as it dawned on me that Ashley and Brittany had landed. How could two people have changed so much in a little over two years since I'd seen them? Where were the zits? The baseball caps and oversize shirts? The sneers?

The cab driver walked around to the trunk and removed two huge bags with great effort. I stared. How could two people have so much luggage? Was there a collapsible dragon boat in among those giant duffel bags?

I braced myself and stepped toward them.

I dug up the best thing I could think of to say: "Welcome to Ottawa."

Okay, that was pretty hokey. Both girls stared back at me. The luggage continued to emerge from what must have been a bottomless trunk. The cab driver grunted and gave them each a dirty look.

"Head on in, you two," I said, "I'll settle up with your cab. I wish I'd realized you were arriving this morning, I could have met you at the airport."

I noticed an exchange of glances. Perhaps I had been expected? Never mind, I was just hoping that in the next few minutes, I'd be able to recall which one was Ashley and which one was Brittany.

I tipped the taxi driver extra. I could only imagine what he'd been through.

"For heaven's sake," Alvin hissed from the kitchen, moments later.

"No need to hiss," I said.

"There is," he said sibilantly. "Why didn't you tell me they were coming by cab? I could have had something ready for them. I could have made their lunch. You know I have this cooking project underway, and it would have been a perfect opportunity—"

"That's because I didn't know they were arriving today, because nobody else, that would be you, remembered to pass on that particular detail."

"Oh sure, blame me for everything."

An attractive head popped around a corner. Ashley (or possibly Brittany) said, "Everything all right in here?"

"Absolutely," I beamed, carefully avoiding the use of first names. "I was just telling Alvin we should make some tea. He said he'd just love to make it, and he apologizes for not thinking of that himself. How about I show you your room? I think you'll be amazed."

Ashley and Brittany loved the red room. "Perfect," they squealed in unison.

Alvin, who had been unable to resist checking their reaction, had followed them upstairs, and now stood blushing in the doorway.

"Great," I said, "toss your stuff in and then we can go downstairs and you can fill me in on the dragon boat races."

"I can make you some lunch. It doesn't have to be just tea," Alvin said

"We'd love that," one of them said, "but we have to meet up with our team. We lost a lot of time at the airport."

"Yes," the other one said. "We still have some serious training to do. We have to practice on the site too, and our team captain managed to get ten practice times booked. We've all kicked in to pay for them. We want to do well in this. We have a ton of pledges."

The first one said, "Dad's really proud of us, and he made sure a lot of people put their names down."

"I'll make a pledge," Alvin said. "Even Camilla might cough up a few dollars. Probably."

"Happy to," I said, looking daggers at him.

"Can we do it later? We have to get out there."

"I'll take you," Alvin said happily.

* * *

I was about to call Ray to tell him his girls had arrived when my cellphone trilled. I considered not answering, but I recognized the number.

P. J. said, "Bad news."

"Spit it out."

"Annalisa Fillmore."

I hate that game of hide the information. "What about her?"

"She didn't kill Rollie."

"Well now, how do you know that, P. J.?"

I could imagine that gotcha grin right over the phone. He crowed. "She has an alibi."

"Oh, pull the other one. How can she have an alibi? Do we even know when Rollie died?"

"We do."

That was news to me. "Are you sure? I hadn't heard anything on the news."

"No, it's not public knowledge yet. But as you know, I'm special. So, when did he die, you ask? Well, he was last seen in Hy's washing down his tenderloin with a bottle of Cab Merlot, so we know he was alive at nine the evening he died. Then he was spotted in the water just before eleven."

"I guess that kind of narrows it down."

"Anyway, the point is she has an alibi for that entire time."

"Big deal. Alibis are easy enough to fake."

"Not this time."

"Why? Did she have an audience with the Pope?"

"Close."

"What do you mean, close? Don't be ridiculous."

"Judge for yourself. Our Annalisa was at a fundraising dinner with a member of the federal cabinet, and not one but two provincial cabinet ministers. Oh and have I mentioned the chief of police?"

"You're kidding."

"Nope. Plenty of media too. And the people at her table say she never left, including our most famous national news anchor."

"Who asked them?"

"I did."

"Maybe they'd just all say that because they don't want to be the one who…" My voice trailed off because I could hear how silly this sounded.

"No one is lying. Anyway, the whole thing was taped by community television and parts of it by one of the major networks. All to say, she could not have slipped out from this event to murder Rollie Thorsten. Even assuming she was capable of shooting him in the legs and tipping him into the water, she didn't have the opportunity."

"But…"

"Whatever else she may have done and no matter how much she might have wanted to kill him, I am afraid she didn't do it. Must have been one of the thousands of other likely candidates, such as yourself."

I could feel myself glowering.

"Don't pout," he said, even though he couldn't see me. "There's still Brugel."

* * *

When I got off the phone, I learned I'd missed a message from Mrs. Parnell. She had some information for me and wanted to share it. Apparently she'd already had some success. No way was I pouting when I beavered in from the parking lot at the Perley and along to her room.

She looked up and grinned when I appeared in the door. "I hear young Ferguson is quite keen on your visitors."

"For me, they might as well be from another planet. He does appear to speak their language. Anyway, they mentioned that they'll be training a lot because they really want to do well in this race to raise the profile of their charity."

"Splendid," Mrs. Parnell said, nodding in approval. "I certainly would like to be able to observe this race. Bit hard stuck in here though. Never mind. Young Ferguson suggested I make a pledge, and I was able to do that. Now, have a seat, Ms MacPhee, and see what I've turned up. Quite a bit on this Brugel character, but nothing that seems to shed light on this situation. There's some on your Roxanne Terrio. And some articles on the accident. Letters to the editor about bicycle safety and the perfidy of automobile drivers."

"She wasn't my Roxanne Terrio, but thanks so much Mrs. P. Boy, that is a lot of stuff."

Mrs. P. smiled her satisfaction. "Let's start with the obituary."

Terrio, Roxanne Gaylene.
October 24, 1965 – April 2, 2009
Tragically in a bicycle accident on April 2nd in Gatineau, Quebec. Roxanne was predeceased by her parents André and Mary Ann. She was a resident of Ottawa and a graduate of University of Ottawa School of Law. She leaves behind to mourn her beloved chihuahua, Moxi, and her colleagues at Terrio and Fox, Real Estate Law.

A memorial service will be held at a later date. Donations to Canadian Chihuahua Rescue would be appreciated.

"A sad life, it seems," Mrs. Parnell said. "Many of us have no family, but not to leave behind a single friend. How tragic that seems. I don't know where I would be without you and young Ferguson."

"And we'd be lost without you. You're still making new friends, but Roxanne seems to have had no one. There's just the chihuahua, not that there's anything wrong with that, I suppose. I wonder who wrote the obit. It seems like they didn't know her well." Someone from work maybe? "You said you found more information?"

"I did find a few items online, but nothing interesting. I've printed out what I did locate. There's a stack of information there, but I doubt if you will find much useful in it. Ms Terrio seems to have led a quiet and uneventful life. She's been in real estate law for a long time."

"Well, you know, that just makes me wonder all the more why her name would be connected with a lousy joke."

"Indeed."

"Worth a bit more digging, Mrs. P?"

"There's nothing I like better than digging."

*　　*　　*

I raced home in time to beat yet another visit from Jacki Jewell, the woman who could not take no for an answer. I was debating whether to let her in or sic the cops on her. As it was, she just wanted to check out the basement and the backyard again. She had a client that she thought could "overlook" some of the issues in the house.

I didn't even know what that meant, although I held Alvin responsible. First Jacki snooped through the basement, complaining loudly about the boxes. Next she did something mysterious with a measuring tape in the backyard, flinching and turning pale at the sight of Alvin's cherished frescoes.

I made myself comfortable in the kitchen and went over the rest of the papers that Mrs. Parnell had printed out for me. The most interesting by far was Judge Robert Cardarelle. I paid close attention to his obit.

Cardarelle, Robert Clément 1943-2009

Robert Clément Cardarelle LLB, retired Federal Court of Canada judge, died suddenly on Saturday, May 23, 2009 of anaphylactic shock. He was born in Hull, Québec and was predeceased by his mother, Marie (Lamoreux) and his father, Aurèle, and son, Alain. Judge Cardarelle is survived by his wife France (Tardiff), and brothers Simon and Rhéal of Gatineau. He was a graduate of University of Ottawa School of Law. There will be no visitation and the funeral will be private at the request of the family. In lieu of flowers, donations to the Jonas Smythe Treatment Centre would be appreciated.

I read it twice. I'd known Judge Cardarelle in my early days practicing law. I remembered him as a remote, unsmiling and difficult man. Some of my classmates had been scared to death of him. Still he'd made a name for himself in the Federal Court. He was perfectly cut out to deal with cases involving federal law: immigration, income tax and maritime law. Except for immigration, his job didn't involve much messy human drama. He wasn't one to mix socially. A good friend of my sister Edwina's lived next door to him in Rockcliffe Park. Coco Bentley had once confirmed my opinion by mentioning he wasn't much of a neighbour. I seemed to remember her calling him a titanic tightwad. He must have turned her down for a fundraiser or something. Still, I was astounded to see this larger-than-life man reduced to a crisp and cold paragraph. And private funeral? Not giving any previously wounded colleagues a chance to gloat at his grave? That might explain it.

I looked up as Jacki buzzed through the back door and into the kitchen, her stilettos tapping on the ceramic floor.

"That's good," she said. "I think the backyard might suit my client quite well. We can paint over that fresco. As for the inside, we're lucky he's colour blind."

I suppose I was staring at her, slack-jawed, because she went on. "So it won't be necessary to cover up the you know."

She must have meant the murals. I noticed that the closer she got, the more attached to Alvin's wall paintings I became. I owed him that much. I made a decision. Maybe I couldn't fire her without provoking World War III with my sisters, but I bet I could make her quit.

She frowned at the pile of papers on the smart little kitchen table. "Of course, there must be no clutter of paper anywhere."

I yawned.

She stared at me. I realized she might not have seen Alvin's handiwork upstairs yet, despite my helpful suggestion earlier. "Have a look at the guest room," I said with a straight face. "I think I mentioned that Alvin's freshened it up a bit."

I smiled at the clack of heels on the staircase. Perhaps I imagined the little squeak. I counted to ten and listened to the heels on the stairs again. I raised my eyebrows in a helpful way as she minced into the kitchen.

"Great colour, isn't it?"

"No, it is not. Red is a big big no-no. Maybe in a formal dining room, but really not even then if you want to sell the house. People polarize around red. We need neutrals. Neutrals!" She yelled this rather like a fireman bellowing for the pumper truck.

"I've heard that red is a neutral."

"Red. Is. Not. A. Neutral."

I shrugged. "Guess I was wrong."

"And aside from the colour, what is going on in that room?"

"In what sense?" I said, radiating innocence.

"In the sense of big duffle bags and underwear and make-up. It looks like an explosion."

"Oh, right. That would be Ashley and Brittany. They're visiting. Didn't I mention that?"

"You'll have to tell them to keep things neat."

"Um, that won't be happening."

I thought her hair stood on end. "What? I can't show a house in this shape."

"I hear you. But I am going to bend over backwards to make these girls feel at home and welcome."

Her lip seemed to quiver. As I watched with interest, it hardened up again. "Well," she said, "I don't know if it's worth my effort to drag anyone in to see this place in its current condition."

"Of course. It's perfectly understandable if you choose not to represent this house."

*   *   *

It had to be done, as much as I hated it. Just after dinner, I slipped into the kind of outfit in the no man's land between what my sisters wouldn't be horrified by and what they would approve of. My lightweight black cotton dress had a bit of stretch, a short-sleeved top and a flared skirt. I squeezed my feet into a pair of cork-soled high-heeled sandals that were neither too sexy nor too comfortable. I knew I'd regret that, but the situation called for them. I transferred everything from my regular Roots shoulder bag to the vast glossy yellow oversize handbag my sister Alexa had given me for my birthday. I drew the line at jewellery.

I headed for Rockcliffe Park and the perfectly manicured lawns, circuitous streets, spacious homes full of diplomats, mandarins, technology wunderkinds, and business people, old money and new. Luckily, through the Coco Bentley connection, I knew exactly where Judge Cardarelle had lived out his days. I found the woman I assumed was Mrs. Cardarelle cutting peonies in the garden. She was humming happily and didn't notice as I arrived. She gasped in surprise as I said hello. Her lustrous silver bob swung in a flattering arc as she turned her head. I smiled and held out my hand.

She shook it uncertainly. I put her at about sixty-five, with the fine lines that go with it. But her skin was soft with a pale glow, and she had the most perfect bone structure I'd ever seen. She was also tall, fluid and elegant, in tan linen pants and a black linen top. I figured her clothes had come from Holt Renfrew, rather than a certain discount outlet like mine. Not that I care a fig about bone structure or where your clothes come from, despite my sisters' propaganda wars.

On the other hand, Judge Robert Cardarelle had resembled a bad-tempered basset hound more than the kind of man I'd expect to be her husband. Of course, he hadn't been as likable as any basset I'd ever met.

I had already worked up a discreet yet sympathetic smile. "Hello, my name is Camilla MacPhee."

Up close, Madame Cardarelle was beautiful, a Spanish Queen perhaps, with a bit of Nordic ice showing in the pale skin and the cool, distant gaze. She tilted her head very slightly.

I felt compelled to add, "I'm a lawyer. I only just found out about your husband's death and I wanted to express my condolences. Your husband was very kind to me."

"Kind?" she said.

"Yes. Very kind."

"Robert?"

"Judge Cardarelle."

"Kind in what way?"

Somehow this wasn't the reaction I expected. "Well, when I was in practice, I had occasion to meet with him to get some information, and I found it most helpful."

Mild interest flickered across her face. "Robert met with you?"

Keep it simple, I always told my legal aid clients, back when I had them. No long stories, no extraneous details, no chances to trip over your own whoppers.

"Oh, no," I said, trying a disarming smile. "I was very new at the law then. I never would have had the nerve to ask for an appointment. I just needed a bit of information."

She watched me carefully. I felt like a mouse in a bucket. "Robert gave you information?"

"Yes. Yes, he did. I just stopped him outside the courthouse years ago. I knew who he was. He just tossed off a bit of information casually, but it was what I needed and it helped me."

"That is truly surprising."

I used the all-purpose line people rely on when they hit a conversational snag after a death. "I am very sorry for your loss."

She glanced around as if she'd just heard a bit of unexpected but not unpleasant news. Why had I thought it would be a good idea to meet Madame Cardarelle?

"It's a very difficult time." I felt that comment was safe enough.

Madame Cardarelle said, "I suppose it is."

I blundered on, "I lost my husband ten years ago."

"An accident?"

"Drunk driver."

She nodded. "Robert hated drunk drivers."

"Did he?"

"He didn't have much use for other lawyers either. Especially women."

By now I knew that I wouldn't be having a cozy chat with Madame France Cardarelle that would reveal the arrival of a lawyer joke one day and the judge's name on a piece of paper the next. I said, "I just wanted to pay my respects."

"You were very young to be a widow."

"Yes, I had just turned thirty. I had a hard time getting over it."

An odd expression crossed her face. "Did you?"

"Yes, but eventually I had to get on with my life. Paul, my husband, left me with some lovely memories."

She furrowed the perfect brow. She leaned forward and clipped a low-flying peony, without acknowledging what I had said. She bent down and wrapped the stem in what looked like a damp paper towel. She echoed my words with a bit of puzzlement. "Lovely memories."

Somehow I suspected she didn't have her own.

I said before backing away. "Again, my condolences. I am sorry to have intruded."

"Thank you," she said, without a trace of emotion.

I slipped back into my car and took stock. Whatever Madame Cardarelle's emotional state, grief formed no part of it. Now that piqued my curiosity.

I got into the Acura and edged the car along until the Cardarelle residence was out of sight. I was grateful for the vast size of the properties on this street as I turned into the next driveway and scurried up to the door. Coco Bentley opened it with one of her usual dramatic gestures. I almost fell off the gracious front step when she screamed, "Camilla!"

"Yes," I said, quietly. I was hoping that Madame Cardarelle hadn't heard, even from half a block away.

"What are you doing here? Come in and have a drink!" Coco is like all my sisters' friends, affluent, with a house that could grace the cover of *Traditional Home*. Unlike my sisters' monuments to obsessive-compulsive disorder, Coco's surfaces are always covered with books, magazines, newspapers, old birthday cards and other lovely debris. The walls are decorated with finds from her many postings with Foreign Affairs and huge outrageous paintings by apparently drunken artists. Coco is tiny, with café-au-lait skin and a wicked glint in her huge dark eyes. She's in her mid-fifties, like my sisters, but she could pass for thirties. I think she must be missing the matronly gene. I should mention that she is also far more fun than all my sisters put together. By now I was sorry I hadn't stopped here first.

I followed her past the cluttered formal living room to a cozy garden room in the back of the house. "Name your poison," she said cheerfully.

"Just soda for me, please."

"Oh, don't be so tight-assed. I finally get a visit from you, and you won't even have a glass of wine. I will not accept it. Will not!"

I agreed to a small glass of red. I sank into a battered leather club chair, which felt quite heavenly, and accepted a red wine goblet filled to the brim. "I was just offering condolences to Madame Cardarelle, and I realized you lived next door." Close enough to the truth. I did have to admit that I sounded as stilted as a stuffed bird.

"Now I'll have to have a double," Coco said, swinging a bottle of something, "because that's just too weird for words. I hope you don't think for one minute that I believe you, Camilla."

"Why not? What's wrong with condolences? Madame Cardarelle seems lovely."

Coco took a sip of her whatever it was, and took a seat in the opposite club chair. She crossed her legs, elegantly. "In an icy, repressed way, I suppose. But he was a gold-plated bastard. Don't bother to deny it."

I didn't plan to deny it. "No kidding. What's the story?"

"Did she seem broken up about it?" Coco arched an eyebrow and giggled.

"Not in the least. No emotion whatsoever."

She said, "And you think she killed him?"

A splot of wine slopped from my glass as she asked that. I snatched a tissue to wipe it up. "What makes you say that?"

She shrugged. "Because you were there. And I know you like to meddle in murder. Every time I open the paper, there you are up to your armpits in one."

"I do not like to meddle in murder."

She shrugged. "Suit yourself."

"Fine. Do you think she might have killed him?"

"I certainly would have bumped off the old bastard. Well, I probably would have divorced him long before I felt like murdering him. And I like to think I wouldn't have married someone like him in the first place." She shivered. "Those jowls."

"But she didn't divorce him."

"No."

"And he treated her badly?"

"I don't mean he beat her or anything. But he was a vile man, cold, manipulative, and I am absolutely certain she never had a happy day in her married life."

"I got that sense too, when she spoke, although she didn't put it into words. So you're insinuating she'd have reason to kill him. Do you think she polished him off?"

She said, "That's just wishful thinking on my part."

"Stop teasing me, Coco. Why not?"

"For one thing, she was in hospital having a hysterectomy. She was still in the recovery room when he died."

"That must be why there was no funeral or visitation," I said.

"It certainly allowed her an out. She wouldn't have had to pretend in front of his colleagues, who were probably glad he died too. I mean he wasn't like any other judge I ever met. Then there was his family. I don't think she got along with them."

"I read that he died of anaphylactic shock."

"Nuts. A long time allergy. He always carried an epi-pen."

"Let's just speculate. Do you think she could have arranged to leave the nuts at home before she went into the hospital? Maybe hid his epi-pen?" Of course, I wasn't sure how a joke would fit into this scenario.

"It didn't happen at home, though. He had gone out for a walk. I saw him leave at least forty-five minutes before they told me he died. He couldn't have eaten any nuts at that point, because he was fine. Not that he spoke to me or even acknowledged my presence."

"Did he forget his pen?"

"I heard that it was found by his hand and that it was working. A fluke, everyone said. I was just kidding about murder. If it was anyone else, I'd have thought what a terrible tragedy. But the world is better off without this man. Don't quote me."

"This is very nice wine." A non-sequitur for sure, but I wanted to get my head around this information.

"Well, it should be a nice wine," Coco said, without bothering to explain. "You still haven't told me why you're here."

I thought for a minute. Coco liked to talk and I didn't want this story spread all over town, at least until I understood it. Finally, I said, "Can you keep a secret?"

"No, not at all. That's why I had a career in the foreign service."

"All right, all right, it sounds like a dumb question." I filled her in on the jokes and the deaths that seemed to be connected, ending up with Judge Cardarelle's name.

She uncrossed her legs and sat forward, staring me right in the eyes. "I see why you wanted to talk to her."

"I thought I could develop a rapport and then sniff out if he'd received any jokes. Then maybe try to learn if there were people who hated him."

"Of course there were," Coco chuckled. "I hated him, and I hardly knew him. France definitely hated him."

"I'm wondering if he had any connection to Lloyd Brugel."

"The nasty creature who's on trial now?"

"The same."

Coco may be small and cute and sexy and glamorous, but she's also sharp. "So you think this Brugel is behind it?"

"There has to be a connection. He's a likely one. Heartless enough to play such a game. I hope it's him. And if it is, he may get away with it too. Who knows how many other people might get a joke."

"What do the police say?"

"The one I talked to from Major Crimes was delighted by the idea. I'm just trying to scrape together enough to get them to take it seriously."

She smiled at me. "I can call the chief if you like. I find him quite attractive, although awfully tall."

"What I'd appreciate even more is if you can find out if the Cardarelles received any jokes. Madame wouldn't have been around on that last day. I am sure that she would have been stunned when she got back home after major surgery, having lost her husband and all, but maybe she would have noticed a joke."

"I'm on the case," Coco said. "I feel guilty about not offering to do anything for France. I think I'll invite her for dinner tomorrow. Impromptu."

"Good neighbour," I said.

"Bad neighbour. Much too nosy." Coco raised her glass and twinkled.

SEVEN

How can you tell when a lawyer is lying?
-Her lips are moving.

It was just past ten when I snuggled into bed with Gussie and the cat and made my nightly call to Ray. The air had cooled enough to leave the windows open and the air conditioner off. Somehow that seemed like a luxury.

"I see you left several voice mails and also phoned a few more times without leaving any messages," I said.

"Just wanting to know how everything is going."

"Great," I said. "Just great."

"And the girls?"

"They got here in one piece. Well, two pieces, not including luggage."

"They're settled in?"

"For sure. They've been training all day and…" I realized I was light on Ashley and Brittany details. In fact, I had no idea if they were even back in the house. I heaved myself out of bed and padded along the hallway to the guest room, leaving a disgruntled dog and cat behind. In the guest quarters, clothing lay jumbled around on one side of the room and folded neatly on the other. I wondered which of the girls was like me and which was like my neat freak sisters. But it didn't matter because they weren't there.

"Can I talk to them?" Ray said.

"Ah, well, you could, but they're not back yet."

"Not back from where?"

"Training, I imagine."

"In the dark? Are you pulling my leg?"

"It hasn't been dark long, Ray. I imagine they're hanging around with the team after—" I wasn't really sure after what, but stopped myself in time.

"After what?"

"Are you fully present in this conversation, Ray?" Sometimes the best defence is a good offence.

"Nice play, Shakespeare. I know when you're stalling me."

"Fine. I don't know where they are. They're grown women. Aren't they both going to university in Halifax? Were you expecting me to shadow them?" I thumped back to bed and disturbed the menagerie once again.

"Just try to show a bit of interest. It's not just a matter of keeping them well-fed and giving them a place to sleep, you know."

Well-fed? That hadn't crossed my mind, although Alvin had cottoned on. It sounded like it was something that Ray took for granted. I was new to this whole *in loco parentis* gig, and there was more to it than I'd imagined. "I hear a note of exasperation in your voice, Ray. I find it very sexy. Don't snort. The thing is, the girls seem amazingly in charge and independent. And this is Ottawa, after all, not the fleshpots of—"

"Okay, you've made your point. They're my girls. I guess I want you to care about them too. I know we've had a lot of issues with them, but they're past that now. They've turned into..." His voice trailed off.

"Women. I hardly recognized them. All those muscles. And very expensive hair. Gorgeous highlights. But you know me, Ray. I have to ease into the situation."

"I do know you. And I guess it's too late to back out now."

"Very funny. No one's holding you captive." As the romantic moment seemed to have fizzled out, I decided I might as well bring up the subject of the jokes and get some advice from my favourite police officer. "Listen, I need to talk to you about—"

"The girls?"

"No. Nothing to do with the girls."

A long peal of laughter from the backyard made me sit up. I dislodged Gussie and the little cat yet again, hustled over to the window and peered out.

"Hang on, they're outside with Alvin, laughing their heads off. I imagine the neighbours will call in the police shortly, but in the meantime, before the bylaw officer shows up, I'll take my phone out to them."

So much for joke talk. I picked up the kitchen receiver on the way out so they could have equal access. After doing my bit for family solidarity, I stomped back to bed, nudging the zoo out of the way. I'd have to discuss the latest on this joke situation with Ray some other time.

*   *   *

In the morning, I noticed the message light on the phone base was flashing. Since I hadn't heard the phone ring, I concluded the call must have come in while Ray was talking to the girls. and they'd just let it go to message. That might also explain why I couldn't find the receivers for the phones. Both turned up outside on lawn chairs. Must be great to be young, I thought grumpily.

Coco Bentley sounded pleased with herself in her message. "I had an interesting talk about you with France Cardarelle. Didn't even have to have dinner," she said. "Call me when you get a chance. No rush. And in the meantime, don't be too surprised if you get a visit from her."

Of course there was no answer when I called her back. I figured we'd have an irritating game of telephone tag for the rest of the day. In the meantime, I had something to discuss with Alvin before I walked Gussie. The dog was as flatulent as ever. Even Mrs. Parnell's little cat had swished out of the room in the middle of the night, and Lester and Pierre looked like they were about to pitch off their perches.

Alvin did not respond well to my inquiry about feeding the girls.

"Of course I got food in for the girls," he snapped. "They're athletes in training. What do you think? I'm going to let them starve? Just because you're happy to eat all your meals in restaurants and never let a vitamin cross your lips doesn't mean that other people are. They'll be well looked after as long as Alvin Ferguson is around. You can pick up the costs."

"Put it up against my tab for taking care of your dog for more than four years. And walking him. Which reminds me, what have you been feeding him? He reeks."

Alvin ignored that. "Who's at the door?"

"I don't know, but as it's not even eight in the morning, it's no one I want to see. Oh wait, I hope it's not—"

Alvin stuck his head out of the kitchen. "It's that real estate lady. She's not as nice and smart as I thought she was. And why is she here so early every day?"

"Damned if I know, Alvin, but you're in charge. I have to walk this dog. He's disgusting. Do your best to discourage her. Show her your tattoo."

I grabbed Gussie's leash and a handful of doggie do bags, and the two of us made an escape out the back door, leaving Alvin to fend off Jacki Jewell.

"Let's go and make it snappy just this once, Gussie. I have stuff to do today," I said as we jumped the low fence.

Ten minutes later, it was obvious that Gussie had only understood the "let's go" part of that directive. We had sniffed our way down Third Avenue to O'Connor and then along to Second Avenue. With Gussie stopping every three feet, we'd worked our way south on Bank, past all the appealing shops, still closed, and over to Fourth. There was a lot to smell, I guess, on Fourth, including the tantalizing aroma of someone cooking bacon for breakfast. I was getting hungry by the time we got ourselves back along O'Connor to our street again.

"This is your last chance," I groused as we approached the house. Gussie slowed at the sound of that, although he did lift his leg to decorate a tire on a Volvo parked in front of our house.

"Sorry," I mouthed with a shrug to the driver. I did a double-take and glanced at the driver again. I stopped and stared.

The door of the Volvo slowly opened. Might even have been a scene from a movie if there had only been a bit of ominous music playing in the background.

Mme Cardarelle stepped out. She was casually dressed this time, in white pants and a black tunic. She had a red cardigan tied loosely around her neck and dark red leather sandals on her feet.

"I'd like to talk to you. I'm sorry if it's too early. I can't sleep since Robert died."

I wanted to talk to her too. "No problem. Gussie won't mind. Shall we walk a bit?"

She stared at me.

I said, "We can go inside if you'd prefer, but I warn you, you may encounter two rowing-obsessed teenaged girls and a truly frightening real estate agent. Plus the world's most annoying office assistant."

"Oh, yes, I think I may have spoken to him on the phone," she said. "Let's walk."

Gussie enjoyed this get-out-of-jail-free card and meandered a bit faster. He pulled on the leash, and I had to hold on to keep from being forced to gallop.

I had said nothing by the time we reached the end of the block. I had no idea why she was there, and I didn't want to spoil it by pushing for information too soon. She kept her gaze on Gussie as we walked, seemingly fascinated. Gussie in turn stopped pulling and sidled up to her, leaning in with that cuddly way that's quite appealing.

"Is he friendly?" she said with a hint of nervousness.

"Gussie has taken a shine to you," I said, "that's why you're being leaned on."

"Oh. I don't really know much about dogs. I never had one. My husband didn't believe in pets. I would have liked a dog. A small one, I think."

"Gussie's very affectionate, but no one's ever accused him of being small."

"I suppose not," she said.

"You can scratch his ears. That will make you popular." I did a demo, and Gussie, the ingrate, didn't so much as cast a glance my way. Madame Cardarelle got the big brown eyes treatment. Heartbreaking. Luckily she missed the gassy output that often accompanied such expressions.

With great concentration, the elegant and dignified judge's widow scratched behind Gussie's ear. Gussie gazed at her with adoration.

"Tell me," she said finally, turning back to me, "why you really came to see me."

"I wanted to learn something about your husband." A passing squirrel caught Gussie's attention, and I held tight to the leash.

"What did you want to learn?"

"I don't know. Anything. I felt grateful to him."

She stopped and turned to me. "That's not entirely true, is it?"

I dug in my heels to keep Gussie from dashing after the squirrel and admitted, "Not entirely."

She said, "I'm here because I had a talk with my neighbour, Coco Bentley. She said she knew you."

I managed to halt Gussie's progress, but only barely. "She does."

"She suggested that I should talk to you and be frank. She said that you are a good person and not as unfeeling as you look. And I should just tell you the truth."

Unfeeling? Look who was talking. But, whatever. "Good idea. I'm in if you are."

"So why did you come to see me?

Still excited by the squirrel, Gussie was definitely pulling me along. I used every bit of my strength to stop him. This wasn't a conversation I could have shouting over my shoulder. When Gussie was under control, I said, "Because I thought your husband might have been murdered."

She stumbled. I reached out and caught her arm. As she steadied herself, the colour drained from her face. The smart red cardigan now seemed harsh next to her suddenly grey skin. She whispered. "Murdered?"

"I'm sorry to shock you." I didn't say that I knew she wasn't grieving for this man. But of course, there's a major leap between not grieving for someone and not minding that they'd been murdered.

She steadied herself. "Why would you even imagine such a bizarre thing?"

"Because of a joke that was sent the day before he died. And a piece of paper that arrived the next day."

"I don't understand. What joke?"

"To tell the truth, I don't understand either. I thought perhaps you had received a joke. Or he had. I am sorry."

She shook her head, then stopped. Her eyes widened. "What was this joke?"

"I don't know."

"I may have seen a joke on a piece of paper in Robert's study. It didn't make any sense at the time."

I said, "Did he mention the joke to you?"

"No. He wouldn't have. He wasn't one for chatting even though it was the day before my surgery and I was apprehensive about it. Never mind, I just noticed it when I was bringing his tea."

"Another question: you took some trouble to find me this morning. Why?"

"I knew you weren't telling me the truth. Robert wouldn't have given a young lawyer the time of day. If you'd asked him for advice, he would probably have enjoyed refusing. Then my neighbour Coco Bentley had some comments that intrigued me, really. But what is your connection to this? Why would someone murder Robert? What does the joke mean?"

I looked her straight in the eye. "I don't know. I am receiving the same jokes. And the next day, I get a piece of paper with a person's name on it, Then I learn that person has died." Of course, this was secondhand from Bunny. "I don't know why anyone would send me those jokes or the names. Strangely enough, your husband was not the only person to be the subject of a joke."

"Other people got them too?"

"They did. Two others that I know of."

She said, "And did anything happen to those people?"

"They died."

Her hand shot to her throat. "How did they die?"

"A combination of murder and a so-called accident."

"My goodness. Who were they?"

"One was the lawyer for the Brugel case."

Her eyes widened. "I heard it on the news. I assumed it had to do with the terrible people he was defending. Robert made disparaging remarks about that lawyer."

"He wasn't alone in that. But there was also a joke and then a note with his name."

"What was his name?"

"Rollie Thorsten. Do you think your husband might have had dealings with him? A connection of some sort?"

She shook her head slowly. "Not if he was a criminal lawyer. Robert despised most of them. He despised criminals too. Didn't even like to look at them. Couldn't imagine that there would be anything of value in such a person. That's why he stuck to Federal Court."

"The third person that I know of was a real estate lawyer named Roxanne Terrio. Does that mean anything?"

She paused, thinking. "No. What happened to her?"

"She was struck by a car while cycling in Gatineau Park."

"But that would be an accident, no?"

"Hit and run, pretty ugly, I guess. She was left to die in a ditch by the side of the road."

"And there was a joke too? That is so horrible. I don't think I want to hear it."

"I don't blame you."

She shuddered. "I was shocked that Robert would die in such a way. But murdered? That's hard to believe. Although I have no idea how he could have ingested any nuts. He was fanatically careful about food."

I paused, wondering how to ask her about what he had eaten before his death, without referring to the autopsy. She saved me the trouble. "They said he had eaten some kind of sweet, a cookie or square. Perhaps two of them. There was no way to know how he got it. No one came forward to say that they'd offered him one. Of course, Robert wasn't one to take anything from strangers. The worst part is that he was found by a group of children."

"I'm sorry to ask this, but I have to know; how did you get along with your husband?"

A flicker crossed the beautiful face. "You can't think that I have anything to do with this?"

"I don't think that at all. But you knew I was lying to you. And I knew that you were not grief-stricken."

A long silence followed. Finally she said, "That's true. Robert was not an easy man to live with, not a loving man. Our only son died at eighteen. Perhaps that would have softened him, but he was never interested in me or my silly emotions. There was no room in his heart for anyone but himself."

"His family? Brothers, I believe?"

She gave a soft little laugh. "They were always in competition with each other. They didn't make any pretense of fondness. They'd each be pleased to have outlived him."

"You must have been married for a long time."

"Forty years."

"But in all that time—"

She cut me off. "In all that time, he lived his life and I stayed in the background. I was a convenience to him. That is all."

"I'm sorry to hear that."

"In the end, I did not love him, I do not grieve for him. I gave him forty years. They were not happy years. I had no way to get out of my marriage. I suppose I lacked the strength. Now I am looking forward to life again. That's a terrible thing to say, but it's true."

"If you think of anything that might have to do with the joke, will you contact me?"

"What sort of thing?"

I shrugged. "I don't know. A person delivering an envelope. A conversation he might have had. A connection with any of these people I mentioned that might turn up. Or a person who might have been angry with him over a judicial ruling, for instance."

"I will, and I'll think about it. I haven't been well enough to clear out his effects. The doctor says it could take up to three months to recover from my surgery. I am just able to drive now after six weeks. I can't really lift anything yet, but if I find something, I will certainly contact you immediately."

"Thank you."

"It must be very disturbing to be getting these jokes and names."

"It is. I am connected in some way, but I have no idea how or why. I am really worried that someone else will die. I have to figure out what's going on."

"And I understand why now that you've explained it. Robert was an intelligent, dignified man. The idea of someone killing him for a joke is astonishing."

"I think it must be some kind of savage bitterness, a desire for revenge."

She nodded, glanced away. "I suppose you must be right. But for Robert to die as a joke! How utterly meaningless is that? What does that say about the value of his life?"

I said. "Perhaps that's at the heart of this."

EIGHT

What's the difference between an accident and a calamity?
-It's an accident if a lawyer's car plunges off the
road into a river. It's a calamity if he can swim.

I had managed to put the girls and the ubiquitous Jacki
Jewell out of my mind, but I was still trying to fathom
the judge's widow as I pulled into the driveway of the small
neat end-unit townhouse on Parkview Circle, part of a
curvy townhouse development in Barrhaven. The grass
was clipped neatly, the door was freshly painted a high
gloss white, and the paving stones in the walkway had been
swept. Someone had been diligent in weeding between
the pavers. A child's bubble gum pink tricycle was visible
from the side gate. The rainbow streamers attached to the
handles made me smile.

As I rang the bell and waited, I noticed fat peonies
exploding into bloom in the small garden. They had
followed the French lilacs. There were only a few of those
left, although their scent was still working fine. The dead
blooms had been clipped. A clump of pom-pom hydrangeas
was coming along well.

Bunny opened the door furtively and checked quickly
to the right, then the left. He beckoned me in to the
immaculate little home, with its wonderful selection of
paintings on the walls, mostly local artists. I could only
hope they'd been purchased. I didn't look too closely in
case they hadn't been.

Bunny put his fingers to his lips. I stepped through the primly furnished living room and saw the reason. A small child, maybe three years old, was sleeping on the sofa. Her little face moved to reflect her dreams. A lock of fair hair hung over her closed eyes. I assumed they would be hazel. She held tight to a rag doll with kinky hot pink hair, green appliquéd eyelashes, and candy pink and purple striped legs.

I followed Bunny into the kitchen, where I sat at the gleaming glass-topped table. Bunny rustled up some coffee and Oreo cookies, and we carried on talking in whispers.

"That's Destiny," he said, pointing back toward the sleeping child.

"Lucky you. I guess I haven't seen you in a long time."

"Three years and a bit." Bunny chewed on his lower lip, something I remembered him doing when I used to visit him in the lockup. "I don't want to be involved in any weird crap. I don't know what they want from me, but I can't drag Tonya and Destiny into it. I have to keep them safe."

That made sense to me. I didn't want to get dragged into any weird crap either, and I didn't have to worry about a child and a spouse.

"If we can figure out what's going on, we can pass the information to the police and go back to doing whatever it is that we do."

"Not so easy, Camilla. How are we going to figure out what's going on?"

"Well, I've been checking around, doing some background work. I think we should do what the cops do. Start by interviewing each other. Taking statements."

He'd stopped chewing his lower lip and goggled at me like I'd lost my mind. He said, "I always hated that."

I said, "We can examine the evidence. Then we'll fan

out and see what we learn that adds to that. Maybe we can form a hypothesis or two. Test them."

"Those interviews with the cops, they always used to really shake me up."

I shrugged. "It's a classic way to proceed. You can't take it personally."

"I did take it personally. Same thing at school with exams. I was really lousy at school. Dyslexic. You know that."

"I know that's made things tough for you. But you have to get past it." I was remembering the time Bunny had gotten his mitts on the security code for a sprawling hacienda on Island Park Drive and strolled through the door with his eye on a couple of paintings by Henri Masson. He'd had a hankering for them, and they'd probably be displayed on the townhouse walls today except that he'd reversed two of the numbers. It had been a close call, but Bunny was outside by the time the cops came by. On the upside, the Massons were still hanging on the walls of their rightful owner. On the down side, Bunny had been carrying burglar tools and no cop would ever mistake him for one of the residents of Island Park Drive.

Despite the best efforts of Ottawa's finest, the Crown couldn't see much sense moving forward on that, especially as some of the Provincial Court judges had a soft spot for Bunny. "Those were the good old days." He grinned his crooked grin when I reminded him. That special grin made you want to buy him an ice cream cone, read him a bedtime story, and tell him not to worry about a thing.

The good old days indeed. Bunny's years as the beautiful burglar, the times when witnesses blushed purple and stammered at the sight of him and in the end most of them couldn't really remember having seen him at all. Best of all, Bunny never had any idea of the effect he had on people. He wouldn't have believed it if someone had pointed it out. I'd got a kick out of those cases even though I am officially opposed to burglary.

The door banged, and a small voice from the living room squealed, "Mommy!"

Tonya entered the kitchen with Destiny, her hair still damp from sleep, clinging to her side. Tonya was tall, tanned and toned. Motherhood hadn't hurt her figure any. From the blonde highlights in her hair to her salon tan, she was as glamorous as any hair stylist whose business requires impressing her clientele.

Tonya glanced at me and raised a perfectly sculpted eyebrow. It reminded me that my sisters would get on my case if I didn't get myself spruced up by the time they got back with my father for our annual Canada Day party.

I nodded.

She opened the fridge, fished out a box of juice, and settled Destiny back in the living room with a TV cartoon. She leaned against the door frame and said, "What do you think is going on?"

I said, "I have no idea. But we'll find out."

"Is someone out to get Bunny?"

I shrugged.

Her eyes misted up. "I can't stand it. Do you think someone's trying to frame him?"

I sloshed my coffee. "Frame him? For what?"

"For these killings. If that's what they are. He'd never make it in prison. Look at him."

"Prison? He's not going to prison, Tonya." Bunny had survived a brutal childhood and a hellish life in school.

He'd probably survive prison too, but I didn't want him to have to any more than Tonya did.

"Tonya thinks someone's setting me up. Sending me the notes so I'll know ahead of time that that person was killed. Then I'll give myself away when the police haul me in."

I said reasonably, "But the police haven't hauled you in."

"Someone will make the connection." Tonya's toned arm muscles tensed.

"If Bunny doesn't tell anybody about it, how could anyone make the connection? I'm getting them too and I don't expect the police to haul me in."

"See, babe? Camilla knows these things. She was always my best lawyer."

"Bunny said you've retired."

Hang on. I'm barely past forty. Retired? "I just haven't been doing any criminal law work or legal aid since I set up Justice for Victims."

"Bunny said you've shut that down."

"It's in process."

Bunny flashed me a nervous glance. "Maybe Camilla can recommend someone else, babe."

"If you're in trouble, Bunny, for something you didn't do, or if someone is trying to frame you, I will be there for you."

"Of course, I didn't do it. I'm a burglar. I wouldn't even know how to kill someone, even if I wanted to."

Tonya balled her hands into fists and almost shrieked, "Bunny is not a murderer."

"I didn't mean to suggest he was."

Bunny got a thoughtful look on his face, "But you know, if my family was threatened, I'd have to do whatever I could."

"Your family's not threatened. If anyone asks, don't volunteer that little observation. In fact, don't say anything to anyone without me present."

"But you're not doing criminal work any more. You just said that."

"I think I just came out of retirement."

"Thank you," Tonya whispered.

Bunny just gave me his grateful little boy look.

"It would help if I could see the jokes."

"I told you they were gone, Camilla, that Tonya is very neat. You can probably tell that just by looking at our place." Bunny had a bead of sweat on his upper lip. "She just can't stand anything that's out of place. She hates clutter and junk."

Tonya said, "Well, I didn't know, did I?"

"It's not your fault, babe. How could you even imagine something like that? I didn't actually tell her, Camilla, because it sounded so crazy. I mean, jokes in the mail and then someone dies, who would believe it?"

"And why would it mean that I couldn't clean up, even if you did tell me, which you didn't," Tonya said with just a touch of defensiveness.

"That's right, babe," Bunny said.

She sniffed. "I can't live in a pigsty with paper all over the place. Don't ask me to do that, Bunny."

"No, no, babe, I'm not, I'm not. It was just a couple of papers and envelopes. I didn't think they'd upset you."

"Really? Then why did you hide them?"

I kept my face impassive. I knew that if Bunny had been a woman in an abusive relationship whose partner didn't let her keep anything private, I would have advised him differently. I wasn't sure what it meant here. Tonya had stood by Bunny through unemployment and sporadic arrests. He might have been my favourite client, but there was no way I could ever live with him. Maybe Tonya was more like a mother.

But how the hell would I know? I'd never even had a mother. And Bunny would have been better off without the toxic alcoholic mother who'd messed up his childhood.

He was biting his lower lip. I wondered if I should tell him later privately that he should adopt less submissive gestures.

I also asked myself if Tonya had picked up her thing with clutter at the same Obsessions and Compulsions R Us outlet that my sisters frequented. Those random papers wouldn't have lasted a New York minute at any of their houses either.

Eventually, I said, "You hid some of them, Bunny?"

Bunny nodded miserably. "Tonya found them. Roxanne and Rollie. She was mad, and she crumpled them up and put them in the garbage."

"I didn't want them in the house," Tonya said fiercely.

"I know, babe. You're right."

"I knew they were bad news. I work hard to keep it nice, to keep it clean, to keep it safe for Destiny." Her voice cracked.

Bunny started to speak, but I cut him off. "Why did you feel that way about the notes?"

She shot him a look. "Because of the way he hid them. Usually that's where he hides items he's fascinated with. Pictures of paintings. Clippings from the newspaper or magazines of some piece of art. Notices about exhibitions. You were his lawyer. You know his weaknesses."

"I do. Or I did. I hope he's reformed. But, anyway, these aren't artworks. They're just pieces of paper."

"But they had an impact on Bunny. He was sneaky about

them. I have always hated that."

Bunny said, "I'm sorry. I promise, it's nothing for us to worry about."

Time to get back to the topic at hand. "So if you get another joke, Bunny, don't touch it. Call me right away, and I'll come and get it. Tonya, you'll just have to give us time to do that. People's lives could be at stake."

Bunny followed me to the door to say goodbye. He looked over his shoulder and said, "I don't still have yesterday's joke, but this came today. I didn't want to say anything in front of her. She's very upset."

I stared at the envelope in his hand. "You didn't open it?"

"Camilla, we both know that whoever it is, it's too late for that person."

I said, "Get me a plastic sandwich bag."

He was back in a flash, and I slipped the envelope in the bag, trying to handle it as little as possible. As much as I wanted to see the contents, it wasn't worth destroying any evidence that might have been inside.

Bunny and I both shivered in the hot June sunlight. I dropped the bag with the envelope into my purse and headed for the car, wishing like hell I could really believe that Bunny and Tonya and Destiny had nothing to worry about. As I was also getting these bizarre jokes and notes, I would have been happier to think I had nothing to worry about either.

*   *   *

Ashley and Brittany were still practicing whatever mysterious things people in dragon boat races do. Don't ask me. Alvin was working on his cooking project, sifting through heritage recipes for fish chowder. Or possibly recipes for heritage fish chowder. Today would be test day.

I called Leonard Mombourquette and got his voice mail. I had no more success with his cellphone. I left messages about the envelope at both numbers and got on with things.

I didn't have much to go on with the killer joke business, so it was important that I follow up on what I had. The little I did know worried me plenty. Plus I was in desperate need of a bit of exercise. If I don't get in a forty-five minute walk every day, my clothes shrink. Luckily I lived in the Glebe, and I could walk to most places I wanted to go. At that moment, I wanted to go to Roxanne Terrio's office.

Half an hour later, I puffed up to an attractive vintage red brick house on MacLeod Street near Queen Elizabeth Drive. The large home had been turned into office suites. There was a brass plaque that said Terrio and Fox, Real Estate. The names Roxanne Terrio and Gary Fox were etched under that. The offices were on the first floor. The first thing I noticed was the scent of spicey pot pourri. The office looked comfortable and pleasant enough in a beigey kind of way. Of course, sharing space with Alvin for a very long time changes how you react to décor.

The woman at reception was in her early thirties. She wore her dark red hair pulled into a high curly ponytail and she sported a startling set of eyelashes. Must have cost her a bundle. Still, it was an effort well worth it, as they framed remarkable brown eyes. She looked up in surprise as I entered. Or maybe that was an effect of the eyelashes.

A small plaque on the desk said Beverly Leclair, Office Queen. "Hello," she said, still smiling.

I smiled back. Some people bring out the smiler in a

person. She was one of them.

"I'm Bev," she said. "Do you have an appointment?"

She knew perfectly well that I didn't and that it didn't matter much to her because she could help me. And she would. But we had to play the game.

"No, sorry, I don't. My name is Camilla MacPhee. I have just put my house on the market, and if my luck holds and it sells in the next while, I'll be needing a lawyer to handle the sale. I don't have anyone right at the moment. And I noticed Roxanne Terrio's name. I'd run into her a few times years back, so I thought I'd—"

She gasped and put her hand to her mouth.

"Something wrong?" I asked innocently.

"You haven't heard?"

"Haven't heard what?"

"She died."

"Died? Really? But she's not even—"

"About four weeks ago. It was an accident. She was on her bike."

"An accident? That's terrible. Was she hit by a car? I can't believe the way that city drivers treat cyclists."

"They said it was an accident, but she was so careful and fanatical about the rules of the road. About everything really, so I can't imagine how it could have been. The road was straight, and she always wore illumination, and she had good lights on her bike and special mirrors. She was riding on the parkway in Gatineau Park near Pink's Lake. They found her in a ditch, with…"

I waited while she pulled herself together. She blew her nose and wiped her eyes. "I heard all about safety concerns from her every single day."

"So what do you think happened?"

"The police seemed to think that an animal ran out in front of her or something, and she lost control and ended up in the ditch. Her neck was broken."

"And you don't believe that?"

She raised her chin. "She was too cautious. I really think that someone must have hit her and then driven off."

Of course, I already knew that Roxanne was dead, but this careful and fanatical element of her personality was news to me. I thought there was a little subtext in Bev's comments about Roxanne. Even so, I wasn't supposed to know anything about Roxanne's death. "I'm stunned. Do you mind if I sit down?"

"Sorry. I shouldn't have blurted it out like that. Did you say you and Roxanne were friends?"

"Um, no."

Bev said, "You look like you've had a shock. Can I get you a cup of herbal tea? I have camomile."

I was taken aback to hear that I looked like I'd had a shock, since I hadn't been in the least bit surprised. My sisters are always insisting that I wear a bit of make-up. I was glad none of them were in the office to hear this. I can't stand camomile tea, but it would allow me to stay there and pump the cheerful and competent Bev Leclair for information about Roxanne.

"I'd love one," I said.

Bev got up and moved to a refreshment station close by.

"I just made it two minutes ago."

"Nice."

"We live the high life here." She handed me a steaming mug and a napkin and said, "So not really friends with Roxanne?"

"More like colleagues."

She headed back to her post behind the desk, wheeled out her ergonomic chair and gestured for me to try the two-seater sofa. "I wondered because I always kept up her Rolodex, and I just transferred everything to her online files and added a lot of business cards, and I'm sorry, but I don't recall your name."

"I don't think we ever even exchanged business cards. I'm not sure if she would have remembered my name. They were just casual encounters. I was at law school a few years after she was."

"Law school?"

"Yes."

She turned to stare at me. "But if you went to law school yourself, why do you need a lawyer?"

"I did criminal law. Thugs and robbers, for my sins. Never had the touch for contracts. In fact, that side of things was almost my undoing. Fell asleep over the small print." I grinned because it was a pleasure not to have to make something up for once.

"Oh. Well, I'm glad I don't have to cope with you around here. It's bad enough dealing with the ones who did choose their living in contract law."

I needed to get back to the main topic. "Poor Roxanne. She was so young to die. What a tragedy for her family too."

Bev pursed her lips. "She didn't actually have any close family. I suppose that's a blessing. It would have been horrible for them, not ever knowing what happened to her."

"Her friends then. They would have been devastated."

She bit her lip.

"Sorry," I added. "Did I say something wrong?"

"Well, you couldn't know, could you?"

"Know what?"

"Well, I probably shouldn't say this, but Roxanne was the only person I ever met who didn't seem to have a single friend."

"Really? When I met her at whatever event years ago, she seemed pleasant enough, socializing with people, chatting."

"Perhaps something happened to her over the years. She didn't go to meetings or networking events any more. She wasn't the warmest person. I don't think she had anyone but us, I suppose, and Moxi."

Ah right, the chihuahua.

I said, "Moxi? A boyfriend?"

"A spoiled rotten little pooch."

"Oh boy, but if she didn't have any family or friends, what happened to the dog?"

A man's voice came from the door to the office behind me. "It's spending its days here in the office, temporarily."

I looked up to see a man with prematurely grey hair and a gentle smile. A small dog danced around his feet. I wondered if he had been standing there quietly thoughout our conversation. "I know all about that kind of thing," I said. "My temporary dog has been with me for years, and his owners are still very much alive."

He said, "Oh, I don't think that will happen. Bev just needs to find a home for Moxi. She doesn't want him to go to the pound."

"Does he stay here at night?" I had learned from Gussie that dogs need their cuddle time.

"He comes home with me," Bev admitted. "My boyfriend's not that keen on the situation, but I hope we can work it out. Poor Moxi."

I was proud of myself that I didn't say, "Get yourself a new boyfriend."

"I should point out that I also have a cat that's been visiting for five years, and more recently some birds that are apparently just passing through."

Bev said to the grey-haired man, "Gary, this lady knew Roxanne and thought she could handle her house sale, so it was a big shock for her to find out what happened."

Of course, he had to be Gary Fox. He said, "For us too. One day the cops just showed up at the door."

"Here? Oh, because she didn't have anyone."

Bev shivered. "Gary went to identify her. I would have had hysterics, someone you worked with so closely. I couldn't stand it."

"Been there," I said.

He nodded. "It's hard to explain to someone who hasn't. The saddest thing was there was no one closer. Her parents died a few years back, one after the other, heart attacks in both cases. There's a brother somewhere out west, but they were estranged."

"That's sad."

"Yes, it is," Bev said. "It's a reminder to put some energy into relationships that are not always easy."

That sounded like a reprieve for the dog-resenting boyfriend.

I thought about my sisters and how I often wished they lived out west or even further away, so they'd stop their relentless age-old campaign to change everything about me into their own tall, blonde, neat, homemaking images. Still, I knew they'd make a real deal out of my funeral if it came down to that.

Bev said, "But anyway, maybe Gary can handle your real

estate transaction. He's great. And I'm first-rate too, in case you're wondering." She grinned. I figured this was not a woman to dwell in despair.

I said. "Sounds good. I'll give you a call when the house sells. Do you have a card?"

"Don't feel pressured," Gary said anxiously. "You came looking for Roxanne, and you don't have to get stuck with me. I'm a big boy."

Bev said, "Sure, he has a card, and you will love dealing with him." She stood up and slipped a business card into my hand.

I glanced at the card and said, "I'm glad not to have to hunt around for someone else. We lawyers have to stick together. Everyone's always dumping on us."

"They are?" Gary said.

I was pretty sure I heard Bev snicker.

I said, "Are you kidding? People even send anonymous lawyer jokes in the mail. Nasty ones too."

He frowned, scratched his head. "They do?"

"Yes, and I'm getting sick of it. Totally uncalled for. You mean that never happens to you?"

He shook his head. "No. I've never received one. I don't know that I'd worry much about it if I did get one."

Bev said thoughtfully, "People do send them."

I said, "Did Roxanne ever get them?"

Bev said, "She did get one, actually. Not long before she died. She tossed it in the trash."

Gary agreed. "And I bet she said, 'what a loser.'"

Bev chuckled sadly. "You got it."

I put in my two cents worth. "Well, that's the right attitude. My office assistant reads them out loud. Lucky me."

Gary snorted.

Bev insisted. "I would never do that. What kind of assistant is he?"

"You wouldn't believe," I said. "So for sure, these jokes got thrown right out? You didn't keep any of them?"

"I only saw one."

"Another thing," I said. "By any chance did Roxanne get an envelope with her name typed on a blank sheet of paper after the joke came in? That's happened to me, and I have to tell you, it kind of creeps me out."

Bev was looking at me differently now.

I sipped my cooling camomile and waited.

Gary said, "That is creepy."

"She did," Bev said reluctantly. "The mail arrived after she left the office that last day."

Gary said, "Crazy world. Some people have too much time on their hands. Nice to meet you, Camilla. I'm sorry you had to find out about Roxanne's death in this way."

I said, "Thanks for the information, Bev. I'll give you a call if and when the house sells. Probably when. We have Jacki Jewell on the case."

Gary rolled his eyes. "Jacki Jewell? She's easy to look at and hard on the nerves."

"No kidding," I said.

"Bev doesn't mind Jacki, but that woman sure gives me a hard time whenever I deal with her which is all too often, because she can really unload properties. All to say, I'd be glad to have your business if you stick with her long enough to sell the house."

"Stay tuned," I said.

Gary waved, but Bev watched me closely as I left. The smile on her lips wasn't nearly as warm and natural as it had been. I was pretty sure she was on to my little tricks.

125

NINE

It's so cold today that the lawyers
have their hands in their own pockets.

I felt a chill as I stepped from the cheerful office. The temperature must have dropped about ten degrees without warning. It looked like rain too. I found myself shivering in the damp air and contemplating what to do next. With Bev's take on Roxanne's death confirming my fears, I knew it was time to go back to the police and to convince them. Best to start with Mombourquette, even though he hadn't returned my calls.

I hurried back home to get something warm and waterproof before heading to the cop shop. I checked the mailbox for a sign of an envelope. Empty. That was good. I checked the hall console which is the agreed upon place for the mail. Nada. I checked the kitchen table. Pristine. I trotted up the stairs and found Alvin on all fours in my bedroom. "I'm installing plug-in air fresheners in every room. I've three for this room, because of the Gussie factor. I hope it's enough. They had a great special at Home Hardware, so I cleaned them out of Sea Breeze," he said.

"Jokes, Alvin," I said, not wishing to be sidetracked by air fresheners. "Did we get a joke yesterday?"

"Um. What?"

"Don't make me repeat myself."

"I've been busy, you know, because of the girls and the real estate person and all that and some of the mail got buried under a magazine and then Gussie chewed it up. There's so much going on here it makes it hard for me to think clearly. And I may be losing my home, so that's weighing on my mind too."

"I take it that's a yes. And where's what's left of it now?"

"Recycle bin," Alvin said, looking aggrieved.

"And did we get a piece of paper today? With a name on it?"

"Lord thundering Jesus, Camilla. Do you ever stop bugging people?"

I massaged my temple. "Did we get an envelope today?

Of course, I'd already spotted the white rectangle sticking out of his skinny jeans pocket. "Don't have to have a hissy over every little thing," he sniped as he handed it over.

"I see that you opened it."

"Gussie chewed up the envelope. I wanted to see what was on the note. Didn't mean anything to me."

Let it go, I told myself. Just let it go.

Since it was open, I checked the name.

It didn't mean anything to me either.

*   *   *

I fished the chewed up envelope out of the recycling bin and used tweezers to put it and the envelope and the sheet of paper with the name on it into a resealable plastic bag. I drove over to police headquarters on Elgin Street, not my favourite place in the world. I found a place to park on Catherine Street and dragged myself over to the front door and into the vast open foyer. At the reception desk, I squared my shoulders and asked for Leonard Mombourquette. If I didn't connect with him, I was going to have to break in some other detective.

127

"Is he here today, or is he out mousing around?" I said pleasantly. No one smiled. There seemed to be a dark undercurrent around the station. Maybe it was my imagination. To reiterate: not my favourite place.

Minutes later, I had been accompanied through the doors into the bowels of the building and up to Major Crimes, currently lurking on the second floor. I figured there must have been some kind of budget cutbacks coming, because everyone had a sombre expression. Constable Kristen Wentzell lumbered by still in her vest, her startling blue eyes tinged by red. What was that about? Late nights in the bar scene? Had P. J. managed to lure her into a date? At his desk, Mombourquette stared at me without smiling. He crossed his arms in front of him.

"Cat got your tongue?" I said.

"Not in the mood today, MacPhee. What do you want?"

"Touchy touchy. I want to talk to you about what is going on. I need you to take these jokes seriously."

"I have two minutes."

"Fine, I've got plenty to do myself. I know it sounds hokey, but there's something really horrible going on. It's not just my imagination. I told you before, I'm getting these jokes, lawyer jokes, and they seem to be tied to people getting killed."

"Don't fucking waste my time."

"Please, language, Leonard. Inappropriate in a man your age."

Mombourquette got up and slammed his filing cabinet drawer shut. My mouth hung open. He can be peevish, even belligerent, but this was a different side of him. What was going on? Pressure of retirement? Whatever. I decided to ignore the drawer slamming and continue. "The problem arises from the fact that the next day a piece of paper arrives with the name of a person. I'm not sure I made that fully clear before."

"You're not making it fully clear now."

"All right. I guess it is pretty bizarre. The thing is that the person whose name is on the paper has just died, by accident in two cases and obviously murder in the third. As far as I can tell, this paper arrives before anyone knows about the death. It seems to be announcing it, I believe, although I don't know why it would be announced to me." I didn't mention Bunny.

"Did you get a joke today?"

"Yesterday. It's here in this plastic bag. Unfortunately, Gussie chewed up the joke as well as both envelopes, so there's probably not much to be learned from—"

He scowled and interrupted. "And did you get a piece of paper today?"

I handed the bag to him. "Maybe you shouldn't open it. Maybe there's some—"

"Don't piss me off," he said.

"Don't want to do that," I said, "and I don't know this person."

"And what person is that?"

"Someone named Steve Anstruther."

That's when all hell broke loose.

*   *   *

"Do you really believe that if I didn't know who Steve Anstruther was when I came in here, somehow I'd find out because you're yelling at me?"

I was still repeating that line of thought an hour later,

only this time in an interrogation room. The detective who had been questioning me had decided to depart. Mombourquette remained, pacing. For the first time ever, he made me nervous.

"I didn't see the joke arrive. I doubt if Alvin saw it arrive either, but you can ask him. I don't know anything. I haven't been able to figure out what's going on. What the hell is the matter with you, Leonard? You can't possibly think I have anything to do with any of this."

His nose twitched. "What is the matter with me? What is the matter with you? You waltz in here with the name of a cop on a piece of paper the same day that cop ends up in intensive care fighting for his life, and you don't think anyone here's going to be upset?"

I was still feeling the knot in my stomach from learning that Steve Anstruther was a police colleague, and I was guessing a popular one.

"Of course you're angry, but why are you turning it on me? I didn't put your friend in the ICU. I'm being used to send a message, I guess."

"What kind of message?"

"Hard to tell."

"Who's sending this message?"

"I don't know that either. How many other ways can I make that point?"

Mombourquette's chin whiskers quivered. "Why don't you try making some kind of a point that might be useful to me?"

"Okay. Here's one. I have rights, and if you are going to keep me here and treat me like a suspect rather than a citizen who is doing her best to help, then I'm going to have legal representation."

"Oh, sure. Get lawyered up."

"That's the idea."

"Why's that? Feeling guilty?"

"You can shelve that old technique. That won't wash with me, Leonard. I've seen too many people get into trouble because they fell for it. I'll make my phone call now."

"Innocent people don't have to worry, MacPhee."

"Give me a break. Tell that line to Marshall. Or Milgaard. Or Guy-Paul Morin."

Mombourquette snorted.

I said, "Or any of the people who found themselves behind bars because of Dr. Charles Smith. I repeat, if you are going to hold me for questioning, I want a lawyer."

"That could work against you."

"Be that as it may. I came to you, Leonard, with this piece of information. It's not the first time that I tried to get you to pay attention to the jokes. You know that. You just laughed before."

"I'm not laughing now."

"And I was never laughing. I'm not responsible for whatever's going on either. I didn't know anything about Steve Anstruther. I certainly didn't know he was a cop until you and your colleagues wigged out."

"Someone's responsible. And they seem to have some connection with you."

"I'm pretty sure you're right about that, although I hate to admit it. Why else would I be getting this stuff?"

"You sure you never heard of Steve?"

"Well, I don't think so. It's a fairly uncommon name. I didn't recognize it. If I'd known why everyone was so upset, do you really think I would have broken it to you that way?"

He turned away and shrugged.

I said, "What happened to him anyway?"

"I ask the questions."

"What do you think this is? A prime time cop drama?" Mombourquette scowled.

I said, "Attempted suicide?"

"No! Where did that come from?"

"Just guessing because you won't answer me."

"Yeah, well, you're sitting in an interrogation room. Do you think I'm going to give you information?" Mombourquette headed for the door. I hoped he was planning to give me back my cellphone.

"Fine. I'll wait and get it on the news. I don't understand why I received a lawyer joke and then the guy turns out to be a cop. It doesn't makes sense to me. The other two were lawyers or in Judge Cardarelle's case a former lawyer."

Mombourquette paused, his hand on the door. He turned and stared at me. "He's been accepted to law school. U of O. He was supposed to start this fall. Just got married too."

"Do they think he'll make it?"

"They don't know. He's in a coma. And if he does, who's to say he'll be all there."

"I'm sorry about your friend, Leonard. I want you to know that. But what happened to him?"

Mombourquette finally relented. "He was heading home to the east end last night. His car went off the road at the foot of the cliff on the eastern parkway around midnight last night, and he ended up in the river."

"And it looked like another accident."

He nodded. "They're checking out the car now. Looks like he might have fallen asleep, although he was a real careful guy."

I said, "You know, except for Rollie, someone has gone to a lot of trouble to stage these so-called accidents."

He raised an eyebrow at me. "If another car hit him or forced him off the road, there will be paint traces on his vehicle. We won't miss those if they're there."

I said, "Did you notice that with Rollie, the whole thing seemed to be set up for obvious drama? But this is dramatic too."

Mombourquette nodded slowly.

I said, "But they're sending the jokes and names to me to ensure that I realize that even the ones that look like accidents are not. And if they know anything about me, they'll be aware I'll try to find out what's going on and even talk to you. So I just don't get it. It's like a taunt."

"Take it again from the top," Mombourquette said. "There has to be something."

I ran through everything I knew once more with feeling, including my short-lived suspicions about Annalisa Fillmore. I admitted that I hadn't felt any great grief about Rollie or sadness about Judge Cardarelle. The world might be fine without them, but Roxanne Terrio seemed a sad story to me and now, so now did Steve Anstruther. I said as much to Mombourquette.

Whether or not it was a wise decision, I still left out the part about Bunny Mayhew.

"Did this Anstruther guy have any connection to Brugel?" I said as we finished up.

Mombourquette's eyes told me that he did. He kept his mouth firmly closed though.

I said, "I know Brugel's behind it. I could see him thinking this joke thing was funny. He's quite capable of directing this vicious farce from the Regional Detention Centre. You know it too. The thing is to find out how Anstruther fits in."

*　　*　　*

I was relieved to get away from Police Headquarters. It was still nippy, but the June sunshine seemed reassuringly bright and the threatening clouds had scurried off. I pulled out my cellphone and called Mrs. Parnell first. She was more than willing to pursue the latest line of investigation I requested. A photo of a Constable Steve Anstruther would be very handy for me indeed.

"This small task will be the best medicine possible, Ms MacPhee," she said. "A person could die of boredom lying around waiting for short-lived social opportunities. I have found a few more items for you that might help."

"Great. I'll swing by later."

P. J. Lynch didn't answer his phone, but I left a message suggesting it would be worth his while to give me a call at the first possible opportunity.

*　　*　　*

What I needed was a wonderful endless soak in the tub to get the interrogation room germs off my body while I had a long soothing chat with Ray, a chat that didn't include anything remotely connected with lawyer jokes, suspicious accidents, ratty detectives or Lloyd Brugel. Our chats always took place later in the evening and anyway, Alvin had other plans. What Alvin wants, Alvin gets. And Alvin wanted to see the girls practicing. "I'm not really in the mood for this, Alvin. I've been interrogated by the police today."

"Then you need something to take your mind off that."

I thought about it. Of course, Ray would want to talk about his girls, so the conversation would go better if I got this chore out of the way. As we insinuated the car into the traffic and proceeded to the nicely scenic Colonel By Drive, I ignored the driver who gave me the finger. I was thinking about Ray. I wished I could bond with these girls of his. What the hell was wrong with me? Sure, they'd gone out of their way to sabotage our relationship and caused several calamities in the process, but was that the only problem? They'd been teenagers, still missing their mother and anxious not to lose their father to a stranger. I could relate to that. I'd been a particularly obnoxious teenager myself. Maybe it was because we had nothing in common but Ray. On the other hand, maybe that would have to be enough.

Alvin was chattering, and I was attempting to tune him out. "Did you know that the dragon boat tradition is more than two thousand years old?" he said.

"It kind of snuck up on me," I answered, hoping to stem a stream of factoids.

"Blah blah…as a fertility rite to avert misfortune and bring rain by worshipping the dragon."

I smothered a yawn. He prattled away about teams from across the country, funds raised and how the races were conducted. I tried not to fall asleep at the wheel as we drove out to Mooney's Bay and the Rideau Canoe Club.

"At least pretend to be interested," Alvin said as we approached the parking lot.

"Don't push your luck," I said as we got out of the car. A gentle wind ruffled my hair. Things were warming up again. The night was perfect, the water was luminous. I found myself glad to be there. Not a soak in the tub, but good all the same. We ambled down and were able to get a glimpse of the team practicing.

The team was fast and furious. I was astounded. I didn't

realize that they sat on the boats that way, practically kneeling. The whole thing looked like a lot of work to me.

I said, "I guess it's like a sport."

Alvin sniffed. "It is a sport. Ashley might even be good enough to make the Olympic team. That's what they're hoping."

"There's Olympic dragon boat racing? Are you kidding me?"

"She's into rowing. She's on the university team. She's got a sports scholarship and Brittany has a shot at one too."

"Really?"

"I can't believe Ray didn't mention it."

Of course, Ray would have mentioned that. It was more likely that my brain had done a big LALALA when he did. My good angel mentioned to my bad angel that it was high time I started to pay more attention. Ray loved the girls, and I loved Ray, and I'd just have to get used to it. In the meantime, until I found a way to like them, there was no choice but to fake it.

Alvin yelled encouragement to the team. I wasn't sure they wanted anything to take their mind off whatever they were trying to achieve. But I echoed his yell and waved. Part of the new me. I was pretty sure Ashley waved back. Or maybe it was Brittany. Alvin had arranged to hang out with the team afterwards. He said they'd find their way home. That left me free to meddle.

*   *   *

P. J. returned my call, and I took advantage of the timing to arrange a meeting. I suggested The Works in the Glebe at eight, but P. J. claimed to have pressing business at that time.

"I can squeeze you in now," he said.

"It's my exercise time, so if you want to join me on a stroll, that'll be all right."

"A stroll? You mean like a walk?"

"Much like a walk, in fact. It's a beautiful night. Cool. The humidity's cleared." There was a pause on the line. I added, "And today I didn't get in my full walking quota."

"So," he said. "What is it you want?"

"I'll tell you when we're on the move. I'll meet you on the canal near the new bridge from the university. I think there's a bench you can lounge on if it takes me a while to get there. I'm heading out now."

P. J. is more of a restaurant booth and car kind of guy, but he was waiting on a bench as I puffed up from the Glebe on the Queen Elizabeth side of the canal.

We settled on crossing on the new Corktown bridge over the canal and headed down the Colonel By side bike path to Pretoria Bridge, then back to P. J.'s bench headquarters. A good walk from my point of view, made better by the scent of fresh cut grass. What's more, even if he wanted to quit on me, he'd have no choice but to keep going.

"Keep an eye out for speeding cyclists and rollerbladers," I said. "Whatever you do, don't drift from your path without warning."

"Can you slow down a bit?" he puffed.

"Time for you to get in shape, my lad."

"I think you wanted something from me. No killing the goose that laid the golden egg and all that."

I refrained from saying that P. J. had yet to deliver any golden eggs, although one could always hope. Instead, I said, "Another joke came in. And another name."

"You're kidding."

"May I add, it's not funny in the least."

"Who was it this time? I can think of a few people who are kind of asking for it."

"A fairly young officer called Steve Anstruther. A detective constable, I think, but I'm not sure about that."

"Steve Anstruther, you said?"

"Yes. Know anything about him? Gossip, people on the periphery of a case?"

P. J. nodded. "He could have been in court or been a court escort or made a minor arrest, anything like that, and it would never be written up. His name does sound familiar. It's not a typical name."

"I'm pretty sure I've never heard it, and I followed all the Brugel stuff. We really need to find a Brugel connection."

"I've got to file a story by ten," P. J. said. "And didn't I follow up on Annalisa Fillmore based on your suggestion? And that was a wild goose chase, so forgive me if I don't want to waste a lot more time on any of your hare-brained ideas. No offence, Tiger."

"None taken," I said, trying to get as close to a purr as I could. "It would be tragic if the day-to-day minutiae and this uncalled for bitterness of yours got in the way of breaking a story connecting Brugel and these deaths."

"You're not exactly subtle," P. J. said.

"Not trying to be. Keep me posted, and I'll let you know what I find out."

"I'll give it some thought, but that's all I can say."

"The thing is I have Mrs. Parnell checking for links between Brugel and each of the victims. She'd be just as effective as you would be on the print and digital front, but you're in a better position to find out who Brugel is connected with in the local sleaze community, who could be hired to cause these deaths. Stuff that would never make it into print."

"Thugs, I imagine."

"I'm not so sure. The jokes are well-presented, nicely printed out on good quality paper. The names as well. Someone has a sense of style."

P. J.'s face puckered in thought. I sure hope he never tries his luck at poker.

I said, "And they'd have to look respectable or non-threatening. Roxanne Terrio was very conscious of her safety. She wouldn't let just anyone get close. Somehow this person must not have appeared to be any kind of a threat. Same thing with the judge. He was a cold and snobbish person. And suspicious, I think. So how did he come to eat a nut-laced cookie in a lonely spot?"

P. J. seemed to be still busy thinking. "Rollie Thorsten wouldn't notice anything. He made his living from the underbelly of society."

"But maybe even Rollie wasn't foolish enough to go off on a boat with someone who might do him harm. So he mustn't have been too worried about whoever it was."

"Then there's the cop, Anstruther. Cops are used to crooks," P. J. said.

"Uh-huh. Ever see a police officer in a restaurant? Back to the wall. Or scanning the room. They're wary. But someone took him by surprise in his car. Whoever it is, it's someone nobody would worry about. And that someone, somehow, goes back to Brugel."

"It would be one helluva story, if you're right. Still not convinced Brugel's behind it."

"Fine. But it's worth considering. This is one story that would be above the fold."

"Can't argue with that. I'll dig around a bit to see who might be associated with Brugel, but who might appear to be pretty tame and harmless and not obviously criminal."

"Great. Stay in touch. We can brainstorm."

By the time we got back to the bench, P. J. decided he would never walk again. I left him panting, and I hoofed it on home.

*　*　*

"They interrogated you?" Ray said. "I can't believe they interrogated you. You're just pulling my leg, Camilla."

I was lounging in the bathtub and enjoying his consternation. Ray's calls and his reactions were two of the reasons I enjoyed the midnight hour. "Well, they did."

"Why haven't you filled me in on this before? It's not like I couldn't help you."

"I'm sure I mentioned the jokes before. I hardly knew whether it made any sense or not at the time. I didn't know if it wasn't just a figment of someone's imagination, but then today kind of proved it wasn't."

I chose not to bring Bunny into the equation as Ray isn't that crazy about burglars.

"I'm going to give Lennie a call anyway, just to get his take on the situation," he said.

"You know what? They're all pretty wrecked because of this young colleague."

"You know what, Camilla?"

"What?"

"Two points. One: when you say, you know what, you are almost always about to tell me a whopper of some sort or divert me from something that I shouldn't be diverted from, and two: if this joker is out there and involving you, then you need some kind of protection, and since I'm not there, I'm going to make damn sure that Lennie takes care of that."

"But—"

"Don't bother arguing. I am fully aware that you've left out some key information. I don't need to know what it is to realize that you've done it."

"Come on, Ray."

"Just don't insult my intelligence, Camilla, although I know that's fun for you. My gut tells me you're protecting someone who may or may not need protecting and that you are as usual needling the local cops for the hell of it. I can accept all these things, but I don't have to take them lying down."

"Are you lying down?" I said, attempting to get the conversation into a more interesting track that wouldn't involve Leonard Mombourquette or me giving Bunny up to the cops.

"Are you?" he said after a pause.

"I am, as a matter of fact, and if you weren't, you will be when I tell you that Alvin and I went to see the girls practice for the race. It was beyond awesome."

"Beyond awesome?"

Oops. I'd overdone it again.

"Well, interesting," I amended.

"Hey, that's great. So, tell me, what was their time?"

Aw, crap. Of course, I hadn't really understood anything at all about it, and Ray wouldn't take long to figure that out. "No technical questions, Ray. But I was really impressed."

"Camilla?"

"What?"

"Promise me you'll never change."

TEN

You're trapped in a room with a tiger, a rattlesnake and a lawyer. Your gun has two bullets. What should you do?
-Shoot the lawyer. Twice.

I opened my eyes to find Gussie gazing soulfully into them. "Not now," I said. "It's too early."

Was it my imagination that Gussie seemed to be staring at the clock? The clock in turn suggested it might be eight o'clock. I tumbled out of bed, dislodging Mrs. Parnell's cat in a pile of sheets.

Ten minutes later, I'd had the world's fastest shower, uncovered Lester and Pierre and changed their food and water, fed Gussie, and slipped the cat some tuna as a way of making amends.

Gussie and I arrived breathless at the dog park. I plunked myself down on a bench and started on the large dark roast coffee I'd picked up at Francesco's. The cooler weather had carried over, and at least this morning, it was still pleasant enough to drink coffee without dropping ice cubes into it. Gussie joined in with a gang of gangly fuzzy dogs like himself. They romped and barked merrily, and I sipped and thought about bad jokes and deadly jokes, deceased lawyers and cops in the ICU.

As I took the first sip, I spotted Madame France Cardarelle. She was unleashing a smallish silky dog with delicate features. The dog hobbled off and stood shyly gazing at the gangly crowd before choosing a King Charles spaniel and a pair of miniature dachshunds to hang out with.

Mme Cardarelle waved and approached me. She was the only person in the dog park dressed in a crisp white shirt and tailored charcoal pants with a snazzy leather belt. I found myself waving back. She sat on the bench beside me. "Coffee," she said, "what a good idea. I'll do that the next time too."

"What kind of pooch is that?" I asked, pointing at the new arrival.

"Her name is Lulu," she said, smiling. "What they call a mix, I believe. Mostly Pekinese, they told me."

I paused here. What I really wanted to know was why Mme Cardarelle, who had no pets, was walking a dog early in the morning in a dog park that was nowhere near her home. I'm not that subtle at the best of times and not at all in the mornings. "Are you walking her for a neighbour?" I asked.

A smile lit up her face. "I am walking her because she is mine."

"Yours?"

"Yes. Imagine. My own little dog. I saw her in the paper. She was advertized by the SPCA of Western Quebec. I read the description, and I saw her beautiful little picture, and I fell in love with her. Those silky ears! I think the person who does those write-ups must have the soul of a poet."

"So you drove over to see her?"

"And I took her home with me the same day. She is eight years old, and that made it hard for her to be adopted. People don't value old dogs. Or old ladies for that matter. I thought we'd be perfect for each other."

"That's great," I said. "She looks like a nice pet, although if you don't mind me saying, you don't strike me as an old lady. Anyway, in my own experience, many people do value old ladies. They are full of surprises."

She said, "Lulu is the first pet I've ever had in sixty-five years. Like me, she was in a cage, just wanting to be out and to love and be loved. Your assistant told me that you usually take Gussie here in the morning. I was hoping to introduce you to Lulu."

"I was wondering, because you don't live nearby," I said.

"I thought about our conversation the other day and the possibility that someone killed my husband for a joke as you suggested."

I nodded. "Not a good way to go."

Across the field, Lulu trotted along with the others, not gamboling like the larger ones, but getting the idea that this was a good safe place.

"You pointed out that I wasn't grief-stricken. That was true. In fact, I'm not sorry that he's dead. It's opened a door for me to enjoy life and be happy with myself."

She kept an eye on her new pet as she spoke. "I didn't hate Robert. They say that the opposite of love isn't hate, it's indifference. He had always been indifferent to others, to their needs and their feelings. Although I loved him at one time, I believe you could say I had become indifferent to him."

"Do you have any idea who might have hated him?"

"It must have been someone he met through his work."

"Did he talk about his work? Any case that he worried about? A plaintiff? A defendant?"

She laughed. "Robert wasn't fearful. He saw himself as right and as unassailable, on almost every issue. It didn't endear him to people, but he didn't believe in wasting time on worry. And of course, as I said, he just didn't care."

"What about friends or family?"

"There wasn't a tear when he died, Camilla. Do you mind if I call you Camilla? At any rate, no one seemed in the least bit upset. He didn't have any friends that I knew of."

I was pushing my luck when I said, "You could have left him. You would have split the assets. I am sure you would have been all right financially and much better off emotionally."

She shook her head. The beautiful bob swayed. "Robert was a man who enjoyed exercising power. I suppose I could have left, but he would have made me pay in some unexpected way. He was not a man to be crossed. So I stayed. From the outside, it may have looked as though I had a wonderful life, but it was anything but that."

"Thank you for being candid with me. Even so, I am sorry to have brought the jokes to your attention. He was your husband, after all."

She stood up and brushed off the back of her tailored slacks. "Don't worry about it. I'm glad I met you and Gussie. Perhaps it was unintentional, but you have given me a way to move on. And little Lulu too. I am grateful. If you hadn't been here this morning, I would have rung your doorbell to tell you that."

I said. "In that case, you should consider yourself lucky that you didn't meet the cat and the birds too."

As Gussie and I strolled home, I decided I wasn't going to let too much more time pass before I moved forward too. This time with the very amiable Ray Deveau.

I chewed over what Madame Cardarelle had said about her life and marriage. This was yet another aspect of this case in which nothing was what it seemed. What else was there to know about the late unlamented judge?

I stuck my nose into the Pub at the Perley before heading up to Mrs. Parnell's room, even though it wasn't even ten in the morning. I wouldn't have put it beyond her powers of persuasion to have convinced the administration to modify the opening hours using her "The sun is over the yardarm somewhere in the world" argument. Apparently this hadn't happened yet. I kept going and found her cheerfully seated in the armchair in her room.

"Ms MacPhee," she trumpeted. "Just in time. I've printed out some information for you. Judge Cardarelle and Roxanne Terrio are considered to be accidents. Of course, it's straightforward murder with this Thorsten fellow. And now as you say, there's this young policeman in critical condition. There's nothing much on that yet, except for a Facebook group that some of his family members and friends have set up. Seems to be a young man who is loved and admired. I was able to get some photos of him as a result. They're in your package."

"That's the opposite of Judge Cardarelle. It sounds as though he was feared and loathed pretty much everywhere."

"And Ms Terrio? What do you know of her?"

"Somewhere in between. Kept to herself, but pleasant enough to people she worked with. No friends other than work and estranged from her only sibling."

She nodded. "That's the sort of information that doesn't appear in print."

I picked up the thick wad of paper and flipped through it. Printouts of newspaper stories, mostly. I knew Mrs. Parnell would be nothing but thorough. I said, "The manner of their deaths is quite different. If it weren't for the jokes, I'd say they have nothing in common."

"Were they graduates of the same law school?"

"The judge and Roxanne went to University of Ottawa, same as me. But Rollie went to school out west somewhere."

"Ah well. What do the police think?"

"They don't think. Or if they do, they don't tell me."

Mrs. Parnell glowered. "They should. Don't they know that wars are won or lost based on the choice of allies?"

"That's my view too. What about connections between these names and Brugel?"

"Of course. Why do you think that package is so thick?"

I had to grin at that. "Spare me the suspense, Mrs. P."

"Several connections, one a passing reference. It seems that Roxanne Terrio represented Brugel nearly twenty years back. Were you aware of that?" She took the package back from me and flipped through it until she found the right printout.

I took the package back and said, "I wasn't. She must have been fresh out of law school then. I didn't know she ever did criminal work. Paul and I were admitted to the bar fourteen years ago, and she was a few years ahead of us."

"As far as I can tell, he was convicted for aggravated assault in that trial."

I glanced over the article and raised an eyebrow. "Looks that way."

"I was surprised to read that someone like that would still receive a suspended sentence, even back then," Mrs. Parnell said. "Aggravated assault is a very serious change. You would think he'd be locked up."

"You would. But that was early days for Brugel too. I imagine the judge had no idea he was sentencing a man who would later become one of the worst that Ottawa has to offer. I've heard that he got into trouble as a juvenile too, but that information would never be allowed into the record. Those files are sealed."

"This young lawyer might have had some idea of what kind of person her client really was." Mrs. Parnell pursed her lips in speculation. "Perhaps it put her off being a defence lawyer."

"It would have put me off."

"Do you think, Ms MacPhee, that Roxanne Terrio went into real estate law to avoid dealing with people like this Brugel?"

"Maybe she did. But if that was her reasoning, it sure wasn't enough of a strategy to keep her from..." My head jerked at a familiar name buried at the tail end of the story.

"Something wrong, Ms MacPhee? You look as though something has shocked you."

"No kidding. I saw a name I wasn't expecting."

"Who?"

"None other than our own Sgt. Leonard Mombourquette."

Mrs. Parnell shook her head in consternation. "How did I miss that?"

"Easy enough. I almost missed it myself. He was Detective Constable Mombourquette back then. He testified at that trial. Roxanne Terrio cross-examined him. So, what do you think about that?"

*   *   *

The Ferguson family's cross-legged dog had just managed to get some relief when I heard the whoop of a siren behind me. An unmarked dark sedan with a cherry flasher had pulled up onto the sidewalk. It stopped, and the passenger door opened. I stuck my head in and waved my nasty-looking and pungent plastic bag in the direction of the driver.

"Hello, Leonard. I see you got my detailed message." I opened the back door to let Gussie in before I slid into front passenger seat.

"Don't even think about bringing that thing in the car."

I hopped out and deposited the bag in the nearest garbage can. Gussie took advantage of the moment to scramble from the back seat to join Mombourquette in the front. That didn't last long. When I got back, Gussie was sprawled over the back seat, and Mombourquette was fuming in the front. Perhaps that's why he pulled back out into traffic apparently without a glance, causing a screech of brakes behind us. Mombourquette used to be a good driver. I decided that Elaine must be a bad influence on him. Or else my message had made him nervous.

The guy in the SUV who'd screeched his brakes now laid on his horn and upped the ante by showing us a good view of his upraised middle finger, a mistake as it turned out. On went the siren. The SUV pulled over, and Mombourquette got out, tail twitching.

I smiled. I planned to enjoy the entertainment portion of the encounter. It hadn't been a great day, so I felt entitled. Five minutes later, he returned in all his soft, grey glory. He pulled away without incident this time, leaving the driver of the SUV behind, routed and shaken. More fun than television, in my opinion.

Mombourquette was quiet as he drove.

I watched and waited. He had that watchfulness that so often predicts trouble. By the time we hit the lights at First Avenue, I caved.

"So, Leonard. What can you tell me?"

He turned his beady eyes on me. "What part of leave this to us would be unclear, MacPhee? Do you want to be interrogated again?"

"Before we go down that path, Leonard, as I said in my message, is there any reason you never mentioned that you were acquainted with Roxanne Terrio? Especially the part where you knew she had defended Brugel in the past—because she would have cross-examined you."

Mombourquette has a genius for turning things around to suit his most rodential purposes. "Something just occurred to me, MacPhee. Does this obsession of yours have anything to do with that tame break-in artist you keep around? He was hanging around the courthouse the day they found Rollie's body. And whenever he's in the picture, there seems to be a batch of trouble brewing."

I did not want Mombourquette connecting Bunny to the jokes or the murders. He'd love to haul Bunny in for questioning on general principles. Of course, I should have counted on his detective's instincts. Now I tried for a bit of damage control. "First of all, I do not keep a tame break-in artist around. And that's not fair to Bunny. You're wrong about him, Leonard. He doesn't break in to anything any more. He has a wife and child and a good life. Those are three good reasons for him to go straight. He's even moved to a location where he doesn't enounter any of the old bad influences."

"I didn't hear anything about a job."

"He's a stay-at-home dad, and he does some part-time work in a framing shop. That's a job in itself. I told you he has a pre-schooler to look after."

"You are such a sucker, MacPhee. So keep this in mind. If I find out that he's put any kind of a foot wrong, or that he knows anything about Roxanne Terrio that hasn't been shared with the police, then—"

"Hang on. Speaking of not sharing, you keep telling me that Roxanne Terrio's death was an accident. Tragic, but no evidence of foul play at all. Although you distinctly failed to mention that you knew her. So stop trying to sidetrack me with Bunny talk and tell me what's going on."

Leonard gunned it at the intersection and swerved past a Jeep that was taking a broad view of what constituted a red light.

I said, "Fine, I'll talk about it then. You know she got a joke."

For once Leonard stared straight ahead. "I made it clear that this joke thing is for the birds. And the official finding is that Roxanne Terrio's death was accidental."

Leonard made an abrupt left turn and shot down Third Avenue. He angled the cruiser in front of the driveway of my fussy and officious next door neighbour.

So call a cop, I thought.

Mombourquette turned off the engine. "We were an item for a while. It was a long time ago, and it didn't last, but she was someone I cared about."

It took a minute to get my head around that.

"Okay," I said after a while. "So did Roxanne have a problem with Brugel after his trial? He got a suspended sentence. Maybe he held her responsible for not getting him off?"

"He made her nervous. She was afraid of him. And, if you must know, I think that's why she went out with me. Because I was a cop, and she thought I'd keep her safe, but it wasn't enough to ease her mind."

I decided to push the envelope. "Did you check out the place where she died?"

Of course he had.

Another little push. "Do you want to show me?"

*   *   *

Mombourquette said nothing as he drove over the Portage Bridge to the Quebec side of the Ottawa River. I love crossing the river and don't do it nearly enough, so I gazed at the scenery while Mombourquette glowered at the wheel and exceeded the speed limit. We headed out through Hull and up toward Gatineau Park. Fifteen minutes later, we were gliding along a wonderful wide parkway fringed by deciduous trees and thick evergreens. Cars were few and far between, although Lycra-clad cyclists laboured up the rolling foothills.

"It's around here somewhere. Goddam trees all look alike," Mombourquette muttered as he peered out the side window. "Give me the city any time."

"Watch the road," I said.

"Feel like a hike?" he said, pulling over, getting out of the car and stretching.

"Sure."

Gussie felt like a hike too. As we set off along the roadside, a few cyclists passed us, some older people off for a gentle spin, others in colourful gear playing out their Tour de France fantasies.

Mombourquette could have done with a bit more quality time in the gym, if his laboured breathing was anything to go by. I didn't think he was a smoker, but he sure wasn't a mover either. We hadn't gone far when he stopped at the side of the road. He pointed out a small makeshift memorial marker, the kind you see at the site of road accidents. A

152

wooden cross was stuck in the ground, some fresh flowers suspended from it.

A stuffed teddy bear leaned against the white cross.

I scratched my head. "She died here?"

He turned and glowered at me. I swear he showed his pointy little teeth. Whatever had happened with Roxanne Terrio, it had gotten under his skin for sure. Despite that, I knew he hadn't constructed that small memorial. Whatever you can say about Mombourquette, and don't get me started, he is a fine and elegant gardener. He would have done a better job than this.

I said, "What's wrong now?"

"What's the matter with you, MacPhee? Is everything some kind of weird riddle to you?"

I thought about that. Was everything some kind of weird riddle to me? I took my time formulating a response. Whatever I answered, Mombourquette would just take it the wrong way.

"It's a beautiful place," I said. "What a shame."

"Yeah. Anything else?"

I glanced at him. What did he want from me? No point in asking. He gets like this sometimes. And it's not like we're the best of friends. "To me, seems like a funny place for an accident."

"Why is that?"

I swivelled around, taking in the lush growth, the wide road, the shallow ditch.

"The parkway is straight here. There is no curve, so no other unexpected cyclist or pedestrian would be appearing as you round a corner. The speed limit is forty kilometres an hour."

He agreed.

"Flat grassy shoulder, nice and wide."

"Yup."

"So if you had to get off the road in a hurry, you'd either keep going until you could stop or you'd land on the grass. A lot softer than the asphalt, so it's highly unlikely that she died dodging a dog or a knot of joggers, because there would be plenty of room for everyone."

He glared at the grass.

"And," I said, "I guess it would make a difference that the road itself is in good shape here. No pot holes, gouges, nothing to destabilize a bike. So what happened?"

"Goddamned if I know," Mombourquette said.

"I suppose there are unpredictable elements, stuff you can't prepare for. A child could run out, and you'd have to swerve. Leaves on the ground making it slippery. Was it raining that night?"

"Day. It was in broad daylight. She'd never do anything as risky as riding her bike here in the night. Look around you. This is a place for the day. And no, it wasn't raining. Calm, sunny."

"What did the witnesses say?"

"Well, that's the thing, MacPhee. There weren't any witnesses, were there?"

"There weren't?"

"None."

"There's always lots of traffic around here. In the spring, people are itching to get out on their bikes. Or just to walk. You can see today how many people have passed us, dozens and dozens. On a Saturday, with good weather, there might be five times this many people. Like a highway."

"Did I say it was a Saturday?"

I blinked. "No. I just assumed."

154

"You should know where assumptions get you."

Good point. I'd forgotten she'd received a joke at the office. "I should indeed. But she had a legal practice, so I figured the bicycle was either transportation or recreational weekend stuff."

"She often went for a ride in the day. The office wasn't really that far from here. You saw it just took us twenty minutes by car. She had a bike rack, she'd park her car and do a loop, I guess."

That was enough information for me to know that Mombourquette had stayed in touch with Roxanne Terrio. Interesting and possibly weird.

He shrugged. "I guess it only took a second for her to fall over. People came by right afterwards, but by the time they called 911 and the paramedics got here, it was too late."

I paused. Weighed my words, because you never knew with Mombourquette. "I'm sorry, Leonard."

He turned his head to stare down at the sad little memorial. "Yeah."

I gave him a bit of space for a couple of minutes until he jerked his head as if to say "get moving, I haven't got all day."

On the slow walk back, I said, "Hard to believe her helmet wouldn't have prevented that."

Mombourquette said, "She wasn't wearing her helmet."

"Oh. I just… But I thought she was so careful."

"She was. But this time she left it in her car."

"So why did she leave without it?"

"I don't know."

"Do you think the jokes have something to do with it?"

"That's the thing, MacPhee. Until you told me, that was the first I'd heard about Roxanne receiving a joke."

I nodded. "Have you asked yourself why?"

He hunched his shoulders and kicked at some pebbles at the side of the road. "What the hell do you think? I'm a detective, not a busybody like you. I know how important 'why' is. I've asked myself over and over. You're right. Roxanne wasn't the type to get into any trouble. She wasn't the type to take a chance. She was lousy in criminal defence because of it."

"She was supposed to be obsessed with safety. Do you know why?"

"In recent years, she was just a bit afraid of life."

"But she rode up here on her own without a helmet that day."

"Yes. I told you that. You don't have to repeat everything I say as if you're giving me a news flash."

I took a deep breath. "Fair enough. But in the end, her fears were proved right. She did have reason to be afraid. As did the other people who died or almost died after receiving these jokes."

Mombourquette's nose twitched.

I said, "We should really try to figure out what they had in common."

"I've been working on that, MacPhee, being a detective and all. But I'll be damned if I can see what Roxanne had in common with that crooked lawyer Rollie Thorstein. She hadn't been a criminal lawyer for years, and as I said, clearly, she was never any good at it."

"What about Judge Cardarelle?"

"He was supposed to be as mean as the day is long. Roxanne was kind and self-effacing if a bit socially awkward."

"And Steve Anstruther? He seems a totally different type again."

"He is."

"How is he doing?"

"Still in a coma. Anyway, aside from the fact that Rollie and Roxanne both represented Brugel at one time, none of these people had anything in common."

"There has to be a connection with the other two and Lloyd Brugel."

Mombourquette said, "By the way, Roxanne was a long time before I became involved Elaine. I want you to know that."

"Of course. It goes without saying. Well, back to our connections. There's going to be something. Surely you can find that out, Leonard, being a detective and all. Check out the judge and Anstruther. Even me, since I'm getting the jokes. Of course, my connection with Brugel is fairly obvious. Laurie Roulay. I made sure he got burned by her."

I didn't mention Bunny, as no good would have come of getting Mombourquette hot under the collar about him. As a peace-keeping gesture, I said, "And I won't mention anything to Elaine. You know that."

I guess that did the trick because Mombourquette said, "Steve Anstruther was on the task force that took Brugel down."

"Thanks."

"I don't know anything relevant about the judge."

*   *   *

Gussie and I were deposited at home first. Mombourquette pulled in and blocked the neighbour's driveway. Sometimes I think it must be terrific fun to be a cop. Eventually, Mombourquette headed back to the Elgin Street station to continue brooding and to do whatever you do when you have less than a month to work in Major Crimes and some serious crap to deal with.

"It will take me a week to air out this car after that dog," he said as I opened the door.

"Forget about the dog, just don't forget about Brugel and the judge, Leonard."

Mombourquette pulled away from the curb, just as my imperious neighbour descended from her designer front porch about to give him whatfor. He never noticed her, which meant a waste of dramatic and accusatory finger-pointing on her part.

Oh, well.

I grinned and headed into the house. By some small miracle, no one was home. No Alvin, no girls, no real estate agents. Just me, the stinky dog, the calico cat and the noisy birds.

Bliss.

I made a pot of coffee and sat at the stylish little kitchen table with a pad of paper. I wrote in stream of consciousness the names of every person who I knew to be even peripherally connected to the recent deaths or the people who had died, or in Anstruther's case been critically injured.

The victims were on one list. Their nearest and dearest on another. Bev Leclair was on the list. As were Tonya, Alvin, Madame Cardarelle and a dozen or so others. One name reminded me of a line I'd been meaning to pursue.

Jamie Kilpatrick. A man who was very afraid of something.

You can't fault the telephone book as a source of information: in this case, Kilpatricks. The same goes for maps. I had the old phone book because Alvin insists on having the latest for his "work". Mrs. Parnell just uses the internet. What can I say?

I found five Kilpatricks in Ottawa. One on Bruyère, J. Kilpatrick, that would be lawyer boy. One in Orleans and one on Island Park. Not likely. Of the others, one was on Carling and the other off Lees Avenue. I just had to check out if any of these addresses featured a small house with a large spreading maple. The same one I'd noticed in the framed photo of Kilpatrick's grandparents in his office.

I had plenty to do to keep me busy. I waited until dark, then fished out a dark baseball cap that Ray had left behind on a visit and a dark long-sleeved T-shirt and black chinos. Naturally, my socks and running shoes were black too. I turned off the back porch light and slipped out into the backyard.

TEN

*It shall be unlawful to shout "whiplash", "ambulance",
or "free single malt scotch" for the purpose
of trapping unwary lawyers in the wild.*

Paranoid? Sure, but it had finally crossed my mind that if someone was not only killing off innocent people, but also delivering envelopes to my home without getting caught, then that someone could be watching the house too. I might not have known much about what was going on, but I knew that whoever was behind this was dangerous.

And may I point out that just because you are pananoid doesn't mean that Lloyd Brugel might not have an interest in you. After all, I had been receiving these jokes too.

I hadn't seen any lowlifes lurking around my place, nor had I spotted anyone who seemed to be watching. But then again, nothing would have surprised me after the weird events that had been happening.

I managed to haul myself over my back neighbour's rickety fence and whipped through that yard and along the driveway to Fourth Avenue. Two minutes later, I was on Bank Street walking north. It wasn't long before I was able to flag a cab. The taxi dropped me off at Mrs. Parnell's apartment. I checked out her apartment as usual, only this time I picked up the little folder with her vehicle registration and insurance and went straight to the parking garage.

Mrs. P. had upgraded her vehicle again, and the Altima slid out the door like a pat of melting butter. The Carling area was fairly close, and I chose that first. I drove along the street looking for the first Kilpatrick address. The house seemed right, one of the many one-and-a-half-storey homes built for veterans after World War II, but there wasn't a mature tree anywhere near it. Next I checked the Island Park address, not expecting that house to pay off. And it didn't.

I made a U-turn and headed for the Queensway, the quickest route to Lees Avenue and the Ottawa East address. Five minutes later, I turned on to Beechnut and pulled over. The street had several such post-war houses, some now with second storeys added, but most of the street had kept its character.

Bingo. I was sure that I was looking at the same house as in the photo, the same massive tree towering over it, no doubt shading it, although at this time of night who could tell. Best of all, a Kilpatrick was listed at that address.

I got out of the car and glanced around.

"Here, Rover," I said. "Where are you, boy?"

I moved along the sidewalk, checking in front of cars and behind bushes. I whistled and called Rover again. Surreptitiously, I checked inside the cars for signs of anyone who could be associated with Brugel. I knew that they didn't need to watch a person every minute to pose an effective threat. Every now and then would be enough, something dramatic. I wondered what they'd suggested that had terrified James Kilpatrick.

"Rover!" I inserted a bit of irritation into my voice. There were no lights on in the house. A FOR SALE sign stood at an angle on the uncut lawn. For sure, Jacki Jewell wasn't their agent. Had they gone into hiding?

"You better show up, Rover, or you're toast."

At that moment, a giant dog leapt at me. I fell back on

the lawn, and the dog licked my face.

"You're not Rover, and you're not fooling me," I said, while attempting to push the dog away.

"I'm so sorry," a woman's voice said. "Sultan! Off!" She had a pronounced British accent and was dressed entirely in Tilley wear as far as I could tell.

Eventually Sultan bounded off, and I struggled to my feet. "Definitely not Rover. But big, a hundred pounds anyway."

"One twenty," she said. "Bernese mountain dog."

"Huh." I brushed the dust off my pants. "I was looking for my dog, but he won't come. I guess he'll show up."

"Maybe he's gone over to the dog park in back of St. Paul's. That's where Sultan goes when he manages to slip from his lead. Unless he's just happy to knock people off their pins."

"I don't come to this neighbourhood very often," I said. "But I remember the Kilpatricks used to live here. Do you know them?"

"Oh," she said.

"Oh?"

"I suppose you haven't heard."

I wanted to scream "out with it" but I said, "I haven't heard anything about them for years. My parents know them."

"I'm so sorry to tell you this, but they're dead."

"Dead? Really? Both of them?"

She nodded sombrely.

I said, "Well, that's a shame. My father will be quite upset."

"It was an awful way to go."

"What do you mean? I haven't seen anything about it in the papers lately."

"Well, of course, it was quite a while ago. A year and a half."

"What happened?"

"They were coming home from church. There was a Christmas concert. The *Messiah*, I think. A drunk driver ran them down."

I chose not to let my mind go down the drunk driver path. I kept my focus. "I'm sorry. Were they killed?"

"Yes." She gave me a look like I wasn't all there, which I suppose I wasn't. I must have had some kind of unacceptable expression on my face.

"Mrs. Kilpatrick was in the passenger seat. I think she was killed instantly. Her husband never got over it, and a month later he was dead too. It would have been their sixtieth anniversary on the day he died."

I glanced at the house and shook my head.

She had begun to take stock of me, I saw her eyes flick from the dark jacket to the dark pants and back to the baseball cap. Not at all right for a pleasant June evening like this.

"Thank you," I said. "I am sorry to hear this. Good evening." I tried to look normal, but I had a feeling that ship had sailed. I pretended briefly to continue my hunt for the mythical Rover. I could feel the woman's eyes on my back as I turned the corner, shouting "Rover" once more for good luck.

* * *

Mrs. Parnell never sleeps. It's one of the things I love about her. I got back into the car as soon as the woman with the Bernese mountain dog disappeared, and I could stop pretending to be looking for my non-existent dog.

"On the double, Ms MacPhee," she said when I called

and asked her to check on the Kilpatricks' accident.

"Thanks, can you call me as soon as you find out anything?"

"I could email it to young Ferguson if there's too much to convey by telephone. If you don't mind waiting, I can see what I can discover with a quick search."

I ended the call and had just turned the key in the ignition when I was treated to the flash of rooflights and the whoop of a siren.

"Good evening, officer," I said. "What can I do for you?"

"License and registration, ma'am," the officer said.

"Any particular reason?" I asked.

"We have a report of a person of your description engaged in suspicious activity, ma'am."

"Really? And what exactly would a person of my description be? Out of curiosity, officer."

"Dark clothing, dark baseball cap shielding face. Engaged in the pretence of searching for a dog."

I refrained from asking him where they learned to talk in that alien way. I didn't feel like ending up at the station again.

"No law against looking for a dog," I mentioned.

"How about loitering with intent?" he said.

"Ah. But I didn't have intent, officer. Clearly."

"Not yet it isn't clear, ma'am. License and registration, please."

He was actually pretty polite, if a bit wordy. I fished in my pocket for my wallet, pulled it out and extracted my driver's license. "This may be an embarrassing moment for me," I said. I opened the glove compartment and pulled out Mrs. Parnell's registration and insurance packet. "This is actually my friend's car, but I have borrowed it to do some errands."

"That so?" he said.

"Yes."

"You just stay put, ma'am, and I'll check this out."

"Go right ahead. It's not stolen, if that's what you're thinking. I can give you the owner's telephone number." Of course, he was out of hearing by then. I imagined he was waiting for me to make a break for it so he could have an exciting arrest or even activate his Taser. I used the time to call Mombourquette at home. Of course, he wasn't at home, but I had better luck when I tried Elaine's number.

"I have half a mind to let them drag you in," he said.

"But that would be a travesty of justice, Leonard. Plays badly in the media, harassing citizens for sport."

The officer began his slow swagger back to the car, and said, "I need you to step out of the car, ma'am."

"Sure thing," I said. "And I need you to talk to Sgt. Leonard Mombourquette of Major Crimes."

"You first, ma'am."

That whole thing would have gone better if Mombourquette had had the basic decency to stay on the line.

*   *   *

"That all sounds very embarrassing. Uncomfortable too. Of course, you can avoid incidents like that by not dressing up as a break-in artist and setting off the neighbourhood watchers," Mombourquette said with a typical twitch of his whiskers as we walked out of police headquarters a very considerable time later.

"Thank you, Ann Landers," I said as we headed down Elgin Street.

The June night was warm and once again humid. Elgin

165

Street, just a few short blocks from the station, hummed with people, music and action. We dodged college boys walking three abreast, without regard to us old folks making our slow way along the sidewalk. Knowing Mombourquette the way I did, I wondered if those foolish kids realized the close call they'd just had. Of course, he had me in his sights at that particular moment.

"You can thank me, MacPhee, because I took time away from Elaine to come down here and explain that you are not a criminal, even though you do a pretty good imitation of one. Lucky they didn't keep you in."

"Last time I looked it wasn't against the law to walk on a city street. And I already thanked you for coming in, maybe even twice, although it did take you long enough. And, by the way, when you say Elaine, would that be the same Elaine who is not supposed to have Roxanne Terrio mentioned to her?"

"Don't push that one too far, MacPhee."

"Let's find a place to sit down and we can talk freely." I headed into Fresco's. A couple who had been seated at a table in front of the large windows open to the street rose to leave at just that moment. I like window seats. I always enjoy watching the crowds on Elgin and I often see former clients. A trip down memory lane so to speak. I scored the table. Mombourquette made that right with the hostess.

Mombourquette got his mitts on two menus, squeezed into his chair and said, "Now that we're out of earshot, do you want to tell me what you were doing there?"

"Where?"

"Now that's just annoying, MacPhee."

"You don't believe I was looking for my dog?"

"The dog that's been home all night with your office

assistant? The one that's not called Rover?"

"You followed up on me, Leonard? For shame. You really should learn to trust people more."

He bristled. "People have been murdered. Do you think that's a joke?"

"I don't actually. In fact, I am taking it much more seriously than you are. And I was checking something out."

"I'm waiting."

"Okay, you remember the young lawyer assisting Rollie Thorsten?"

Mombourquette slapped the menu on the table. "Don't drag this out, okay?"

Our server arrived, and I ordered a diet cola, because I still had to get back, pick up Mrs. Parnell's car and return it. Mombourquette had an Upper Canada Pale Ale.

"Get on with it," Mombourquette said when the server left.

"He has withdrawn from the defence, although he's the only person who really knows whatever final arguments and appeal strategies Thorsten was cooking up. I'm guessing he did all the work. It would have been a great chance to make a name for himself."

"He couldn't really pull off a trial like that alone."

"Agreed, but he could have taken it to one of the other local stalwarts. Eisenberg or McCarrol, to name just two."

"And he didn't. Get to the point."

"I figure Brugel wants yet another delay so he can frighten off any remaining witnesses, so he orchestrated it. This kid's scared shitless. He was so nervous that he was dropping papers on the floor when I was talking to him."

"You can have that effect," Mombourquette muttered.

"Anyway, I figured his grandparents had been threatened.

There was a picture of them, and there was something about the expression on his face when I noticed it."

Mombourquette rolled his eyes. "And they tell me that cops go off on tangents without evidence."

"I just wanted to get a look. See whether anyone was watching the house or if they seemed to be vulnerable."

"That was just plain dumb."

"I can see that now. Especially since the grandparents have been dead for more than a year."

"Oh. So you misunderstood the look on his face. Jumping to conclusions. Why am I not surprised?"

"I wasn't just jumping. I was pushed. I think Jamie Kilpatrick wanted me to think that."

"Hey, I'm glad that mind-reading hobby you took up is working out well for you, MacPhee."

"Cute. He deliberately misled me in a very subtle way. And I'd like to know why that was. Although I have a theory."

I glanced out the window at that moment and did a double-take. Was that Ashley and Brittany with a couple of lads? Indeed it was, their heads were thrown back in laughter. A good time was being had by all.

"What the hell is it now, MacPhee?"

"It's—" Before I could say another word, Ashley happened to look my way, although it may have been Brittany. She elbowed her sister in the ribs, and they both turned and stared at Mombourquette. The two girls whispered something to each other, although why anyone would feel the need to do anything but shout on Elgin Street on a summer evening was beyond me.

Belatedly, I waved. They gave a me a look that could have meant anything and moved along.

"Who was that?" Mombourquette said.

"Ray's kids. They hate me."

"I can't imagine why."

"And now apparently they hate you too, Leonard."

"Guilt by association. I must find myself some better associates."

"Do you think they'll be all right here? I'm sure Ray doesn't know they're partying on Elgin Street."

"Aren't they going to school in Halifax?"

"Yes."

"Halifax is a real party town. Ray must have come to grips with that by now."

"I'm not so sure. He thinks they're studying hard and training for the Olympics."

"MacPhee, give it a rest. Now back to this Fitzpatrick."

"Kilpatrick. Jamie Kilpatrick. I told you I think he misled me. He figured out that I thought he was afraid for his grandparents, and he decided to let me continue to think that."

"You complicate everything so much. Why the hell would this what's-his-name want to mess with your head?"

"My best guess? He knows something he shouldn't. What if he actually spotted Rollie in his car with some associate of Brugel's? Kilpatrick is smart enough to put two and two together, and he knows that if he says anything, he'll be next."

"These are all speculations on your part. Let *us* take care of it. If Brugel's threatening witnesses or even lawyers, we need to follow up. And as irritating as we in Major Crimes find you, we don't want to end up investigating your murder. We have too much work as it is."

"That's so sweet, Leonard. So you'll check out my idea about Kilpatrick?"

It was after midnight when I finally got home after returning Mrs. Parnell's car and waiting a ridiculously long time for a taxi. Alvin greeted me with enthusiasm for once. "Did you hear the one about the parrot and burglar?"

I held up my hand in the international symbol for "don't want to listen to a joke." I said, "Where are the girls?"

"Practice, I guess," he sniffed. "Tomorrow's the big day."

"It's after midnight, Alvin. If they're practicing, it's nothing to do with dragon boats. I saw them on Elgin Street."

He shrugged. "I think their teammates were going out for a drink after their session. So what? They're young. They can have fun. They asked me to go with them, but I wanted to drop in to see Violet at the Perley."

"I'll be glad when she's home again," I said, heading off for bed.

"I almost forgot. Ray called. A couple of times. And someone else too."

I ignored the throb in my temple. It had been a long day and I didn't want to lose my temper. "Who else called?"

"It's late. I can't remember the name. It'll come to me."

"Try to write down messages, Alvin," I said with admirable calm.

"Yeah, I did write it down. It's around somewhere. When I find it, I'll show it to you. Oh, it was that real estate woman. She wants to speak to you. She says it's urgent."

"Fend her off, Alvin, and I'll forgive your message-taking lapses." That was the best I could get out of that conversation. I didn't care. I didn't really feel like talking to anyone anyway. Except for Ray. I crawled into bed and pressed 1 on my phone. That was automatically set to call Ray.

"Hey," I said.

"You're late," he said.

"Well, you know."

"Did you have a nice evening?"

"No." Was there something funny in his voice? Maybe he was just tired. It was an hour later down there. This didn't seem like the best time to mention I'd spent another spell in the police station discussing my so-called loitering with intent.

"Anything interesting happen?"

"Not really. You?"

"Nope."

I decided to change the subject. "Our real estate agent is still trying to hound us. I don't know how to get rid of her. She keeps dropping in and leaving messages and getting Alvin in a flap."

"Did she do that while you were sitting in a bar with some guy?"

"What?"

"You heard me. You were seen."

I started to laugh. "Your kids ratted me out? That's hilarious. I wasn't going to spill the beans on them, and they call you and tell you this. I knew they didn't really like me. They're still trying to break us up after all these years."

"That's not the case. They—"

"Of course, I love it when you're jealous. For the record, I was having a soft drink with your cousin Leonard."

"At midnight in a bar?"

"Are you listening to me? Your cousin, Leonard? The least attractive man on the planet. No, better make that the—"

"Why?"

"Why what?"

"No games, Camilla."

"Fine. There may have been a small misunderstanding about my presence in a certain neighbourhood and Leonard may have had to stick up for me at the cop shop. Nothing serious, really. Then we went off to have a chat. Don't you feel silly now? Not that I don't appreciate it and feel flattered. I didn't squeal on your girls for partying with a crowd of drunken louts."

"Promise me that you are not going to get involved with anything dangerous," Ray said. "Let me hear you say it."

"Sure thing. But make sure you get jealous for no reason every now and then. It's good for my morale. I have a great big smile on my face. You should see it."

I wore that smile all night. I was lucky to have Ray. I might have been luckier if he hadn't lived so far away, but I couldn't think of anyone else I'd rather be with, even at a distance. With more luck, the girls would grow up, finish university and move to the States or even Europe. Maybe become astronauts. That was worth smiling about too.

At three o'clock, I woke up in the middle of a dream about Brugel. For some reason, in a serious betrayal by my subconscious mind, I found myself in court defending him against a brace of new charges. "I'm innocent, as you know," he kept saying.

My eyes popped open and the dream stayed fresh in my mind. Innocent? Lloyd Brugel? Not bloody likely. I knew he was guilty of the charges he was facing, and I was pretty sure he'd be convicted. Did the dream mean anything?

By some astounding possibility, was Brugel not the bad guy here? What the hell was my subconscious up to? Just making trouble?

It was nearly ten in the morning when I thundered into the kitchen. No sign of the two girls who had been so keen to undermine my relationship with their father.

Alvin picked up where he left off.

"Good afternoon," he said. "This will creep you out. So this burglar breaks into a house in the middle of the night. He's tiptoeing through a dark room when he hears this eerie parrot voice saying, 'Jesus is watching you.'"

"Not in the mood for a: burglars b: parrots c: jokes. Especially this week, Alvin. You should be able to understand that."

In fact, I knew the joke. It had circulated to great merriment a few years back. I left that out of my comments. Alvin was looking crushed enough, and I was beginning to realize that sometimes I might be a bit rough on him. He sniffed and turned away. I watched his skinny back as he retreated to the kitchen.

"Fine, I take it back." I called out kindly. "I'm sorry. Tell your stupid joke, if it makes you happy."

At least three minutes passed before Alvin swanned back in and started the joke from the beginning as I bit my tongue. The burglar in this particular joke was pretty snotty, nothing like Bunny.

"Hang on," I said, as a feeling of dread swept over me. The hair on the back of my neck prickled. "Where did this joke come from? The internet?"

Alvin shook his head. "In case you haven't noticed, I'm a bit too busy lately to waste my time looking for jokes on the computer."

"Tell me it's from a joke book."

"If I don't have time to look up jokes on the net, what would make you think I would go get a joke book? So let me ask you a question, Camilla. Where have we been getting our jokes lately?"

"Oh, no."

"Well, yeah. Except it's a bit different from the others. It's not a question and answer sort of a joke and..."

"It's a burglar, Alvin. What part of that is unclear to you?"

Alvin pouted. I ignored him and reached for the receiver which was naturally nowhere near the phone. Instead of hunting for it, I whipped out my cell and pecked out the number of Bunny's number. Pick up, I thought, pick up pick up. Bunny, Bunny, Bunny, where are you?

I snapped it closed and tried again. And again. Was he out? Was he avoiding calls? Was he somewhere with blocked reception? My heart thundered. Or was he already dead? That joke ended with a Rottweiler called Hey-soose, which was very bad news for the burglar. Not remotely funny in my opinion, but I asked myself how could that translate into danger for Bunny? What was the joke connection?

"Dogs, Alvin. How could they kill you?"

"What?"

"In the joke, the burglar is about to meet Jesus, pronounced Hey-soose, like the Spanish pronunciation. Only Hey-soose turns out to be a Rottweiler. Okay, dog dangers, fast." I snapped my fingers.

Alvin said, "Greyhound bus. Remember that other old joke, just the dog, man. Just the dog."

Would Bunny take a Greyhound bus? How could he be enticed onto one? I flicked open the cellphone and tried again with no more success. "I can't reach him to tell him to be careful. I need to get Tonya's number. She'll know how to locate him. She has a hairdressing business called, I think, The Cutting Remarque. "Where did you put the phone book, now, Alvin? It was right here last night."

Alvin, pale-faced, produced the phone book, instantly, for once. My fingers actually shook when the phone was answered at the shop. I said, "Tonya please." Then, "It's an emergency, can you please get her to the phone." Followed by, "It's personal, it's not Destiny, but it is urgent. Her client can wait one short minute, trust me." Finally, after a bit more stonewalling by the receptionist, I snapped, "Why don't you leave it up to Tonya to see if she'll come to the phone? Hold the receiver for her if you're so damned worried she'll get colour on it."

Alvin stared at me. I chewed on my lower lip as I waited to see if Tonya would respond.

"Hello?" she said, fear in her voice.

"Tonya. I need to know if Bunny's out of town. I have to talk to him. Did he take a bus?"

"Who is this?"

"Sorry, it's Camilla MacPhee. You know me. I was at your place the other night. I really need to reach him."

"Did you try at home? He's there with Destiny."

"He didn't answer."

"Maybe they're in the backyard. Sometimes Destiny has a morning nap. He might turn the phone off not to wake her up."

"Is there another number where I could reach him?"

She hesitated.

I said, "If he has a cellphone, I really have to get that number."

"He doesn't want me to give it out."

"Tonya, that doesn't apply to me."

A pause. "I can't give it to you. I'm not going to."

"Fine. Can you call him and tell him to contact me right away on my cell. He has the number. I need to talk to him urgently."

Tonya's voice had developed a little shake. "What is going on? I'm going to go home right now."

There was no point in dragging her into it. One more person who could be in danger. "I'm sorry, I don't mean to alarm you. He has my number. Please, just ask him to call me, that's all."

As she hung up, I said to Alvin. "We have to get to Bunny's place, now. You'd better come with me in case."

"In case what?" Alvin said.

"I don't know. In case of something awful."

Gussie perked up.

I said, "No, not you, Gussie. We have enough dog trouble."

ELEVEN

You're supposed to be a first-rate lawyer! If I give you $5000,
will you answer two questions for me?
-Sure thing. What's the second question?

One minute later, Alvin shot out of the garage in the
Acura. I leapt into the passenger seat, and we careened
down Third Avenue, heading for Barrhaven. I used the time
to keep trying to reach Bunny.

No answer.

I had tried twenty times by the time we screeched to
a halt in front of Bunny and Tonya's tidy townhouse on
Parkview Circle. I jumped out while Alvin kept the car
running. I rang the bell and pounded on the metal front
door for emphasis.

Nothing.

I glanced around. Something was different. What?

"Alvin, what do you see that's changed here?"

"Well, the pink tricycle's gone."

"Right. Maybe they went for a—"

An apple-cheeked young woman emerged from the
house across the street. She was pushing a baby stroller the
size of a subcompact car. She paused by a leafy maple tree
and looked up. I dashed across the street.

"Rotten squirrels," she said. "They're always plotting to
get my birdfeeder."

"That's a shame," I said. "I'm looking for my friend, your
neighbour across the street. I need to get some papers to

him quickly and I'm late. Any idea where he and his little girl would go with the tricycle?"

She smiled trustingly. "Bunny and Destiny will probably be at the park. It's not far. Just go back to the corner and hang a quick right then a left. You can't miss it."

A lovely person, so far not acquainted with the evil ways of the world. I really should have told her not to give that kind of information to a total stranger.

Alvin had heard and moved the Acura closer. I hopped back in the car, and we peeled rubber getting to the park. "I hope to hell," I said, "that it's not a dog park. Can't you go any faster?"

"Not without getting airborne," he grumped.

Bunny was pushing Destiny on the swings when we panted up to him.

"Hey! What is it, Camilla?" he said.

"Push, Daddy!"

Bunny pushed.

"I need to talk, privately," I said.

"Daddeeee, push!"

Bunny gave the swing a mighty shove and Destiny squealed as the swing soared high.

"Take over, Alvin, and keep an eye out for dogs," I ordered. "Bunny, come here."

Bunny followed me. "What?"

"Why don't you answer your phone? What is the matter with you? I've been trying to reach you."

"Lots of people try and reach me, but you know I'm trying to leave my old life behind and be a family man. People say they just want to talk, just need a favour, just going to take a minute and the next thing you know you're—"

"Okay, don't tell me that. I don't need to know about

anything illegal, and I take your point about moving on. But we got another joke. Did you get it?"

"No. Oh, maybe Tonya took it."

I kicked myself for not grilling Tonya about this. I should have known.

"I got a burglar joke."

"What?"

"Push me higher, Daddy!"

I spoke clearly and distinctly. "I received a burglar joke."

Bunny turned the colour of old library paste, more grey than white. "But they've all been lawyer jokes. Why would you get a burglar joke?"

"I don't know, Bunny. I don't really know what this is all about, but I think you are going to have to be careful."

"I am careful. I'm a stay-at-home dad. We go to the park, we read Dr. Seuss, we colour in little books. I put in a few hours a week at the framing shop. How can I be more careful than that?"

"I don't know. Is this a dog park?"

Bunny stared at me.

"Daddeeeee!"

"A dog park? Why?"

At the edge of the park, a man in a baseball cap was just arriving with a large frolicking mixed-breed. "So that probably means yes," I said. "We have to get out of here."

Bunny grabbed Destiny from the swing, setting off a series of howls that drowned out our conversation for several minutes.

"Get in the car," I yelled and popped the tricycle in the back seat. "We'll get you home and try to figure out what to do."

Destiny screamed the entire time. Bunny did his best to

cuddle her and croon soothingly.

As we pulled into the driveway, I said, "Destiny!"

She stopped shrieking and stared at me, her huge eyes even larger than before.

"When I was a little girl…"

Destiny's stare turned to a frown. Perhaps she didn't believe I'd ever been a little girl. Maybe she was worried that little girls could turn out like me. I didn't let her expression stop me. I repeated, "When I was a little girl my sisters used to make me a tent with the dining room table, and if I was very quiet, they used to let me eat my lunch there."

Mostly so they could have quality time with their boyfriends, but never mind. I'd loved the magic world the blankets created the instant they were tossed over a table. I kept talking as we scurried toward the house.

"Do you want to make a tent?" I said to Destiny.

"I am so jealous," Alvin said.

I asked, "Are you allowed to do that?" I felt fairly certain that with Tonya as a mother, she wasn't.

"It's a special treat," Bunny said. "Just for today. Don't tell Mommy."

Destiny sniffed. "Tomorrow too?"

Bunny said, "All right. Tomorrow too. And the next day, because you were a very good girl and came right home."

A good girl? There was still more proof that I'd never make much of a parent, although I was proud of remembering the tent trick.

The child bought into this idea. "Destiny is a very good girl."

Destiny took Bunny's hand as we walked into the house. I returned the tricycle to its regular parking spot in the walkway. The front door hadn't even been locked. What had Bunny the burglar been thinking? I secured the door behind us and tapped my toe until he was ready to talk. Bunny busied himself using a blanket to make the tent. He said, "I never thought of that. What a great idea."

I knew that Bunny's childhood had not included playtime, parks or reading with a stay-at-home parent. And apparently no tents using dining room tables. But then he'd done more parenting for his alcoholic mother than he'd ever received. There was something comforting about seeing that this pattern was changing with Destiny. If Bunny could stay alive, that is.

"Okay," I said in a low voice when he finally joined us. "We're going to get you out of here without anyone knowing. I need a plan. And it would help if you would be straight with me about who might be behind all this."

Bunny shook his head frantically. "I have no idea who's behind it. But anyway, we can't leave here. We'll be safe if we stay in the house."

I hated to burst his balloon, but I said, "Remember Rollie? Roxanne? Judge Cardarelle? And now Anstruther. They thought they were safe too. If it's Brugel, he's capable of anything. You should know that. He's obviously engaged accomplices who appear to be trustworthy."

Bunny said, "But…"

"We need to let the police know you're involved, Bunny. We can't take any more chances."

"No police! No. They'll take Destiny away. What are you doing, Camilla? I trusted you and—"

Alvin said, "They won't take her away, Bunny."

I bit my lip. I wasn't so sure. If the wrong cop showed up, then connected with CAS, and if Bunny seemed to be involved with a crime and not a fit parent, who knew what could happen, at least in the short term.

"Fine," I said. "Pull yourself together. Leave it with me. I know who to call."

Elaine picked up the phone on the tenth ring. "I can't talk to you now, Camilla. I'm having my carpets cleaned."

"It's incredibly urgent."

"Call me back. I can't hear you anyway over the sound of the machinery. It's like being in a tornado."

That was true enough, because even over the phone line the racket from the carpet cleaning procedure was clearly audible.

"Bunny's in danger," I shouted.

"What?"

"Bunny's in—" I was counting on the fact that Elaine loved Bunny as much as I did.

"Actually I heard you. My eardrum is still suffering from it. What kind of danger?"

"You're not going to believe this." I moved into the living room to be more private, although I was almost shouting.

"Try me. Wait a minute," I heard her bellowing in the background. "Joe, can you turn off the equipment for a minute. I have an emergency call here."

It took a while to fill her in on the background of the new and obscure but creepy threat to Bunny. His fear that Destiny would be taken away from him if the cops got involved.

"You're right, that is unbelievable, Camilla. Why would anyone do such a thing? It sounds like a straight-to-DVD movie."

"I know how weird it seems."

"Even so, I think you should tell Leonard."

"Leonard's aware. But not about Bunny. I don't want to draw attention to him. You know how hard he's trying to go

182

straight. And there's Destiny, remember."

"Of course, I remember," Elaine said with what sounded like a flash of irritation. "But really, Leonard would appreciate that. He wouldn't put that little family at risk. He's very kind-hearted."

I stifled a snort. Kind-hearted Leonard, my fat fanny. I'd heard his remarks when we saw Bunny in the courthouse. Never mind, love is blind. And Elaine is stubborn by anyone's standards.

"Leonard's not the only problem. The police just aren't taking it seriously at all. Maybe because of the jokes. Who can blame them? Lots of the guys in Major Crimes had a real hate on for Thorsten, seeing as he'd sunk so many of their cases."

"I don't know what you think I can do," Elaine said grumpily, "with wet carpets and all that. Anyway, the whole thing sounds totally paranoid and otherwise crazy too. Have you been mixing medications, Camilla?"

If there is one thing I have learned from my sisters, it's how to guilt trip people. I usually try to avoid this. However, the situation called for desperate measures. I lowered my voice.

"I don't take medications, and you know it. This is Bunny, Elaine. Paranoid crazy idea or not, you should want to help. You want to go together to his funeral? You could do a touching eulogy. Dead at twenty-nine? Never had a chance in this cold and uncaring world where even social work professionals refused to—"

"Cut it out," Elaine snapped. "That's not fair. Bunny's not going to die."

"But that's the thing, Elaine. He is. And he will. Maybe his sweet little family too." I didn't look in Bunny's direction. I heard him dash from the kitchen into the dining area where

Destiny was once again playing happily under the tent.

"Let's go downstairs to the playroom, pumpkin," Bunny was saying. "Away from the windows."

Destiny began to wail. "I want to stay here, Daddy. You're ruining everything today."

"That is so unfair," Elaine said. "Emotional blackmail. Call 911, Camilla, and stop jerking people around."

"911 will only be a stalling technique. Listen, who's doing your rugs? Did I hear you say Joe?"

"Joe Jeremiah. He always does them. You know that."

I also knew that Joe Jeremiah owed Elaine beyond bigtime for the work she'd done as a social worker with his two crazy teenage boys back in the day, before they became more or less solid citizens. Better yet, he'd always been grateful to me for the legal work I'd done for those out of control offspring.

"Put him on," I said, loudly, because Destiny was screaming at the top of her lungs that she did not want to leave her tent.

I heard a loud sigh from Elaine. That was a good thing. A short chat with Joe Jeremiah confirmed that he could be with us in about an hour earliest or an hour and a half latest. I was grinning as I hung up. Of course, that was until Tonya burst into the house.

Great. One more target for whoever was behind this.

Tonya ignored me and got straight to the point of pounding on Bunny's chest. By the time Alvin and I intervened, she had him slammed against the wall.

"Family violence, Tonya," I said. "Bad experience for the child."

She shrieked, "Putting my baby in danger. That's worse." She turned to see Destiny, who had stopped screaming and was standing staring, her thumb in her mouth, fat tears running down her cheeks. Tonya choked out, "Go play, honey, Mommy wants to talk to Daddy."

"You're hurting him."

"No, no, it's just…" Tonya sank onto the chair and put her head in her hands. "It just looks that way."

Alvin took Destiny's hand. "Do you have any Frosted Flakes?"

Destiny nodded.

"Do you have any Count Chocula?"

Another nod.

"What about Pop Tarts?"

"Yes."

Alvin said, "No one will mind if we eat them now. Let's mix them all together. We could put the Pop Tarts on top."

"I want the biggest bowl," Destiny said.

I turned to Bunny and Tonya and said, "You two better pull yourselves together. This is serious, Tonya. If you touch Bunny like that again, you will find out how the courts view a mother hitting her spouse in front of her child."

Tonya said, "What's so urgent, Bunny? Why is Camilla so worried? What have you done now?"

Bunny wrapped his arms around Tonya, who sat shaking on the sofa. "But, Camilla, Tonya was just upset. She thinks I put Destiny in danger. I don't know how I did, but I understand how she was feeling. She'd do anything to protect our daughter."

"Yeah well, understand this, Bunny: if you want to protect your daughter, don't ever let her see you accept violence to your person because someone else doesn't like what you've done. You both sent some powerful messages today, and you'd better make goddam sure you send better ones in the future. I'll have Elaine Ekstein talk to you as soon as this is over. She'll chew your ears off. It will serve you both right. Now, get upstairs and pack up what the three of you need for a few days, maybe even a week. Clothes, toiletries, medicines, toys, books, the works. Make-up, I suppose, for Tonya. Don't leave anything important behind."

Bunny said, "But where are we going?"

"I'm working on that."

Tonya said, "And how?"

"Don't ask."

*   *   *

I took Alvin aside while Bunny and Tonya were packing. Destiny joined them to pack a bag for her dolly. Alvin had been asked to dollysit in the meantime.

"Alvin, it just occurred to me that even if we get them out of here, there might be some kind of an attempt. Especially as no one will know that they aren't here."

"And what can we do about that?"

"Surveillance."

"You mean we should watch the house?"

I looked at his unmistakable beaky profile. "Nah. We'd get spotted, and anyway, we need to be free to get around. But remember, Justice for Victims had that surveillance camera when we were worried about clients being harassed?"

"Sure. I remember it. It's in a box in the basement along with a bunch of other junk."

"That device needs to be plugged into an electrical outlet and attached to some kind of recorder."

"It's old, so I think there should be a VCR with it in the box."

"Great. That one will do for the backyard. And we'll

need something for the front too. We should mount it somewhere with a clear view of the front door, but at an angle so we might be able to catch a glimpse of a face. That maple across the way should be perfect. Our joker might be expecting some security at the house, but probably not from across the street."

Alvin peered out the window and nodded. "We had two cameras, but one didn't work. Anyway, there's nowhere to plug it in over there."

"Never mind. I'll stay here for a while, and you head out as fast as you can. Grab the one from the basement and swing by Spytech on Bronson and pick up a model that's battery-powered, that will record from a distance. I'm sure they make them now. I don't care how much it costs, but we have to be able hide them quickly. I'll call and have them get something ready, and I'll give them my credit card number. You just have to pick it up and get it here as fast as possible."

"And then what are we going to do?"

"Our joker might make a move. It would have to be either the front door or the back. With luck we'll get an image. This could be the break we've been waiting for."

Alvin abandoned the doll to me and made tracks.

I said, "I'll be watching from the window until you get back."

* * *

Alvin returned in very good time, obviously having violated the highway code in transit. He had two smallish boxes and some instructions. He said, "This model's new. It works on batteries, and it should be good for about ten hours. It saves the images to DVD. It's really neat. It cost enough, but—"

I said, "You did well."

As Alvin installed the old camera near the back door, well-hidden behind a lattice with a climbing rose, I took the new gear, motion detector camera, battery pack and recorder from their packaging and stuck them in my purse. I headed across the street, where the apple-cheeked young mom was arriving home with her sleeping baby in the stroller.

She said, "It takes him forever to fall asleep."

I smiled. "Your bird feeder looks like it's about to fall down. Would you like me to fix it for you?"

"Oh, thank you," she grinned. "There's a ladder by the garage. Since the baby came, I find I can't keep up with things. Would you mind refilling it with seed when you're up there? The squirrels knock it sideways and eat most of the seed. It's impossible to keep it filled."

I followed her to her cheerful red front door and took the plastic bucket of birdseed. I climbed the ladder and quickly attached the motion detector camera on a branch about eye level. I thought it afforded a good view without being easily seen itself. I climbed higher, refilled the bird feeder and returned the bucket to the front step. There was a reasonable chance that anyone watching me would have been fooled into falling for the bird feeder trick.

Back in the house, I positioned myself to keep watch in the front window until Joe Jeremiah arrived. His white van with its grinning bullfrog logo pulled up to Bunny's place. I opened the door, and he backed the van right into the garage. Tonya, Bunny and Destiny were waiting out of sight as instructed.

Joe approached me on the doorstep and nodded politely. I nodded back, also politely, held the front door open for him and pointed inside.

Alvin ignored him and headed for the car. If anyone was watching, they should take us all for complete strangers. So far so good.

"What now?" Alvin said as we pulled away.

"Joe will spend the amount of time in the house that he normally would for a rug-cleaning job. He'll probably really clean the rugs too."

"They seemed spotless to me. I think you could probably eat on them."

"That's Tonya. But he'll do it. That way it will sound right to anyone keeping watch on the house. I don't think they will try anything with Joe Jeremiah on the premises."

"No kidding. The guy's a giant."

"When he's done, he'll get the three of them and their bags into the back of the van where the machinery is, without having them be visible to anyone who is watching the place."

"Is that possible?"

"That's why he backed right into the garage. When he leaves, he'll make a big show of waving to them as though they're still there."

Alvin nodded and thought hard for a minute. "But what if the person is smart enough to catch on and follow them?"

"That person will have to be very lucky to catch up with Joe Jeremiah if he doesn't want to be caught up with."

*　*　*

I wasn't expecting Mombourquette's voice when I picked up.

"Sorry to disappoint you, MacPhee," he said.

"Disappoint me about what?"

"For starters, your nutty idea that James Kilpatrick might have witnessed something about his boss's murder."

"Why?"

"Because it turns out that this Kilpatrick was a witness to something else entirely."

"What's that supposed to mean?"

"It means there was some kind of an argument near his home with some neighbours, and he was drawn into it somehow and one of them is a bit unstable and she accused him of threatening her."

"Threatening her? Kilpatrick? Are you pulling my leg?"

"Nope."

"Well, that's laughable. Kilpatrick couldn't threaten a hummingbird. Have you seen him? He looks like a stick drawing."

"So I gather, but a couple of uniforms were dispatched, and I guess they thought he got a bit lippy. All to say he ended up cooling his heels at the station. He was in an interrogation room screaming about a lawsuit at the key times between when Rollie Thorsten was last seen and when he died."

"He has my sympathy then. I've been on the wrong side of your interrogation rooms, and I know how you guys can trump things up."

"So here's my point, MacPhee. We are on it. And you are not."

"Well, thank you, Leonard. I appreciate your keeping me up to speed."

"No need to be sarcastic," he said and hung up.

*   *   *

Although I knew deep down Mrs. P. would give thumbs up to my plan, I wanted to clear it with her first. But she didn't answer her phone. She didn't answer her cell either. Perhaps she was having her daily visit to the Physical Terrorist as she called the excellent young man who was helping her get her groove back.

I checked with the nursing station to see if she could be tracked down. Surprisingly, someone answered and suggested that Violet must be outside on a Benson & Hedges break.

At that moment, my own cellphone rang and I snapped it open. "Yes."

Joe Jeremiah said, "Heading out to my next appointment."

"That's great."

"Thanks for the referral. I hope you and your friends are happy with the job I did."

"I imagine they are." I tried not to picture Bunny, Tonya and Destiny wedged in the back of the truck for the mystery trip with Joe who usually drove like the hounds of hell were after him. And for all we knew, they were.

I added, "Did you have any trouble getting into the place we discussed without being seen?"

"Are you kidding? I could get into 24 Sussex if I tried. Piece of cake."

Maybe, as Elaine suggested, I was paranoid, but I wasn't giving details out loud in my car. There was no way anyone could have known about Joe and his secret mission, but still. I wouldn't put it past Brugel to arrange to have my car bugged. He wouldn't be hampered by pesky legislation like the police would be. Anyway, everything about this case was so bizarre and creepy that I thought it better to be discreet.

Joe would have been buzzed in to the garage of Mrs. P.'s building by the super. He would have transported Bunny, Tonya and Destiny safely to her empty apartment. I imagined that Bunny and Tonya would be dressed as workers. Maybe Destiny would be undercover with his equipment. I was glad that the super had been willing to say yes to my request for the locked service elevator so that Mrs. P.'s carpets could be cleaned during her absence.

"Always glad to help Violet out," the super had said. I knew the same wouldn't apply to me.

Joe was still speaking. "I made sure none of those close-circuit security cameras caught their faces."

"Thanks, again, Joe. I owe you."

"You don't owe me nothing. A father never forgets," Joe said before ringing off.

I said to Alvin, who was chewing his nails. "The package has been delivered. Now we just have to take care of that other small matter."

"What matter?"

I mouthed, "The dog."

Alvin gazed at me more blankly than usual.

I mouthed "In the joke." Alvin continued to looked unutterably baffled. Before I could clarify, my cellphone rang again. With luck it would be Bunny telling me his family was enjoying a comfortable stay in Mrs. P.'s place. I hoped she hadn't cut back on her extended cable package. But of course, it wasn't Bunny. He'd hardly have been settled in.

"Ray!" I said. "How um…"

"Right, it's definitely um."

"Cute. Even at a distance."

"That's me. My kids are cute too. Or they used to be, anyway. I'm just checking to see that's still true."

Oh, right. The girls. I hadn't been paying much attention to them what with all the murder and mayhem and the fact that they'd once again tried to make trouble between me and Ray. Of course, Ray didn't know anything about Bunny's getaway. For sure, he wouldn't want Brittany and Ashley caught up in whatever was going on.

He didn't usually call during the day, but I guess there are different rules for parents.

"Can I talk to them?"

"Well, they're not here. I'm not home."

"I figured that. I called there first."

"Right. Alvin and I are on an errand. The girls aren't with us. They'll be…" I thought hard. Where would they be? Yet another practice? Alvin probably knew. Was I supposed to keep up with their every move? Was that one of the things that other people seem to know instinctively? That you have to keep an eye on teenage girls who are larger and stronger and most definitely meaner than you are yourself? Was there a human being less suited to being a stepmother than me? Off the top of my head, I couldn't think of one.

"Where?" said Ray with that tone he gets.

"Getting ready for their race." I felt pretty safe with that response. They seemed to be practicing all the time. Well, maybe not practicing, but doing something to keep out of the way. Up until this moment, I'd thought that was a good thing.

"So they're gone already."

"That's what I thought," I fibbed. "Something with the team anyway. Working out, whatever. They all seem to be quite friendly."

"They are. They all had…" Ray cleared his throat. "They each lost a mother or an aunt to cancer. It gives them a special bond."

"Oh right," I said. "It would." I felt like banging my head on the steering wheel. My mother died when I was born, but it didn't mean I couldn't imagine what it would have been like to have known her and lost her.

"I was calling just to wish them luck. They'll be pretty excited about the race, and I might not have access to a phone during this course."

Right. The damned course.

He said, " So I was calling to talk to you too, by the way. Although that's not always straightforward."

"It isn't? Hey, why are you laughing, Ray?"

"No reason."

"Okay. I'll tell them you called."

"Sure thing."

"Bye, Ray. I'll miss talking to you this weekend."

"Bye, Camilla."

Alvin glanced over as I clicked off and frowned. I said, "Am I supposed to be watching Ashley and Brittany?"

"They are over eighteen. Adults, and pretty independent adults at that," Alvin said. "Why?"

"Maybe I'm falling down on the job. This whole joke nightmare has been pretty intense and distracting. I should have been thinking more about them and keeping a closer watch on them while they're here."

"I imagine they're glad you are distracted."

That struck me as suspicious. "Why do you say that? Do you think they're up to something?"

"No."

"Do you think Ray thinks they're up to something?"

"I think parents always assume you might be up to something."

I said, "Humph. Well, I know for sure that sisters do."

My sisters have always stuck their noses into every aspect of my business. They are truly unclear on boundaries. I didn't want to be like them, but I wasn't sure exactly what Ray wanted from me. Understanding family dynamics has never been my forte. Even if it had been, I had way too much to think about without adding the girls to the package.

Still, I did wonder how Alvin seemed to naturally pick up on these things.

"Okay, well, that's enough about that. We have to figure out what to do about you know who. He can't stay you know where for sure."

Alvin stared at me and wrinkled his beaky nose. "There you go again, not making any sense. By any chance, have you lost your you know what?"

I made what I thought could be a universal symbol for "maybe someone has bugged our vehicle."

Alvin countered with the universal symbol for "you've lost your marbles" and upped the ante by mouthing the words paranoid paranoid paranoid, followed by the phrase "just plain nuts."

I did my best to mouth back, "Just because you're paranoid doesn't mean they're not out to get you."

He countered with, "Just because they're out to get you doesn't mean you haven't lost your marbles."

*   *   *

Back at the house, Alvin busied himself on a baking bender. He was testing a traditional recipe for scones to see how it compared to the Fergusons' favourite. I wasn't sure where that left the chowder project. Never mind, I like scones, so I was willing to show support for either food group. In the meantime, I was feeling restless. Where was Bunny? Why didn't anyone ever phone me back? I checked out the house and located all the wayward phone receivers, two in the girls' room and one in the bathroom. I paced waiting for the phone to ring. Of course, I wouldn't have answered the phone if I'd known it was Jacki Jewell. I was hoping for Bunny and some signal that things were all right.

"I visited your house yesterday," she accused.

"Did you?"

"It's still full of suitcases and sports gear. Running shoes everywhere. Unmade beds, towels on the floor."

I waited.

"And boxes of feminine products in clear view," she added pointedly.

I said, "I have visitors. I'm sure I told you that. My friend's daughters are with me. They're here for the Dragon Boat Festival."

"It's just that I can't show the house when it's like that. Surely you are aware that neat, uncluttered houses sell faster and get a better price."

"Just tell them I have visitors. What are you so worried about?"

"Camilla, it's a buyers' market now. Even though you have visitors, any potential purchaser is going to look around and decide you don't have enough storage if there's not space for their clothes and suitcases and toiletries."

"There's plenty of storage."

"Well, you must insist that your guests use it."

I had a difficult enough relationship with Ashley and Brittany without adding housekeeping inspection to my routine. Besides, there were few humans who cared less about maintaining a spotless abode than I did. And oddly enough, I felt that the girls didn't merit this kind of overbearing behaviour.

"Look. Why don't you wait until they've gone back to Nova Scotia and then bring people around?"

"It's not that simple." I noticed that Jacki Jewell had developed a slight edge to her voice in the course of our conversation. I wondered if I should suggest that she try to work on that.

"It's simple, really. They're guests and they're young, and I'm not going to hound them about their stuff."

"Here is the situation: I have potential purchasers in town. They have cash, they love the Glebe and they need to find a place quickly and oddly enough, as they adore Italy, they may not even mind the murals." I suspected Jacki paused to shudder delicately. "But they don't have children, and she's quite fastidious and so far storage has been an issue with them in all of the places we've visited. You take my point."

"I do, and I hope you take mine. I don't plan to tie myself in knots over the house."

"Fine," she snapped. "I'll bring them over, but it's probably a complete waste of time."

Somehow I felt it wasn't really fine, but that was so not my problem. The house could sell whenever. Or never. Jacki Jewell and my sisters could go up in flames over it if they wanted to. I definitely had other fish to fry.

And other calls to answer. "Elaine? What is it? Are you crying? Calm down!"

"Oh, my god, Camilla! Have you been watching the news?"

"Since when do I watch the news? Why are you asking? Is there some political bullshit going down? A big announcement by some level of government? I have a lot of more important stuff happening here."

"Bunny."

"What about him?"

I heard a lot of snuffling down the phone line.

"Elaine. Pull yourself together and tell me. What about Bunny?"

"I saw it on television. Why didn't I listen to you? How could I be so selfish? What was I—?"

Elaine blubbering was a truly disconcerting phenomenon. I said as calmly as I could. "You what exactly?"

"His house. I recognized it. Little Destiny's bike is still lying on the path," Elaine wailed. "You were right, Camilla. Bunny's beautiful little house burned to the ground. Nobody could have gotten out alive."

TWELVE

What is the biggest difference between
a tick and a lawyer?
-A tick will fall off when you die.

Even from the kitchen, Alvin heard Elaine wailing over the phone. He stuck his head around the corner of the kitchen.

I said, "That's shocking, Elaine, but Bunny and his family weren't there. You know I got Joe to take them to a safe place." I hadn't told her where Joe Jeremiah had taken Bunny and his family in case she accidentally spilled the beans to Mombourquette.

"Are you sure they didn't go back? I don't see how anyone could survive an inferno like that."

"Trust me, they're all right." I aimed a calming gesture at Alvin, who was swaying in alarm.

"The entire house is destroyed," Elaine said with a catch in her voice. "Everything. They're still fighting the fire. The neighbouring families had to be evacuated. And a woman was taken away by ambulance."

I sat down.

"I'll never forgive myself for not taking you more seriously. Oh my god, Camilla. Do you think it was Tonya? I talked to Joe Jeremiah after his, um, task, and he said she didn't really want to go with him. The little girl was crying too. What if they went back?"

The same thought had run through my mind. Destiny

crying for her doll. Tonya insisting that she needed certain clothing or toiletries. Bunny deciding he couldn't live without some watercolour.

"Elaine, talk to Leonard. Make him find out what they know about that woman. It's important." Elaine likes a mission and she was off on this one.

Alvin grabbed my arm. "Lord thundering Jesus, what is it, Camilla? Are you trying to drive me crazy?"

"Bunny's house burned to the ground. Elaine is afraid Bunny and his family might have gone home for some reason because emergency workers took a woman, injured or dead, from the house."

Alvin goggled. "Burned?"

"Yes."

"To the ground?"

"Yes."

"And a woman may have died?"

"Exactly. It's too horrible to imagine. What if it was Tonya?"

"But we got a joke. The joke didn't say anything about fire. It was a dog. We were supposed to be worried about a Rottweiler named Hey-soose."

"The whole point of that joke is the burglar meets his maker, and the maker is a surprise. I'm going to head out and try to check up on Bunny. You better go see if you can retrieve that surveillance camera without the police catching on."

* * *

It seemed like a year had passed before I pulled up into the parking lot of the building on Clearwater Crescent. I stayed out of sight behind a pillar in the garage for a while to be on the safe side, until I was sure no one followed me in. I took the service elevator to the 20th floor and walked down to the 16th. Anyone watching the elevator wouldn't know what floor I'd chosen. These spy antics seemed silly even as I was engaging in them. If Bunny's house hadn't just burned down, I might even have laughed. What I had recently considered paranoia, now just seemed like a plan. I opened 1608 with my key after knocking. I walked into the apartment.

"Don't panic. It's me, Camilla."

Empty.

No Bunny. No Tonya. No little Destiny.

Nothing but echoing empty rooms.

They had been there. I found a few chocolate bar wrappers in the garbage can. Nothing Mrs. Parnell would ever eat. Behind the black leather club chair, I saw the pink and purple arm of Destiny's rag doll, lying there, stretched out as if reaching for the little girl. I picked up the doll and stuck it into my immense yellow handbag.

Where had they gone?

And why?

I sank into Mrs. Parnell's black leather chair. The only sound in the empty apartment was the thundering of my heart. Praying is not my best thing, but I prayed that the three Mayhews hadn't gone back to the neat little house in Barrhaven.

*   *   *

P. J. answered his cellphone in his whisper voice. "Can't talk now. I think I'm on to something."

"This is important. Did you know that was Bunny Mayhew's house that just burned to the ground, P. J.?"

"The fire in Barrhaven?"

"That's it."

"Are you sure? The house is in the name of a Tonya Riendeau."

"That's his wife. I need to know if she was the woman who was injured."

"Can't talk."

"Sure, but who is the woman they found?"

His voice dropped to the point where I could scarcely hear him. "They don't know yet. Told you, I can't talk now."

"Yeah, yeah, where did they find her? Inside?"

Sounded to me like P. J. had something caught in his throat. I said, "What? I can't understand you."

"If I answer this question, will you leave me alone? A badly injured woman was found outside near the front entrance. The front door was open. Looks like she tried to escape, but it was too late."

"That's horrible."

"It sure is. Goodbye, Tiger."

"Where are you? Can you find a way to see her? Find out who she is? You must have contacts in ICU."

"Are you completely out of your mind? You are really crossing lines here. Even by your standards. I am hanging up now."

"But I need to know."

Still whispering, P. J. said, "Well, it's too late anyway. I guess I can tell you the woman died a half-hour ago without regaining consciousness."

"And they haven't identified her yet?"

"I told you, no. I believe everyone in the surrounding

houses is accounted for. It was pretty crazy right after the explosion, but the cops have had time to narrow it down. They seem to be fairly sure it's not a neighbour. I talked to Constable Wentzell."

"Right. The big blonde cop you have the hots for. So what did she say? How did the fire start?"

"I don't know, but I'm working on getting someone who will talk to me off the record. You just have to wait."

I felt a catch in my throat. I decided to confide in P. J. "Off the record, and I really mean this to be off the record, Bunny and Tonya and their daughter were hiding out."

"Where were they hiding out?"

"Listen, you don't answer my questions. Why should I answer yours? Tonya was pretty mad because we got a burglar joke. She didn't want to go into hiding. She was really angry at Bunny. She thought he'd involved her in something."

"A burglar joke? You mean this fire was connected with the other deaths? Holy shit."

"But when I figure it out, you will be the first reporter I tell. It will be a huge story, but if you let anything slip about Bunny at this stage, you won't get another word out of me. Clear?"

"Clear. But was Bunny involved? How?"

"That's the thing, P. J. I haven't found any common ground in this weird joke situation. Returning to our issue, what if Tonya went home to that sweet little house that she loved so much and someone set fire to it? You have only about two minutes to escape from a burning house. She could have been trapped. We have to find out right now who that woman was. We can't waste any time."

"Hey, I said that I'm working on it."

"You're sure no one else was found?"

"What is the matter with you? I'm not sure about anything. The fire is still smouldering. They won't know if anyone else was there for a while. There will be a police briefing at some point, but it's way too early. You think Bunny's in there too?"

"I don't know. You never saw three people so reluctant to leave a place. Can you go and talk to the cops? Find out if there's any sign of…" I struggled to say the words, "…a child."

P. J., tough reporter that he is, gasped.

I shivered in the hot air. An image of Destiny reaching for her dolly kept flashing through my brain.

*   *   *

Alvin stormed back into the house, bleating. "I can't get near Bunny's place, Camilla. There are still cops everywhere. The street is closed. They're keeping everyone out who doesn't live there. I think they're even checking ID. The traffic is backed up for blocks."

"Thanks for trying, Alvin. We'll just have to wait for a while, I guess."

"And it won't be easy. I think the neighbours will be very suspicious of anyone they don't know."

"I can try to retrieve the camera later when things settle down."

"Bad idea. You were asking about Bunny, remember? Not that long before the fire?"

"So?"

"Lord thundering Jesus, Camilla. Remember you asked that woman with the stroller if she knew where Bunny was? She saw you clearly, and I'm sure she will have described you to the police. Then you even talked to her about the bird feeder. If you show up and try to get that camera, you'll be back in an interview room for the third time this week. Bet you anything. Anyway, you'll miss the girls' race. They're on this evening."

"No choice, Alvin. I'll wait until the traffic dies down, but I must get that camera. No need for that expression on your face. Don't they have another race tomorrow?"

I found myself pacing. I needed to do something. I called Mombourquette. He didn't answer his cellphone. Never mind. I had a plan.

*   *   *

I waited until after seven that evening when I figured the traffic would have eased up. I assumed that the unfortunate citizens of Parkside Circle would have been allowed back to their homes by this point. I drove back to Barrhaven, parked a couple of blocks away and walked to Bunny's former house. I spotted Mombourquette's distinctive sillouette in the distance. Why was he still hanging around?

The thing you don't expect about a fire is the smell, like a campfire with plastic thrown in. Apparently, it's worse when it smoulders. The stench of burned vinyl clogged my nose.

The uniformed officer was disinclined to let me stroll over and inclined to have me hit the road. I stood my ground and said, "Better let the great detective decide for himself if he wants to see me. I have information pertinent to this case. Tell him it's Camilla MacPhee."

Two minutes later, I was nose to nose with his royal furriness. "Leonard, I need you to tell me how many bodies were found here."

He stared at me. "I thought you had information."

I said, "All in good time. I need you to—"

"You need me to? Guess I seem to have missed the memo where I take orders from you, MacPhee. You better print me out a copy of that directive, otherwise I just might take exception to your tone."

"Maybe that came out wrong, but, listen, this was Bunny Mayhew's house."

"What the hell?"

"As far as I can tell, Bunny went into hiding. Tonya and little Destiny were with him, and now none of them can be found. And their house just burned to the ground."

"I know about the fire, MacPhee. I'm standing next to you in front of the shell of the house. I'm retiring, not slipping into a coma."

"Let's not argue about everything. I need...would sure appreciate finding out if other bodies were found."

"And I'd sure appreciate it you told me why."

"I'm worried they might have gone back to the house."

"You always share way too much information and not nearly enough facts. Why were they hiding? What did they have to worry about?"

"Maybe they were worried someone would burn down their house."

"Hmmm. But not worried enough if they would go back."

"Bunny was worried. Tonya was really angry at him for getting her into it."

"Into what? Call me nosy."

"I don't know. Whatever caused their house to burn down, Leonard. Someone set that fire and that person has something against Bunny or wants to send a message or is just plain sadistic. Who would set fire to a house that usually has a small child in it? Well, aside from Lloyd Brugel."

"I still don't know where you come in, MacPhee."

"I'm not giving up until I find out."

"You are loyal to your former sleazebag clients, that's all I can say." Mombourquette's whiskers quivered.

"First of all, Bunny was never a sleazebag, Leonard. And he hasn't done anything wrong except ask me to help him. Secondly, his wife and child are completely innocent of any crime whatsoever. So forgive me if I care about this little family. You might try a bit more of that yourself."

"Get out of here, MacPhee, before I have you arrested for interfering with an active investigation."

I held my head high as I stomped back toward my car. Across the street, I paused briefly to lean against the maple. I took my shoe off and pretended to shake it out. "A stone in my shoe," I shouted to Mombourquette, who was watching me.

He turned away in irritation. I took advantage of that to reach up into the maple tree and yank down the camera and the small recorder. I stuck the whole thing into my oversize handbag and I beat it the hell out of there. Even from across the street, I could still smell the chemical odours.

*   *   *

I was amazed at the quality of the image that the pinhole camera was able to capture. Who knew that the technology was so advanced? There was very little action on Bunny's street, so the time dragged as I watched. After what seemed like a month, a woman walked into the camera's view and along to Bunny's house. She wore a floppy bush hat and large sunglasses, a longish flowered skirt and a loose overblouse. She marched confidently up the paving stone walk, past the pom-pom hydrangeas, the peonies and the tricycle, and up the front steps, a large green stuffed toy dog dangling from her right hand.

She knocked confidently at the door. Waited. Knocked again. Waited. She tried the latch, and sure enough, the door opened. Wasn't it just like our Bunny the burglar to keep forgetting to lock his front door before departing?

The woman glanced around furtively. Then she stepped through the door and into the house. She may have been in disguise, but I was pretty sure I'd know that back and that walk anywhere. I didn't need to see her Sunny Choi suit or three hundred dollar pumps to know this was Annalisa Fillmore.

Minutes later, I sat watching, mesmerized, as a red glow showed through the windows. Curtains on fire? Where was Annalisa? The front door opened and a human figure, hat and clothing blazing, staggered from the burning house. My stomach lurched as she stumbled and lay writhing on the neat paving stones of the walkway a foot away from the pink tricycle.

A frantic man, a neighbour perhaps, ran up to the figure, now lying still, and backed away, hand over his mouth, seemingly repelled by the heat from the house.

As the emergency personnel arrived, I turned away from the image, but I knew I'd have it in my head for a long time.

What the hell had happened inside that house? The more I thought about it, the more Annalisa appeared to be the author of her own destruction. But why?

By midnight I was still mulling over the huge green stuffed dog she'd been carrying. A dog named Hey-soose? Now I knew who the body was. But where the hell were

Bunny, Tonya and Destiny? More to the point, were they still in danger?

Needless to say, Mombourquette did not respond to my calls.

I could have used a bit of advice and soothing talk from Ray, but he was on his course and incommunicado.

*   *   *

Jacki Jewell's eyebrows rose. For a fleeting moment, I wondered if she found us as difficult as we found her. A second too late, she unleashed a blindingly toothy smile. "I'm so sorry," she said. "Did I get you out of bed? I'm having trouble reaching you it seems. My messages aren't returned."

"I'm awake now," I said.

"Yes, of course."

"I had a late night," I said, not liking the fact that I seemed to be offering excuses to her. I hadn't bothered to pick up when I saw her name on call display or return her messages. It's not like she was Bunny.

She paused. "Are you alone?"

"Alvin's here. He's cooking up a storm in the kitchen." I figured from the air it was to be another chowder day, starting with poaching a few pounds of haddock.

"That couple I mentioned, the ones who liked the Italian-style murals, they're with me in the car. I took them by to show them the neighbourhood and the exterior, and they'd like a more detailed viewing."

I opened my mouth to say it wasn't such a good time, but she steamrollered ahead. "Did I mention they'll only be in town for a few days? This could be your best chance of a sale in this market."

209

I blinked. Really, this woman was too much.

"How many people are in the house? Are those visitors still here? Is it possible that you could all go up to Bridgehead for a coffee for an hour? Put the pets in the car?" She wrinkled her nose as she said "pets".

"No, it is not possible," I said.

"But..."

"Not going to happen."

"We'll have to do something about this. I don't know how I'm expected to sell this property when it's always crawling with people and animals. Animals make it very difficult to move a property." Again with the nose wrinkling.

What the hell? "The animals stay. The people too."

"Well, you really should consider making some kind of arrangements so that the house shows well, because—"

"Take it or leave it," I said.

Her lips thinned out with the effort of saying, "Fine. We'll be in shortly."

*   *   *

"Less than ten years old," Jacki Jewell was saying. "Designed by one of Ottawa's foremost architects. It's a beautiful example of upscale infill housing that respects the original neighbourhood and the character of the Glebe. Very very very easy to redecorate. Just a bit of paint here and there, that's all."

The couple nodded, looking around, acknowledging Alvin and me. Her eyes went right to Alvin's mural. She smiled. She was hooked all right.

"There's still a warranty on the roof," Jacki Jewell said to the husband, as the wife was busy mooning over the faux stone walls with the grapevines. No one paid much attention to her. "The furnace and air conditioning are well-maintained."

The young woman continued to smile. I was pleased to note the smile reached her dark eyes. She leaned over and scratched Gussie's ears.

She pointed at the walls. "I just love these paintings. I'm crazy about anything Italian."

I was startled to hear myself saying, "I'm glad you like the murals. I'll pass it on to the artist."

I refrained from mentioning that the artist, Alvin Ferguson, hailed from Sydney, Nova Scotia, and was about as Italian as your basic haggis.

The husband gave a gentle pat to his wife's backside, meaning let's get a move on. Maybe they were as irritated by the real estate agent as I was.

Jacki Jewell shot us a critical glance as she followed her clients into the kitchen. Her chipper voice grated, "The kitchen is totally up-to-date with granite countertops and high end appliances. The French-door refrigerator is a nice feature and the stainless is a true classic, don't you think?"

I tried not to listen to appreciative murmurs from the young couple, but they were drowned out by the latest blast from Jacki Jewell.

"And you have a lovely view of the deck and the garden. It seems to extend the kitchen beautifully. Step outside, and I think you'll see how pleasant and private it is for meals on the deck, surrounded by greenery."

I supposed that they stepped outside.

Jacki shot her head around the corner, and I swear she hissed. "Please stop making fishy foods during the showing of the house. It's hard enough with all those murals and

Tuscan trinkets. Fresh-baked cookies. That's a good aroma. Flowers. Or anything with cinnamon. Even barbecue smells good to some people. We just don't need them thinking about fish heads in the garbage or anything disgusting like that."

"Point taken," I said. "Now can you excuse me, please?"

What did I care? I wasn't running for Miss Congeniality. I guess it took more than that to deflate our ace realtor.

She said, "I realize this is very hard for you to grasp, but there's an art to getting the best price. It means money in the bank for both of us. Please tell your guests not to leave their luggage open and their sports gear strewn around. It's also quite inappropriate to have undergarments hanging on chairs in full view of clients during a viewing. Between that and the revolting smell of fish, it will be almost impossible to move this place. I'm not sure I should bother."

The young couple had returned from the backyard. "I love the fountain fresco, and the potted rosemary is wonderful."

Alvin had chosen that moment to make an appearance. He said, "Thank you," with great dignity.

"And I can tell you really use the kitchen."

"Why don't you head upstairs?" Jacki Jewell said. "I'll be there in a second."

I called up to the prospective buyers. "By the way, my friend's daughters are here for the Dragon Boat Festival. They are accomplished athletes. Alvin is making a giant vat of fish chowder for them. I don't intend to fuss over a bit of luggage strewn around. Or the chowder. We have to keep living here as usual."

Jacki flounced up the stairs after her clients. She stopped briefly as soon as she was out of sight. I figured she needed to have a silent and private hissy fit.

No problem for me. I returned to the living room where I pressed PLAY again on the DVD player. I wanted to revisit the scene of Annalisa Fillmore's death, and to try to figure out what I might learn from it. The clunk of feet on the staircase put an end to that. The young couple entered the living room, smiling broadly. Jacki Jewell followed, not smiling.

The young woman grinned from ear to ear. "I love that this is a house that my sisters can come and visit. It seems so comfortable upstairs, but private for guests too."

"They have their own bathroom up there," I said. "They're guests, and I'm letting them relax while they're here." I refrained from giving Jacki Jewell the finger.

"We are so tired of houses that don't quite look real, aren't we, honey?"

Her mate had that buzzed-out look that husbands get sometimes in intense situations. No one expected much of a response from him.

She reached over and shook my hand. "We'll be in touch. Or Jacki will. Thank you and we're sorry to interrupt."

"Fine with me," I said. "And with the artist who did the murals."

Alvin blushed to the tip of his ponytail.

She said, "I love them all. That's what makes the house really special."

Jacki Jewell cleared her throat. "Well, we have a couple more really special houses to visit, so we'll be off now."

The young couple prepared to leave. The young woman leaned over and gave Alvin a huge hug. "I know you will have a successful career as an artist and as a chef too, if that wonderful chowder is anything to go by."

By this point, the tips of his pointed ears were glowing like embers.

213

As Jacki Jewell, significantly more purse-lipped than she'd been when she arrived, shepherded her buyers out the door, Alvin said, "I think that went well."

Jacki turned and said, "You may be hearing from me. I'm not overly hopeful."

Alvin snorted. "I don't know why not. They were ready to sign on the dotted line before they even left."

Jacki Jewell slammed the door. Not that we cared.

"Will you make me a copy of that DVD quickly, Alvin? I have an idea of how to find Bunny, and he has to see it."

THIRTEEN

What's the difference between a lawyer and a pothole?
-People will swerve to avoid hitting a pothole.

What conceivable connection could Bunny have with Annalisa Fillmore? Or, for that matter, why would she, a high-powered crusader, have wasted her time trying to harm a tame former burglar? She usually set her sights on cabinet ministers or influential media types. It just didn't make sense. She was the most resolute anti-crime crusader anyway. She was in favour of bringing back capital punishment. She would have been able to reduce Bunny to a solitary speck of lint on Tonya's spotless carpet. He might have died of fright, no fire necessary.

I got P. J. on the phone. "Me again, and don't interrupt. Are you sure there wasn't any way that Annalisa Fillmore could have stage-managed that 'alibi' for the time of Rollie Thorsten's death?"

"Hello to you, Tiger. And no, there isn't any way. I've been checking and rechecking. The people she was with are rock solid. And none of them had any reason to love her, let alone lie for her. At best, she was like a permanent hangnail for most of them. Endless harassing letters and time-wasting calls. Most of the people who can vouch for her would have been overjoyed to see her as a viable suspect in a murder case."

"Did they know that's why you were asking? It's not like the police suspected her."

"I may have suggested the possibility of something tasty if we could put her somewhere else at that time, without revealing what. They were all tempted, but the fact is she was there. All evening. Mind telling me why you're pushing this?"

"Soon. I promise you will be glad you helped me."

"High time. I'm always helping you."

"I just need to check out one small detail, then I'll let you see something that will blow the top of your head off."

"Make sure it happens. I'm getting tired of all this one way—"

I hung up and planned my next move. Bunny was the only person who might possibly be able to answer the question as to why Annalisa Fillmore was lying in the morgue. If they had already identified her, that might explain Mombourquette's lack of cooperative information sharing. And, more worrying, the police would now be actively looking for Bunny. Sure, his house had burned down and he was a victim, but they didn't believe in him the way I did.

If Bunny wasn't dead, and now I felt confident that he wasn't, where the hell was he holed up? His townhouse was toast, and from the stories I'd heard over the years, every member of Tonya's family and all of her friends had hated the idea of a smart, hardworking girl with her own successful business saddled with a dyslexic, art-loving burglar. According to Bunny, Tonya had cut off contact with most of them. Therefore, it was unlikely that they'd go running to that side of the family.

Bunny had sworn he'd never go back to his old life, that he was steering clear of any lowlife colleagues who could drag him back. I'd believed him. Just to stay grounded, I reminded myself that this wouldn't be the first time I'd been fooled by a former client who talked a good story. Even so, I couldn't figure out how Bunny's recent troubles came from his criminal past. Brugel had never figured in his life.

Mrs. Parnell's place would have been perfect, yet Bunny hadn't stayed there long. And stranger still, he hadn't found a way to let me know where they'd gone or even that they were all right. Why not?

What would have motivated him to hide from me? Elaine and I were the only two people in the world who always stood by him, aside from Tonya, and even she had threatened to walk away if Bunny was involved in something shifty. She was raising a child, so I got that, no question. But I couldn't imagine what circumstances would cause me to abandon Bunny.

He should have known that. So where the hell was he?

Bunny could have been anywhere.

Or nowhere.

*   *   *

I whipped over to Clearwater with the copied DVD and a new plan. The execution started in the mailroom on the first floor of the building I'd called home for years. I turned my attention to the mailboxes. I had Alvin's copy of Mrs. Parnell's keys and decided to use picking up her mail as a cover. I waited until no one was in the room, then began at one end of the mailboxes and moved along. I was checking for boxes that were stuffed with paper, signs of mail not collected for a while. By the time I'd reached the end of the bank of mailboxes, I'd identified two dozen of them, all conveniently identified by their apartment numbers.

I checked as I got off the elevator and hustled down the hallway on the third floor. My hunch was that Bunny had felt exposed in 1608. Too many people knew about the connection with Mrs. Parnell and me, and he didn't want to take a chance. Now that I'd seen what had happened to his home and what could have happened to his neighbours, in retrospect I couldn't blame him. If it had been my family, I wouldn't have chosen an apartment on one of the higher floors. If he needed to get out fast, close to ground level would be better.

The third floor seemed like the place to start. I tried not to berate myself for giving a known burglar the run of the apartment building. After all, this was an emergency and an unusual one at that.

I tried the door of 306.

No luck. The door didn't budge when I turned the handle. There wasn't much I could do about that: I didn't own burglar tools and wouldn't have been inclined to use them if I did. The door at 310 held fast. There were extra locksets on each of these doors. I figured these people probably also invested in deadbolts that were too much for the casual break-in. By the end of the hallway, I was no better off. I took the stairs to the fourth floor and started again. At apartment 428, I paused. There was a crack of light at the edge of the door. I stuck out a finger and gave the tiniest of pushes. The door swung inward, and I popped through it without waiting. Bunny never was much for locking doors.

Inside, Tonya's face was swollen from crying. She slumped on the sofa in this stranger's apartment with a blanket over her shoulders, Destiny snuggled beside her.

"Hello," I said, glancing around for Bunny. "Where's—?"

Bunny stuck his head out of the bedroom and began pacing, pale and agitated. "You found us."

"Hi, Tonya. Destiny."

"I lost my dolly. Daddy's going to get me another one."

"Guess what I found?" I said, putting a finger to my lips. "He won't have to."

I pulled the ragdoll from my big yellow handbag. Destiny squealed and hugged the doll, then put her hand over her mouth. "We're not supposed to make any noise."

I said, "Do you and Mummy want to take your dolly into the bedroom so she can have a nap while I chat with Daddy about big people stuff?"

"So," I said when they'd closed the bedroom door behind them. "Thanks a lot for giving me all this grief, Bunny."

"Sorry, Camilla, but I had no choice. I have to protect them. I didn't know who else might know where we were. I didn't know that carpet guy, or if I could trust him. His kids were once in trouble with the law. They might still be connected."

"They're not connected, but anyway, you can trust me."

"You can't be everywhere all the time."

"I'm here now. And you are going to be arrested for being unlawfully in this apartment. You had access to Mrs. Parnell's place. You didn't have to worry about breaking the law."

Tonya yanked open the door to the bedroom and blurted, "You're here unlawfully too, Camilla. Probably none of this would have happened if you hadn't gotten involved. I think the police will have to know that."

I rolled my eyes, "Good thing you're an honest citizen, Tonya, because you don't have what it takes to make a criminal. I know that you're stressed, but I need you to work with me. Try to remember that I have your best interests at heart."

Tonya sniffed before retreating to the bedroom and closing the door softly. Bunny paused in his pacing. "Did you see what happened to our house? I had the TV on with no sound just to keep Destiny amused. Tonya freaked. I hope no one in the next apartment heard her carrying on."

"Lucky for you, most people here work during the day. Look, I'm sorry about your house, Bunny. I know your paintings would have been destroyed too but it was a good thing that the three of you got out of it. You had a close call."

"Tonya and Destiny are safe. That's all that matters. But on the news they said a woman was badly burned in the fire. Who was that? One of our neighbours?"

"I thought it was you at first, or Tonya. I was terrified there might be three bodies. Do you have any idea how I felt about that?"

"I never thought about it," Bunny said. "I'm sorry, Camilla."

"By the time I heard about the news, I already knew that you weren't where you were supposed to be, so guess what went through my mind?"

"I told you, I couldn't stay there."

"Whatever. You sure can't stay here."

"How did you find me?"

"I used to be your lawyer, remember? I knew your MOs."

Bunny's hazel eyes teared up. "I thought I'd never have to use any of those again. I'm really serious about going straight. This was a matter of life and death for..." He stared toward the closed door.

"We have to get you out of here and into somewhere safe. You're going to do what I tell you and not try any tricks."

I hoped like hell I wasn't being a gold-plated patsy

falling for Bunny's tales. Of course, I knew if he'd planned it, he could have found a better hiding place and one that wouldn't come with a spell in the slammer.

"I don't know if anywhere is safe. I saw people checking out the building. We've kept the lights off in the apartment just in case. But it looks over the parking lot, and I can see people watching the windows."

"You're a tad too paranoid lately, Bunny, even for this weird situation," I said. "Of course, who am I to talk? I've been worried that my phone or car could be bugged. Conspiracy theories dance in my head. Anyway, let's get down to work. How about if we get you all out of here? My sisters are away, and you'll be all right at one of their places. I have keys."

"I bet they're watching you too, Camilla. Someone probably followed you here. They'll just track us, and we'd be sitting ducks. I'm not going to risk it."

"Unlikely, Bunny. They, if there is a 'they' and whoever 'they' might be, will be looking for a family of three. We can outfox them on that front."

"Maybe."

Bunny was the picture of misery. For the first time I noticed the pronounced shake in his hand. I sat down and looked him straight in the eye. He managed to evade my scrutiny. I said, "Before we go anywhere, I need to know what your connection is with Annalisa Fillmore."

"Who?"

"Oh, come on, Bunny. Anyone who reads the paper knows…"

"Dyslexia, remember?"

"You watch television. You must see the news from time to time."

"Yeah, but I don't know who she is."

"She's the crusading mother who has been lobbying for stiffer sentences for people who injure or kill other people while commiting a crime. She's been advocating a return of the death penalty."

Bunny stared back at me uncomprehendingly.

"Ring a bell?" I said.

"No, and anyway, why would it? I've never hurt anyone in my life, Camilla. You know that's true."

I did.

"Death penalty?" he said with a shiver.

"This would be a good time to quit dicking around, Bunny. Who is after you? And what the hell do they want?"

He shook his head. "I don't know anyone who would want to hurt me. I mean, the guys I used to hang out with, they're just losers, small-time crooks. They want a fix or a few bucks to blow on a weekend. They're not evil. They might kill a person in a bar fight, or if they felt trapped in an armed robbery, but they wouldn't chase my family. So I don't understand. But I'm really scared."

"What about Brugel?"

"What about him?" Bunny was practically gibbering by this time.

You can't really throttle a terrified father, so I fought off the urge. "Is there something I should know, Bunny? Something that connects you and Brugel? The kind of thing that could get your house burned down and someone killed?"

Bunny bit his lip until it bled.

I couldn't say I blamed him. I was coming up empty trying to find a reason to connect Brugel and Annalisa and Bunny too.

"Well, there must be some connection. Think."

"But Camilla, I already thought about it."

"Well, you'd better think harder."

He stared at me, panic clouding his features. "What is the matter with you? Why are you asking me about Brugel and this woman, whatever her name is?"

"Because she walked right into your home just before it burned down. And I believe that her body was found outside what was left of your house. Is that a good enough reason?"

"Why would this woman that I don't know and don't have anything to do with have been in my house?"

"You tell me."

His voice rose like the whine of a chainsaw. "But I can't. I don't understand. I didn't know her. I can't think of any reason at all. She's a stranger."

I did a little hard thinking myself. I did know that Bunny was dyslexic and never read anything he didn't have to unless it involved the art world or Destiny. All to say, maybe Bunny did know her and didn't know he did.

I said, "Is there a computer here? Or a DVD player?"

Bunny shook his head. "No DVD player and I guess whoever lives here took their laptop with them. There's a TV, but we're trying to keep the lights down so the people who are watching from the parking lot don't catch on that we're here."

I let that go. No point in arguing with a paranoid person.

"Hang on a bit," I said. "I'm going to go to Mrs. Parnell's place. She has a DVD player."

"Be careful, Camilla."

*　　*　　*

A few minutes later I reached Mrs. Parnell's door, yet again. As I went to stick the key in the lock, the door swung open. I gave myself a brief tongue-lashing. Had I been so unnerved when I'd found out that Bunny and his family were gone that I'd forgotten to lock the door when I'd left? I didn't think so. A closer look revealed jimmy marks on the lock. Mrs. Parnell had never been nervous enough to install better security despite Alvin's urgings. I stepped inside and glanced around. There hadn't been an ordinary burglary, that was for sure. Mrs. Parnell had more electronic gadgets than anyone I knew. Even though she had a cluster of toys with her at the Perley, there was plenty left behind in the apartment. Her high-end stereo was still there as well as her computer, two of her three printers, her everyday laser and her inkjet, and the bulk of her CD collection and the DVD player I was looking for. Her digital camera sat on the console in the hallway. No burglar would have left without that, at the very least. Therefore, maybe he or she was still in the apartment.

If that was true, I needed to find out and fast. But I didn't plan to walk in there to see if someone was ready to pounce on me from the bedroom or the bathroom. In my experience, burglars are a cowardly lot and not likely to be a threat, but you never know what a panicked felon will do when cornered. Plus, my instincts told me that this was no ordinary break-in. First, I called the super. Luckily, I hadn't had time to forget his number after all the years I'd lived in this building.

"Get up to 1608. On the double," I said to the super.

Then I called 911.

The super was nothing if not quick. He had a soft spot in his heart for Mrs. Parnell and a general wariness of me.

Together, we checked the bedroom and bathroom. I held a lamp as a weapon. He had his wrench.

"Okay," I said, "The police are on the way. I'll wait outside for them."

I was thinking fast throughout this. Had someone seen me return to the first floor to check out the mailboxes? Had that person—perhaps the parking lot watcher—then taken advantage of my absence to dash up to 1608 to pick the lock? Was that person looking for Bunny and his family? Who were the watchers in the parking lot, if indeed they were real?

Were they still watching from somewhere, waiting for their chance to catch Bunny? For what reason?

I snatched up the digital camera, took the elevator to the ground floor and dashed out the door and into the parking lot. I walked behind the last row of cars, snapping shots of the vehicles and the license plates. There were at least twenty cars parked there. By the time I reached the first row, which I figured would give a good view of the windows on Bunny's side of the building, a mustard-yellow Mustang started up. I jogged toward the front of the row to catch the plate before the Mustang left the lot. It revved its engine and shot forward, turning toward me. I leapt back out of the way and tripped over one of the cement parking barriers fringing the lot. I fell toward the giant dumpster that serviced the building and felt a wrench as my shoulder hit the ground. I huddled between the concrete wall of the building and the dumpster and listened to another rev. Pain shot through me as I forced myself to roll as far from the dumpster as I could get. I managed to hide myself behind the tall blue recycle bins. The car hit the dumpster, reversed and shot forward and hit it again. A door slammed. I made myself as small as I could and tried to think how to use the recycling bin as a weapon. The footsteps came closer. Stopped. An image of Rollie Thorsten, shot and drowned, flashed through my brain. Whoever had killed him wasn't afraid to use a gun.

I had nothing to lose. Using my good side, I threw my body and gave the bins a mighty heave towards my unseen stalker. I heard a satisfying "oof" as I sprinted toward the low fence at the near end of the parking lot. So close and yet so far away.

You gotta love adrenaline. I barely managed to stumble over the fence. I landed on my nose in the soft grass in the area known as the dog walk. I glanced up but saw no one coming after me. No arm raised with a gun. No joker. Good news. On the other hand, if a shoulder could scream in agony, mine would have. My nose hurt like hell too.

Sirens were the best music in the world at that moment. I heard the pounding of feet, the slam of a door and the rev of an engine behind me.

I got to my feet, my knees wobbling under me. As the first squad squealed into the parking lot, the Mustang shot out, nicking the cruiser as it went. The crash hurt my ears. A second car, roof lights flashing and siren shrieking, tore off in pursuit of the Mustang. A third cruiser followed. I was impressed with the number of cars that had arrived as a result of my 911 call, even though it had taken them long enough. I didn't think they usually used their sirens for a mere break-in either. I limped toward the police car to see if the occupants had been injured. The airbags had deployed. A young officer was stepping out, looking dazed and holding his head.

The officer blinked at me when I got close.

"You're bleeding," he said, pointing to my nose.

"Look who's talking," I answered, pointing to his head.

He stared at me. "What? I'm not…" He raised his hand and felt his forehead. He brought his hand down to have a look at it. He gazed at the hand in confusion, probably surprised to find it all red and sticky.

I said, a bit more kindly, "I sure hope you don't have a concussion. They're going to haul you off to Emerg. You have my sympathy if you do. Concussions are a real bitch to deal with."

He swayed, which is a bad sign.

"Hang in there," I said, "Here come the paramedics. You go first. But maybe you shouldn't try walking anywhere."

"I'm all right," he said, as his knees buckled and he sank to the ground.

I grabbed onto him to break his fall. My shoulder didn't thank me. I said, "Sure you are. And in case I don't see you again, thanks a lot for saving my life."

"Job," he said, closing his eyes.

"Better keep those eyes open," I said. "Tell me, what made you drive into the parking lot instead of heading in the front door?"

The eyes opened part way. "Got a call."

"Sure. You got my 911 about a problem in apartment 1608."

"No, parking lot."

Hmm.

I looked up and saw Bunny staring down from a fourth floor window. He may have given me the thumbs up, hard to tell at that distance. Sometimes it's good to have a burglar in your corner, I suppose, even one that doesn't do what he's told, like hide in a safe place such as Mrs. Parnell's. I stopped that thought mid-stream. I'd told Bunny earlier that Mrs. Parnell's place was safe. I'd been wrong.

I no longer knew what I knew. I had no idea who'd been in the mustard-yellow Mustang and why they'd been watching the building. Maybe they weren't connected to this, maybe they were a pair of lowlife drug dealers who wanted to avoid arrest. Maybe it was just a coincidence. There are lots of coincidences in life, but something, maybe the searing pain in my shoulder suggested that this wasn't one of them. This was not only up close but also very personal.

As the paramedics headed rapidly toward me, I gestured to the cop, who was now sitting down, resting his head against the body of the cruiser. His eyes were closed again.

"Better take care of him first," I said. "He's one of the good guys."

*　*　*

I figured the police officer had a concussion for sure. I hate head injuries, and I've had more than my share. but I had to admit this shoulder thing wasn't much better. To make things worse, I spotted the familiar face of Dr. Abdullah Hasheem when I got hauled into Emerg by the second ambulance. Just my luck he was on duty. Of course, when wasn't he?

"Haven't seen you for a while," he said. "I thought you must have moved to another city."

I decided to sidestep a chat about how I spend more time getting patched up at the Ottawa General Hospital emergency room than the average lawyer. I wasn't the only person in the world with that kind of track record. "How's the police officer doing?" I said, conversationally. "I believe he had a concussion."

"Why? Is he another relative of yours?" Dr. Hasheem asked as he looked up from my shoulder.

I considered the utility of a fib at this point and decided against it. I did say, "No, but let's say I have a legitimate interest."

"Do you." Usually that's a question, but I've had a few too many dealings with Dr. Hasheem over the years. In this case, I took it that he meant "you don't."

"Never mind. I've got connections on the force. I'll find out for myself." I followed this with a yelp as he examined my shoulder.

"Good idea," Dr. Hasheem said. "But speaking of concussions, did you happen to hit your head when you fell?"

"Just my nose. It's stopped bleeding. No hits to my skull."

"Well, that's a first. Perhaps you're turning over a new leaf. Even so, I think you'll need an ultrasound and an X-ray."

"Is that absolutely necessary? I've got quite a few things to take care of today."

Dr. Hasheem didn't answer until he'd written up his notes and what looked like a couple of requisitions. When he clicked his pen closed, he said, "Good to see some things never change."

He was gone with the usual flap of his white coat before I could come up with a suitably huffy reply.

FOURTEEN

How many lawyers does it take to change a light bulb?
-Lawyers can't change light bulbs. But if you're looking
for a lawyer to screw a light bulb...

Eventually, after being shuffled from lab to lab, I found myself back in hospital never never land. Dr. Hasheem's soft grey replacement showed up, tail twitching. I'd been expecting Leonard Mombourquette. He was not amused, no surprise there. Even the bizarre tale I had to tell him didn't help his mood.

I did my best to look him right in his bright beady eyes.

"Start at the beginning," he said. "Explain what were you doing in the parking lot again."

"I've told you a half-dozen times. I was just checking it out to see if there was anyone suspicious there. Someone had broken into Mrs. Parnell's apartment, and I thought I might be able to head off their confederates before they got away."

"Right. You did tell me that. Now, why don't you tell me a story that makes a bit of sense? Don't overdo it. I don't want to pass out from shock or anything."

"Why don't you believe me? Did you check out Mrs. Parnell's apartment? It's obvious that someone broke in there. You can clearly see the damage to the door frame. I have a key, as you know."

"That part makes sense. It's why would you run out to the parking lot and check out the vehicles there, that's what I don't get."

"I didn't want her stuff to…"

Damn.

"Right. You mean the stuff that wasn't taken?"

"I didn't take time to search for everything. She keeps a bit of money and some credit cards hidden here and there. She has items of sentimental value."

"Tell you what. Keep sticking to that story, and I'll keep you here talking."

"Come on, Leonard. Give me a break. You know I haven't done anything wrong."

"I know you cost the province a good bit of money today and took some poor devil's spot on a gurney and I also know that you're harbouring that greasy little con."

"What greasy little…? Oh, you mean, Bunny? I'd hardly call him greasy. He's actually very fastidious."

"Go ahead. Keep it up. I got all night. In fact, I got every day and night until I retire. I might even sit here as a volunteer afterwards if you want to stonewall me that long."

"Look, Leonard. Bunny wasn't there. He used to be a burglar and a good one. He never would have left the door looking like that. This was some person that didn't have the skill level and finesse of a… Don't make that face. No matter how you feel about him, Bunny didn't burgle Mrs. P.'s place."

It might have been the right time to tell Mombourquette that Bunny had the keys to the apartment making burglary unnecessary, but that was one can of worms I didn't care to open.

"In that case, I'd like to hear exactly how his prints got in her apartment. I'm sure you could come up with a good story for that."

I have to admit I blinked. I wasn't about to say uncle though. "Bunny knows Mrs. Parnell. I think he might have been in her apartment legitimately. He's not on a wanted list. You have a bit of tunnel vision where he's concerned."

"Maybe that tunnel vision is what made me notice his fingerprints turning up in her bedroom, bedside table and in the bathroom. What else you wonder? Let's see. There's the fridge, the toaster, the oven, the air conditioner and… Shall I continue?"

"Fingerprints are not against the law. I'm telling you that Bunny didn't break into that apartment. I don't know why you don't believe me."

"Me neither. Especially since you always tell the truth."

"Leonard, you have to trust me. Bunny didn't run me down, and he's not the person who was in that apartment. I admit he may have been there at some other point, but he was not there today when this happened."

"Here's the thing: this fastidious criminal you seem to be so fond of is the number one suspect in a case of premeditated murder. So if you know where he is, you'd better spit it out, or you are going to find yourself charged with obstruction and anything else I can throw at you. You don't have many friends in the Crown Prosecutor's office, so they'll probably come up with a few doozies themselves."

I raised my hands in defeat. "Hey, Leonard, go ahead. Throw the book at me. Bunny didn't kill that woman. He was the intended victim, and I believe I can prove it. He was due to be home with his family at the moment his house caught fire. He would have been killed. His wife and child would have been too. The real question is: what was Annalisa Fillmore doing there?"

There was a sharp intake of breath on Mombourquette's part. "What makes you think that Annalisa Fillmore was there? What would she be doing there? What's her connection with Bunny Mayhew?"

"I don't know."

"Where did Bunny go? Did you take him somewhere?"

I could handle this without actually lying outright. "I saw him that day at his house, but I left before the fire and explosion. I thought that perhaps the whole family had died. Annalisa Fillmore never crossed my mind."

"Where is he now?"

Good question. "No idea, Leonard. And I am happy to say that's the truth. But I would like to know if the investigators found the remains of a toy dog anywhere near Annalisa Fillmore's body? Maybe a huge green dog?"

"Okay. You do go too far, MacPhee. You're not too badly off to get hauled into the station. Maybe we'll have to beat it out of you."

Dr. Hasheem reappeared at that key point. He stood behind Mombourquette, cleared his throat and said, "I don't think either of those two things will be happening."

I said, "Leonard here is just being whimsical. However, on the off chance he's not, I'll trust you to remember this conversation, Dr. Hasheem."

"I could hardly forget it," Dr. Hasheem muttered as he left the room. He turned and said, "Speak to the nurses before you leave, and make sure someone lets me know if this person tries to take you in for questioning before we get your results back."

After he left, I said, "You see. Good citizens take care of each other. Here's the deal. I haven't been straight with you, Leonard, mostly because you wouldn't believe me about the joke situation. So you can be mad if you want, and you can take it out on me if it makes you happy. You can even arrest me, but I have some information for you. You'll have to work with me, though."

Mombourquette was silent for a long while.

Finally, I said, "Evidence doesn't interest you?"

"What is it?"

"You'll find it of interest?"

"Talk."

"It's surveillance footage of Annalisa Fillmore heading into Bunny's house after he left and while the house is empty. And afterwards. It's pretty grim."

"How do you come to have that?"

"I knew someone was going to go after Bunny today, so I installed a camera in the tree across the street to catch anyone trying to go in the front door. There was one by the back door too, but the fire probably destroyed that. I have a DVD. I would have told you about it if you hadn't practically thrown me off the scene."

"Why would you have something like that? It doesn't make sense. Even for you, MacPhee."

"Because I received a burglar joke. And you left me no choice."

"Forgive me if, as usual, I don't follow your thinking."

"Three people are dead: Rollie Thorsten, Judge Card-arelle, Roxanne Terrio. Your police colleague Steve Anstruther is seriously injured. As far as I can tell, they all received jokes. I got the same jokes. So did Bunny. The day they died or were injured, he and I received their names, including Steve Anstruther. Remember? I have always figured it was Brugel. He's capable of doing it. Completely. And there's no way that Annalisa Fillmore would do anything for him or with him. Don't you think I'm right there?

Mombourquette nodded dourly. "Love her or hate her, she wasn't the front woman for a gang lord."

"But she was involved somehow. We need to find out how she was connected with any of these people."

"She was definitely connected to Thorsten. We all accept that. I myself checked that out. She couldn't have killed him. She was with a number of people who couldn't stand her and would have loved to point the finger.."

"Well, maybe she had someone to do her bidding. We thought that Brugel could use others to do his dirty work. Why couldn't Annalisa?"

"First of all, for the last time, there is no 'we'. Second, I want that DVD."

"Sure thing," I said. "I'll ask Alvin to bring it over."

"Never mind. I'll send a uniform for it."

"Good idea," I said, thinking fast. "I'll ask him to let your officer in and hand the DVD over."

Lucky for me, Mombouquette had to go to the little boy's room. That meant I could tell Alvin, when I got him on my cell, to make sure to copy the DVD before the uniform showed up to get it.

"You're where?" Alvin bleated.

"Emergency. Don't even ask. Better yet, can you pick me up here and bring a copy of that DVD for Sgt. Mombourquette? That's a copy. Don't forget. Don't mention it to anyone. Bring the original too. We need to show it to Mrs. P. And hurry up."

"Good news," I said to Mombourquette as he returned. "I reached Alvin. He'll bring the DVD here. By the way, how's the officer who hit his head? He seemed to be pretty badly injured. Will he need surgery?"

"I don't know," he said.

"What about the guys who hit him? That Mustang must have been damaged after that."

His eyes narrowed. "We haven't found them yet."

"But you will," I smiled encouragingly. Of course, Mombourquette was pretty well immune to deceitful types like me.

"We will. We got the car."

"You did? Really?" I said admiringly.

"Not me personally, so you don't need to lay it on quite so thick, but it's been found. Abandoned. They must have fled on foot."

"But you know who owns it? The Mustang, I mean."

Mombourquette watched me with narrowed eyes. "It was reported stolen earlier today. But there will be a link to whoever was driving. For sure. Fingerprints, hair. Something."

"Of course, although they don't usually do any amount of forensic follow-up on stolen cars, do they?"

"This isn't usual. This was an attack on a police officer."

"Right. Of course. Sorry, I was just thinking out loud, and face it, I have my own interest in it. Those guys tried to run me over. They were coming after me when the first police cars arrived. I owe you guys a lot."

"That's weird, isn't it, that a pair of complete strangers would try to kill you. You sure you didn't know them?"

My jaw dropped. "Of course, I didn't know them. The people I know don't try to kill me. They just get pissed off."

"They sure do. Don't go anywhere. I'm going to make some calls. I'll be back."

After about twenty minutes, I was really glad to hear Alvin's voice.

"Alvin, I need something else from you."

"You could say hello first," he sniffed. "And what happened to you, anyway? Do you know that you missed the girls' second race?"

In the interests of redeeming myself, I filled him in on events, perhaps adding a bit of drama here and there, in case the missing burglar, the invaded apartment, the injured cop, and the attempt to run me over weren't enough. Alvin can set the guilt bar quite high. Sometimes he's worse than my sisters.

Finally, he sniffed, "I guess if you were in the hospital, it would be understandable. I'll make sure the girls hear the story behind it."

"Perhaps I should call Ashley and Brittany to apologize."

"I don't think so, Camilla. You'll probably just make things worse. You know what you're like."

"Fine. Okay. Can you take me over to Clearwater to pick up my car? While you're there, we can look for my digital camera. It got knocked out of my hand when that Mustang came after me. I'm hoping I captured a picture of the people who hit me. I'd like to get a look at that. Oh wait, here comes Leonard now. Do you have the DVD for him?"

"Why don't you get him to pick up the camera?" Alvin said.

"Shh. Don't mention the camera to Mombourquette because—oh hi, Leonard, how are you?"

Mombourquette just shot me a look. I made a big deal out of accepting the DVD from Alvin and passing it to him.

"Don't thank me," I said.

"I don't plan to," he answered. "You could have saved us a lot of trouble if you'd told me about it and don't bother to pretend I wouldn't let you."

I just shrugged and turned to Alvin. "Let's head home.

Dr. Hasheem told me to take it easy."

Dr. Hasheem, whishing past at that moment, said, "And try to stay out of fights."

Alvin was driving Mrs. Parnell's former vehicle, the seemingly indestructible 1974 LTD that she'd given to him. It practically knew its way back to her apartment, leaving Alvin and me time to argue.

"I still don't see why you didn't just tell the police where in the parking lot your camera is and leave it to them."

"If Mombourquette gets the camera before I do, he won't let me see anything. He doesn't want me interfering in his so-called investigation, which I have to say would be going nowhere if you and I weren't involved. And Bunny is the second reason. I don't want the cops around the building any more than they have to be. I'm willing to take the risk. Illegal, I know, unwise for sure, and possibly even insane. But Bunny went to the wire for me when I needed him, and I would do the same for him. Anyway, the camera might be behind the recycle bins or maybe it dropped when I jumped over the barrier at the end of the lot. It could be on the patch of grass by the edge of the parking lot. Let's hope it's still there and that there's something worthwhile on it. If we find it, I'll tell Mombourquette that I forgot all about the camera in the shock of being attacked."

"The fun never ends," Alvin said.

*   *   *

The camera turned up on the grass, just as I'd hoped. Alvin scooped it up. I peered at the indistinct image on the small screen. I could barely make out the cars, let alone who might have been sitting in them.

"Fine. We'll drop off one of the cars at home and take the camera to Mrs. Parnell's. She'll be happy to print out my shots for us. She might be able to improve the image of the guy in the Mustang. And there are a few more things I'd like her to look up."

"Okay. But are you sure you should be driving?"

"I've had lots of excellent painkillers. Unless you've figured out how you can drive two cars at once?"

Alvin sniffed. "Fine. But I hope I don't have to drag you back to Emergency."

"Not everything's about you, Alvin," I said as I hurried off before he could respond.

We chose to drop off the LTD first. As we both pulled up to the house, Jacki Jewell was just getting out of her black Mercedes SUV.

"Wow," Alvin said. "She's had her photo and name vinyl-wrapped on her car. That's so—"

"Egotistical?" I muttered.

"Well, looks like I caught you," she said with just a hint of accusation.

"Likewise," I said. I tried not to stare at the giant scary vinyl teeth on the side of her pricey vehicle.

"We have an offer," she said, the way anyone else might say the patient died.

"Told you," Alvin muttered.

"Why the long face? I thought that was what we wanted," I said.

"Well, I'm certain we can get a better price," she said. "Give it some thought."

"Is it much under what we asked?" I said.

"No. They didn't quibble about price at all. But that's a sign. Perhaps we can get a higher offer from someone else and then get a bidding war going. That's where…"

"Is it that couple who were here earlier?" Alvin said, "Because they were lovely and I don't think that Camilla wants to rip them off. Do you?"

"Of course not. We're in a hurry, Jacki. Can you give us the offer, and we'll take it with us to read it over before we sign it."

"I've indicated those items you need to note," she said haughtily.

"Camilla can never forget she's a lawyer," Alvin piped up.

"Is it a conditional offer?" I asked. "Maybe we shouldn't get too excited, Alvin."

"No conditions," she said in clipped tones. "They have the money. They won't even need a mortgage. They sold their house in Vancouver. Could have bought a much more expensive property if they wanted."

"Possession date?"

"Flexible. Up to three months if you need it."

"Is there anything unreasonable?" I asked.

"Not really, but I do believe we could have gotten a better price if you—"

"Thank you, Jacki," I said extracting the envelope from her hand. "I'll go over it tonight, and you can pick it up tomorrow. And now if you'll excuse us, we have to get out to visit our friend before it's too late. Alvin, do we have any good quality photo paper?"

"Don't be ridiculous. We don't even have a decent printer. But we can get some on the way."

"Did you ever find the wires to connect the camera to the computer?"

"Lord thundering Jesus, Camilla, you're the one who's always losing things."

Mrs. Parnell had no trouble uploading the images from the camera to her laptop and displaying them on her large screen television. Apparently, it's easy if you know how and have thousands of dollars worth of the right kind of software.

We were crowded into her small space in the Perley, mostly because the Major and the Colonel had decided to join us. We were more than a little sombre as we had all just watched the surveillance DVD of Annalisa Fillmore's approach to Bunny's house and her horrifying fiery exit.

"I got good shots of all the cars in the parking lot. They were all empty, but I'm not certain I actually got an image of the Mustang before it tried to run me over," I said as Mrs. P. quickly clicked through photo by photo. Sombre or not, she was enjoying the task.

Click click.

There were pictures of a silver Mazda 3 and a black Acura, almost a twin of my own, only with Manitoba plates.

She clicked onto the candy red Yaris, then the black cherry Honda Accord from the late nineties, a ribbon of rust showing around each of the wheel wells. All were empty, all had Ontario plates.

Click.

The glossy Ford F-150 King Ranch truck had no plates in the front, meaning either it was straight off a dealer's lot with a temporary plate or it was registered in Quebec. I'd stepped behind it to check that. Sure enough, Quebec plates. Click. I'd been approaching the mustard-yellow Mustang, starting to wonder if I had been wasting my time when all hell had broken loose.

Click.

"Did you see anyone in the car that tried to eliminate you, Ms MacPhee?"

I shook my head. "No. It all happened so quickly. I barely saw it coming at me. I guess I heard the engine rev before my brain recognized what was happening and I ran for cover."

"There's an image of the license plate, so surely we can trace the owner. I might even be able to hack in and—"

"Won't do any good, Mrs. P.," I said hastily. "The vehicle was stolen earlier."

Alvin said, "You can see the profile of a person on the passenger side."

"I don't even remember seeing him. I was just clicking away. These shots are not too well focused."

Mrs. Parnell swirled her mouse. "I can enhance that shot a bit more. It's somewhat blurry, but my photo software can produce miracles."

I squinted. "It's not quite enough to identify anyone though."

Alvin said, "Give Violet a chance."

Mrs. Parnell beamed and swirled her mouse again. All too technical for me. The picture sharpened. I stared. "That's funny. That person looks a lot like…"

"What?" Alvin said.

"Who?" Mrs. Parnell added.

The Major or possibly the Colonel said, "Don't hold back. It's not sporting."

I said, "Well, that just doesn't make sense."

"Who?" Alvin raised his voice. The other three reminded him that we were in a medical facility, and we didn't want to get turfed out.

"It looks like Jamie Kilpatrick."

Mrs. Parnell glanced up sharply. "You asked me to research the demise of a pair of Kilpatricks."

I sat on Mrs. Parnell's bed and stared at her. "I did indeed. His grandparents. They were killed by a drunk driver. But that doesn't explain why he would be in the passenger seat of a stolen Mustang that tried to run me down."

"From my time in Intelligence," the Major said, "I learned that things are not always what they seem."

"Very astute, Major," Mrs. P. said. "Very."

So if things weren't as they seemed, what were they? I'd been sleuthing around Kilpatrick's grandparents' house, and someone had called the police on me. What if it had been Kilpatrick himself and not the English lady with the dog? But what would that accomplish? Unless he didn't want me looking too closely at anything to do with him. If people weren't as they presented themselves, who were they? Annalisa had presented herself as a campaigner against crime, and yet as far as I could tell, she'd had a plan to murder Bunny and his family. The people in this strange game of cat and mouse, victims and villains, were connected somehow. Would I ever figure it out?

"I don't know why he'd try to kill me, but he was Rollie Thorsten's assistant, and he is definitely connected to Brugel. I don't think there's any link between him and Annalisa, but it's worth exploring. I think I need to sit back and think of everyone who is even vaguely related to this and then perhaps, if it isn't too much trouble, Mrs. P., see if we can find photos of them and print them. It's time to talk to the people who knew the victims."

Within fifteen minutes, we had several decent photos printed out: a shot of Brugel, thuglike, one of Annalisa Fillmore, giving a speech, another of Judge Cardarelle gazing frostily into the camera at a formal event. Madame Cardarelle, elegant as usual, stood beside him with a pro forma smile on her beautiful face. Roxanne Terrio standing by her bicycle, shielding her eyes from the sun. Bev Leclair was waving in the background. Rollie Thorsten striding out of the Courthouse, and Constable Steve Anstruther at his swearing in ceremony. We came up empty on Jamie Kilpatrick. Eventually, even Mrs. Parnell gave up.

I didn't though. I pulled out my cellphone.

"P. J.," I said merrily. "Glad to catch you. I think I have a few scraps of very newsy stuff for you."

"You're always saying that, Tiger, and yet, to date? Big fat zero."

"Take heart. I was almost run over today, and it looks like the passenger in the car was the junior lawyer in the Brugel case. I think he's involved in this whole joke set-up and these deaths. I don't know why, but his grandparents were killed a year and a half ago. There has to be some connection. His name is Jamie Kilpatrick. Do you have a shot of him? Maybe leaving the court? I know you take lots. I noticed one you took of Rollie Thorsten made the paper after his death."

P. J. sighed.

I said, "By the way, the cops aren't saying anything, but that body outside Bunny Mayhew's house? That was Annalisa Fillmore."

I enjoyed P. J.'s gasp more than the preceding sigh. "You can ask if they'll confirm or deny it. I suggest starting with the lovely and talented Sgt. Leonard Mombourquette." I added, "That might get you something before the paper goes to bed tonight. Make sure you send me that photo soon. The best address is Mrs. Parnell's, but send it to me too. Just in case."

P. J. said, "I'll see what I can find, and I'll email you. Just give me a bit of time. This is smokin'."

"You're welcome," I said, smugly.

The group was watching me as I finished making sure he had the right email addresses. When I hung up, Mrs, Parnell said, "I wonder why it is that you would be receiving these jokes, and why your former client Mr. Mayhew would have been at risk?"

I said. "The questions are the easy part. What I need is answers."

"Perhaps it's not the only question," the Colonel said. "It's important to ask the right questions in order to produce the best answers."

Frankly, while I thought he was just trying to keep up with the Major in Mrs. P.'s estimation, he went way up in mine.

"You're right," I said. "We should all be trying to find relationships between and among each of these people. Let's work on that on our own. Use your imaginations. Let them run wild."

"Oh, that reminds me, Ms MacPhee. In all the excitement, I quite forgot to tell you that I have learned that Annalisa Fillmore and Judge Cardarelle owned adjacent rental properties in Lowertown. Condos in that new development on George Street. Not sure if that's a fit, but it's a fact."

*   *   *

It was after nine when we got home, a bit later than I'd hoped because Mrs. Parnell, the Colonel and the Major had been keen to offer opinions and suggestions and because I was waiting to see if P. J. actually could send the photo. If the staff hadn't given us the boot we might have been there until midnight.

The girls, big surprise, were out.

Alvin said, "They invited me to go with them and their team, but I couldn't leave you here high and dry."

"Why don't you go now? There's nothing I'd like better than to be high and dry," I said, checking my phone. "Oh look, P. J. sent me a photo of Kilpatrick. Can you take a minute to print a couple of copies? Don't whine about the quality of our printer or the paper, just do it."

I walked Gussie quickly while Alvin managed to print the photo on our crappy printer. That boy can move fast enough when he puts his mind to it. I waved goodbye to him and plunked myself down on the sofa to try to connect the dots. I was really pleased to be home alone. The photo had turned out fine. There was a clear shot of Kilpatrick, slightly dwarfed by Constable Wentzell outside the courthouse. I figured that P. J.'s real goal had been to get a shot of the amazon-like Wentzell, the girl of his dreams.

The day seemed to have been about forty-eight hours long, but by ten o'clock I was frustrated. I knew I'd never be able to sleep. I hadn't connected a single dot. Annalisa hated Rollie with good reason but couldn't possibly have killed him. Jamie Kilpatrick had tried to run me down, but had been in the cop shop at the time of Rollie's death. He was definitely involved somehow, but until I'd seen the photo of his face on the passenger side of the Mustang, I never would have thought he was capable of anything. But who was on the driver's side? Yet another player with no clear relationship?

I paced around a bit and drew arrows and question

marks between people, then scratched them out. I would have liked to get Ray's take on the situation, but you can't have everything. Sometimes you can't have anything.

Of course, I needed to talk to people who might identify relationships between any of the individuals whose photos I'd collected. That would make sense. I glanced at the clock.

Was it really too late to call? My sisters would have said yes, but they were out of town, weren't they? Anyway, I was a big girl, even if I couldn't connect the dots, and all the people I cared about were unavailable, as were most of the people I didn't care about.

What to do?

I picked up that proud low-tech device, the telephone book, and took a look to see if I could locate Bev Leclair, the office manager at Terrio and Fox. Sure enough, I found a couple of listings for B. Leclairs, none too far away. Was it best to call first or try surprise? I opted for surprise. It wasn't like I had anything else to do.

There was no luck at the houses of the first couple of B. Leclairs, and half an hour later I was checking out the third, cruising through the leafy neighbourhood of Sandy Hill, not far from Mombourquette's own tiny mouse house. I took a slight detour and drove past it. The lights were out, his car gone. I popped a set of the photos into his mailbox. I imagined he was at Elaine's place for the evening, surrounded by clutter and non-stop chatter. Clean carpets too.

Oh, well. As Mrs. P. would say, nothing ventured, nothing gained.

I called Mombourquette and imagined him sitting on Elaine's new orange leather sofa, surrounded by stacks of political books and staring at my number on his call display as he didn't pick up. I tried twice more and left a helpful message telling him about the set of photos in his mailbox and suggesting that he find a way to show them to Constable Steve Anstruther if he regained consciousness, taking special note of Anstruther's reaction to Annalisa Fillmore and James Kilpatrick. I felt a bit better after that.

Bev Leclair lived in a well-maintained building with a small lawn that someone must have cut with nail scissors, it was so precise. The lobby smelled of citrus cleaner, and I could practically see my reflection in the polished marble floor. It was exactly the type of place I would have expected for Bev. The leather sofa and pair of matching club chairs also looked well-cared for. Maybe this was the kind of building I'd like for myself once the house sold.

B Leclair appeared on the list of residents. I pressed that button and waited. A disembodied voice said hello, a hint of surprise in the tone. Or was it apprehension?

"Camilla MacPhee," I said. "I have information that might shed light on Roxanne's death, and I would like to know if you could help me by looking at some photos. You could meet me in the foyer if you're more comfortable."

"Come on up," she said. "Apartment 843."

The door was open when I arrived. Based on my years as a victims' advocate, I wanted to suggest that a woman at home alone might show more caution, but of course, this wasn't the right moment for that. Moxi, the bouncing chihuahua, greeted me with a blizzard of barking.

The apartment was like Bev herself, bright, colourful and neat. Her dark red hair was in a French twist, and her black jersey cotton dress and glittery flipflops showed a sexy side I hadn't noticed in the crisp office manager. She wore her curiosity like a piece of jewellery. The man who stood behind her sported baggy plaid shorts, a T-shirt and an expression that indicated he'd be happier if I was vaporized on the spot.

"Won't take long," I said.

He nodded grimly, took his shaved head and his Celtic tattoos and swaggered out to the balcony, along with a package of cigarettes and a glower. Moxi scampered after him. The boyfriend tried and failed to keep Moxi inside.

I plunked myself down next to Bev on the striped IKEA sofa and spread out the photos.

"I need to know if any of these people look familiar, if they might have had a relationship with Roxanne, business or personal, or if they'd ever come to the office."

She nodded. "Sure. Do you think that one of them caused her to crash her bicycle?"

"I think so. I wasn't entirely up front with you and Gary the time I came by the office. Let me go through the whole thing for you: Roxanne died just over a month ago, a Judge Cardarelle died a few weeks before that, Rollie Thorsten was murdered several days ago and a police officer was critically injured this week. Someone set fire to another person's home yesterday. I and one other person received a lawyer joke before each of these deaths. It didn't sound too serious to us until the next day when a sheet of paper with the name of the victim arrived. I think the victims also received the jokes."

"You asked about the jokes and I told you Roxanne got one that I knew of."

"I believe someone is sending a message. Every victim is connected with the legal system in some way, hence the jokes. And the pace is picking up."

Her hand shot to her throat. "You mean you think someone killed poor Roxanne because of some twisted idea of revenge? That's too horrible."

"Yes, it is," I said.

"The jokes were some kind of message to the person?"

"I believe so."

"But Roxanne wasn't upset by that dumb joke. Annoyed maybe, but not upset. She had no idea it meant anything."

I searched for the right words to reveal what I had concluded during my long stretch of thinking. I took a deep breath. Bev stared at me, her brown eyes huge.

I said, "I wonder if she didn't learn it at the end."

"You mean the person would have told her she was going to die and why?"

I shrugged, apologetically. "It makes sense to me."

"Well, not to me. It's horrible!"

The man on the balcony reacted to the sound of her raised voice. He stepped toward the door, and she waved him away again. He turned his back to us. Sulking, I thought.

"Your friend doesn't like me much."

The grin made it all the way to her eyes. "Don't worry about it. I don't think he's a keeper. Unlike Moxi. Moxi's here for good."

I said, "That's terrific. So, now that you understand where I'm coming from, let's have a look at these pictures." I passed her the one of Rollie Thorsten.

She said, "I saw his picture in the paper recently, but I'd never seen him before. And never in person. Next."

I passed her a shot of Annalisa at her most impassioned, and accompanied it with the grainy image of her heading up to Bunny's door.

Bev shook her head. "She's quite memorable. I wouldn't be able to forget her."

"This next guy also had a bicycle, so that may be a connection. I produced the photo of Jamie Kilpatrick, small and stick-like next to the strapping Constable Wentzell as they exited the courthouse. P. J. was so besotted that the shot was really of Wentzell with Kilpatrick as an unfortunate addition.

Bev stabbed a French-manicured finger at the photo. The patio door opened, and the non-keeper boyfriend stepped in, cigarette finished, leaving Moxi yipping on the balcony. Bev didn't give him a glance.

I said to Bev. "Thank you. That's what I need, a connection between him and Roxanne. Did you see him around here? He said he rides his bike everywhere. Did he used to ride with her?"

"Not him," she said, firmly, pointing to Wentzell. "I've seen her talking to Roxanne. On a bike too."

FIFTEEN

A bad lawyer can let a case drag out for several years.
A good lawyer can make it last so much longer.

I had trouble adjusting my mind to this new idea. I wanted to implicate Kilpatrick, since the snivelling little creep had nearly run me down. But what did Wentzell have to do with all this? Was Bev mistaken? Even as I had that thought, I knew it was wishful thinking. No. If Bev said she'd seen her, then Wentzell was definitely involved. But how? What the hell did she have to do with Roxanne Terrio?

"She's quite a bit younger than Roxanne was. Were they friends?"

"No. I just happened to see them having a conversation about bikes one day. That big blonde girl wasn't in a police uniform that time though. She was in that stretchy biking gear you see. Roxanne wore that kind of gear too. I got the impression they had just struck up a casual conversation."

"Was it around the time Roxanne died?"

The amazing eyelashes fluttered. "No. It was a long time ago. Maybe last fall? Before Roxanne put her bike away for the winter."

I sat there mulling over that. Did it mean anything that Roxanne had met Constable Kristen Wentzell? If so, what?

The boyfriend was getting restless, and on the balcony Moxi was flinging his little body against the glass and yowling like a coyote. I could see that it was time to call it quits. But first, I asked Bev, "Do you think that Roxanne would have been nervous around this woman?"

Bev paused. "No. She looked quite comfortable. Not worried at all."

"I wonder if that's what got her killed."

*   *   *

Of course, I was wide awake with this new information. Beyond wide awake. With all the stuff swirling around in it, my head was quite a bit bigger on the inside than on the outside. I now knew it was likely that Wentzell had some involvement. And she'd first met Roxanne the previous fall. Did that mean that whatever had been planned had been in the works for a long time? Wentzell and Kilpatrick had been in the photo together. Had they known each other aside from Court? Could Wentzell have been the driver of the mustard-yellow Mustang?

I climbed into the car to head home. I tried Mombourquette's cellphone number a few more times. It went straight to voice mail. I tried Elaine's too. I checked the clock. After eleven. Late, but not impossibly so. Would Madame Cardarelle still be awake? I figured it wouldn't cost anything to check and drop off her copies of the photos. I was more or less halfway to Rockcliffe at that point, give or take. If the lights were on, maybe Coco Bentley would be at home and willing to bounce around some theories. I could also pop by Elaine's place later on to share this new information with her and her mouseketeer.

Rockcliffe exuded opulence, even in the dark. There was a sense that all was well with the world, although I knew it wasn't. Madame Cardarelle's traditional home was in darkness, which was disappointing. However, Coco

Bentley's huge modern house was lit up like a small airport. Was she having a party? I hurried up to the front door, opened it and yelled hello. Coco was thrilled to see me. I suspected she had already had a snootful, an enviable state of being. However, I needed to keep a clear head and drank only what Coco referred to as "mix". It seemed harmless to ask her to have a look at the photos. Maybe, while lurking snoopily in her garden next to the Cardarelles', Coco had spotted one of these people. Perhaps even Wentzell.

Coco slooshed her G & T as she sat cross-legged on her vast, and I do mean vast, leather sectional. Most of it was scattered with reading material, but if it had been decluttered, it could easily have seated ten. I took the neighbouring chair.

She tossed aside the photos of people she didn't know, but stopped at Annalisa Fillmore's image. "Annalisa. Of course. Such a bitter and annoying woman. The pitch of her voice could give you a migraine. She's everywhere, it seems. I've never seen her on my street, though. If I had, I'd have hidden under the bed. Who's that horrible looking man?"

"Lloyd Brugel."

"Oh right, the thug. Never seen him before and I think I'm glad of it."

"Consider yourself lucky."

"And this skinny kid? He looks like he's afraid of his shadow. But there's something very familiar about him."

"What about the woman he's with?"

"What about her?"

I considered removing the G & T from her hand. "Have you ever seen her around here? With or without the uniform?"

She shook her head emphatically. "Not likely to forget

254

an amazon like her, am I?"

"Okay, fine. What about him?"

"Him, yes. I've seen him somewhere."

"Could it have been on a news clip? His senior lawyer was murdered, and I'm sure he was—"

"Nope. I think it was in the neighbourhood."

"Talking to Judge Cardarelle perhaps? Or Madame?"

"I can't imagine him having the nerve to talk to his godship. And France is pretty icy herself when you first meet her. It will come to me. Sure you won't join me in a drink?"

"Gotta go. Let me know and would you mind showing these photos to Madame Cardarelle tomorrow morning? Once your hangover wears off."

"Very funny. I'd be glad to, though."

*   *   *

I banged on Elaine's door for a while, but no one answered. Voicemail would have to do. I could only hope that Mombourquette actually listened to these messages when he finally got around to checking. His looming retirement had definitely eroded his work ethic.

"Leonard," I said, "I've emailed you a copy of a photo of the man who was in the Mustang that tried to run me over. Draw your own conclusions. And by the way, can you find out which police officers were involved in the detention of Jamie Kilpatrick the night of Rollie Thorsten's murder?"

Excellent.

By now it was midnight. My painkillers were wearing off, and my shoulder was aching like crazy, but never mind, I was following a hunch. The door to 1608 had been

255

repaired and was locked. That was a good sign. The key turned easily. Also good.

I opened the door and stuck my nose in. The hunch paid off. There was nothing but soft breathing sounds from Bunny, Tonya and Destiny, all flaked out on Mrs. Parnell's bed. As I'd hoped, they'd returned to the one place the police and pursuers thought they'd cleared out of. I chose not to wake them up. They were probably exhausted. I left a package of the photos with a note to have Tonya and Bunny check them out and call me in the morning if they recognized anyone at all.

For some reason, I felt tired. There was not much chance of finding anything else out that night. I drove straight home, took Gussie as far as the closest tree, swallowed two painkillers, and pitched head first into bed. There was no sign of Alvin and the girls. It was just as well that my house didn't catch fire, because it would have taken way more than that to wake me up.

*   *   *

What is worse? A cold wet nose on your ear? Pungent dog breath too near your mouth to be healthy? Or an incessantly ringing phone?

I reached blindly for the receiver. My hand came up empty.

"Someone answer that stupid thing," I snarled and slammed the pillow over my head. The stabbing pain in my shoulder woke me up but good. Endless rings later, I heard a short chirp that indicated a message was being recorded. So no rush.

I had just dozed off again when the next call came. This

time Gussie put his paw on my chest to indicate that, as I had to get up to answer the phone anyway, I might as well take him out to attend to pressing business. I squinted blearily at the floor. No receiver there.

I staggered outside with Gussie. The next door neighbour shot me a glance of frosty contempt. Perhaps she'd noticed that my shorts were on backwards and my T-shirt was inside out. But then she's frosty at the best of times. Not like I cared.

Back inside, Alvin was standing in the kitchen, yawning. At least he'd put on coffee, and it did smell heavenly. I fed Gussie and Mrs. Parnell's cat. Not a moment too soon apparently. They gave the impression they were at death's door.

"Any reason you didn't pick up the phone, Alvin?" I asked in a neutral tone.

"I was outside working in the garden. There's a lot of weeding needed, not that you'd ever notice. Where are all the receivers?" he griped.

"You tell me. Oh damn, there it goes again."

Of course, I suspected one or two of the receivers might be in the girls' room. Or Alvin's for that matter.

"Are the girls still asleep?" I said as I stared at the coffee pot, willing it to speed up or be tossed against the nearest mural.

"Asleep? Are you kidding? They were up and gone early. Even though their team didn't qualify, not that you would know that, they still wanted to see the Sunday morning races. Then they're—"

"Unbelievable. What time is it now?"

"It's after noon. Twelve thirty, in fact. I thought you were gone too, it was so quiet here."

"Twelve thirty? That's impossible. I never sleep late. It must have been those painkillers. I'm so groggy I can't focus."

"You have to focus because we're having a kitchen party tomorrow night."

"We are?"

"The girls are finished their events, and they'll be returning to Nova Scotia on Tuesday. It's hard to believe they've been here almost a week. I'll do all the cooking and logistics, but I can't be in two places at a time and I have a list of things for you to…"

I suppose he kept droning on.

Five minutes later, coffee finished and painkiller popped, I hit the shower, and the combo of warm water and green apple shampoo seemed to help. I emerged squeaky clean and slightly less out of it. The downside of all that pleasantness was that, as my mind began to focus, the matter of murder returned.

I sat on my unmade bed and Mrs. Parnell's little cat snuggled in. I stroked her fur and thought hard. Something Alvin had said was twitching in my brain and clamouring for attention. What was it? Something about the kitchen party the next night. Why would I pay any attention to that? Party preparations wouldn't lodge in my brain, even when I'm not groggy.

The little calico nudged my arm. That's code for "keep stroking". Gussie jumped back into bed too and nosed my leg. Why should the cat get all the attention? "You guys sure can work as a team to distract me. It's quite a talent," I said, glad I had two hands, one for each pet.

My hands stopped mid-stroke. The cat and the dog glanced at me with reproach.

"That's it."

The cat nudged again.

"Teamwork," I said. "That's how they did it. Holy shit. That's it! Alvin! Where are you? Get moving! Find me a phone!"

One receiver turned up buried in the sofa cushions. I may have been responsible for that myself. Alvin continued to radiate resentment as he searched for my cellphone. "Other duties as required," I said. "Never forget that job description."

I called Mrs. Parnell, praying she'd be in her room.

No answer.

I called the nursing station and pleaded family emergency. Three minutes later, Mrs. Parnell came on the line. "Is young Ferguson in any difficulty?"

"He won't be if he finds my cellphone. I need some help from you. The photos you printed out last night were amazing. Great quality. Thanks for printing extra copies."

"Splendid. You are most welcome, Ms MacPhee. Glad to be of service."

"As a result of those photos, I think I understand something more about what's going on. I think several people are involved: Annalisa Fillmore, James Kilpatrick, and now, I believe, Constable Kristen Wentzell."

"Fascinating."

"Yes. I need you to dig around and see if you can find any connections between them. For instance, do they have anything in common?"

"All of them?"

"Yes."

"Will do. I'll get on that immediately."

As soon as she disconnected, I checked the messages.

Bunny. Breathless. Agitated.

"Why aren't you answering any of your phones? We can't stay here any more. If you could find us, anyone can. Please try not to put my family in any more danger. I don't know why

259

you left those pictures here. Someone might have followed you. That really creeped me out, Camilla. And I didn't even recognize any of them except for Lloyd Brugel and Rollie Thorsten. And did you know you left the package with the offer to purchase your house here with those photos, and Tonya thinks I should let you know. By the way, she recognized somebody, but she thinks it's probably not connected."

Thanks, Bunny. You're the person who drew me into the investigation anyway, I thought crabbily, and you couldn't even mention which person Tonya thought looked familiar, let alone where you are going now.

*   *   *

I made a quick trip back to Clearwater Crescent to pick up the offer on the house. In apartment 1608, there was no sign of Bunny anywhere. I couldn't blame him for hiding out, but I hoped he hadn't made a pact with some devil to get him to a safer place. My footsteps echoed eerily on the parquet floor of Mrs. Parnell's apartment as I walked to the dining room table to get the document.

I glanced around the apartment sadly. Was our old friend and ally ever going to be able to return to her home? It seemed like the right time to visit her again.

I wasted no time in gettting off to the Perley, determined to look on the bright side where she was concerned.

"Ms MacPhee!" she cheered as I found her in a wheelchair having a Benson & Hedges at the specially designated smoking area outside. I'd wondered how she'd adjusted to that.

"Caught you," I said with a grin.

"I have something for you, Ms MacPhee." She waved the cigarette holder with her usual drama.

"Let's have it. I already know there's some kind of connection between Constable Kristen Wentzell and Roxanne Terrio. Anything else on them?"

"Not really, although I will certainly continue to try to ferret out additional information. This is just a reference really. I wasn't able to find a lot of connections, but I'll keep at it. Guess who I found?"

"Constable Kristen Wentzell and Jamie Kilpatrick?"

She shook her head. "Give it another try."

"Annalisa Fillmore and Bunny Mayhew?"

"Keep guessing, Ms MacPhee."

"Rollie Thorsten and Steven Anstruther? Judge Cardarelle and…?"

"I see I have you bested. But of course, it wasn't really a fair fight." She grinned at me.

I did my best to grin back, but I was truly exhausted by the strain of the last few days and the worry about Bunny and his family. "I admit defeat," I said. "Let's have it."

"Well, I found a document from an organization called Shattered Families. It's dated eighteen months ago and appears to be a group of people who have had terrible things happen to loved ones. This seems to be an agenda for what was an initial meeting. As far as I can tell, the terrible events or tragedies all involve crimes."

"Really? What did you…?"

"Patience, Ms MacPhee."

"Okay, but not much."

"It merely listed members attending the meeting and the name that had been chosen for the group. All the names rang a bell. And the major one of interest to you is of course, A. Fillmore."

"Who were the others?"

"One was K. Wentzell."

"Oh! And Kilpatrick?"

"There was a J. Kilpatrick too. And you may find this interesting, someone called F. Cardarelle. The coincidence of the last name is striking, is it not?"

I sat back on the bench, stunned.

"Ms MacPhee? Are you quite all right? You're shockingly pale. Should I call for a nurse?"

I fought back a wave of nausea. Who and what else had I misjudged? Was anyone else going to die because I couldn't grasp what was going on?

"Anything else about this organization? Are there more names on the list?" I croaked out.

"I've searched around for minutes or other documents from the organization, but I haven't been fortunate enough to find them yet. Of course, they'd hardly be sharing documents that indicate any kind of conspiracy. I assume this initial attendance list just escaped their notice. However, I shall keep ferreting about. I've just taken a brief break, but I'll be back at my station in a minute."

"Great. Keep doing that. We must find links. Okay, I know that Annalisa Fillmore lost her son as a result of a street racer, and she was really devastated that Rollie got him off. Jamie Kilpatrick's grandparents were killed by a drunk driver. I don't know what happened to him. We need to know who killed them. Do you think you can you locate that information for me? Same thing with Kristen Wentzell. Did she lose someone? Who? And Madame Cardarelle. She lost a child. I'll check that out with Coco Bentley. She'll probably know the details."

I counted off on my fingers. "There are four names here. But so far, there are five people who appear to have been targeted, including Bunny. That would indicate that a fifth person is involved. We need to know who the fifth one is."

Mrs. Parnell reached out to touch my hand. "If you will forgive me, Ms MacPhee, you have been receiving the jokes too. We must consider that you may be a sixth intended victim."

I was already on my cellphone, hoping like hell that Coco Bentley was still lounging around. To my relief, she answered. "Coco! Don't show those photos to Madame Cardarelle. Whatever you do."

"Hello, Camilla. I couldn't have anyway. She doesn't seem to be home this afternoon."

"Oh. Promise me you won't mention it to her. I'll explain later."

"Over drinks?" Coco is always hopeful for an extra social situation.

"Sure. But I need a bit of information. You mentioned a tragedy with a child. I need to know about this. What happened? A traffic accident?"

"Oh no. A drug overdose, I believe. Terribly sad. Alain was a difficult teenager. Always so rebellious and challenging, in trouble in school from a young age. The father was stern and uncompromising. He was close to fifty when Alain was born, and France was in her forties. I believe he came as a complete surprise. His mother did her best, but when he hit his teens he went right off the rails. He found the wrong companions and tried every drug going, including crack cocaine. France managed to get him into treatment and then tried to bring him home. I accidentally overheard a discussion between the parents one night from my garden. My French isn't too bad, you know. France was pleading with the miserable old swine to let the boy come home. He wasn't having any of it. Two weeks later, Alain was dead. Would it have made a difference to that troubled lad if he'd been able to stay with his parents? If he'd felt any love and support from his father? Who's to say?"

"But it certainly made a difference to his mother."

"You said it. If she hadn't been in surgery at the time of his death, I wouldn't have put it past her. But of course, she couldn't have done it."

"Sure she could have, Coco. With the right team."

"I don't understand."

"Never mind. At last, I've figured out that part. Whatever you do, just stay away from her."

"I remembered where I saw that young man."

"Let me guess. Visiting France Cardarelle in her home?"

"Close. Having a cozy coffee together in a little bistro, if that's any help."

Another confirmation. Always helpful.

*   *   *

I clicked off, asked Mrs. Parnell to check back and see who Kristen Wentzell might have been grieving for, said goodbye, and bolted for my car. On the way, I tried to reach the spectacularly unavailable Leonard Mombourquette. I'd given up on expecting him to check his phone. I drove to the Queensway, got off at Metcalfe and headed for the Police Station.

Mombourquette was not at his second floor desk. Not too surprising on a Sunday when he had only a few weeks to serve. Undeterred, I explained my conclusions to one of his fellow officers in Major Crimes. He took a few notes. This guy had raised his technique for looking bored to an art form.

"They're in it together. Jamie Kilpatrick, Madame Cardarelle. Annalisa Fillmore was too. There may be others. That's why they have alibis. I believe they are seeking revenge against a justice system that failed them. Lawyers, judges, police officers, like your own Steve Anstruther." I was talking faster than normal and sounding a lot less rational than I needed to. I didn't mention Kristen Wentzell. No point in getting tossed out on my ear just when things were going well.

"We'll look into it," he said, meaning he would not give it a moment's thought, and the notes would end up filed under N for Nutcase along with those unfortunate souls whose hobby is confessing to crimes they haven't committed.

*   *   *

I thought that a visit to Loreena Holmes was next in order. For years, she'd been running Ottawa Bereavement Services with a gentle touch and a heart full of hope and caring. Of course, OBS would be closed on Sunday and Loreena's home number was unlisted. Luckily, we'd been chummy enough because of Justice for Victims that I knew exactly where she lived. She was warm and hospitable to her friends and colleagues too, and I'd been invited more than once to her home. I was back on the Queensway in a flash and on my way to Foster Street. I found Loreena in the vine-festooned backyard, relaxing in a lawn chair, and enjoying what was not the first glass of ruby red wine with a woman friend she introduced as Gillian. A heavenly aroma drifted from the charcoal barbecue on the patio. The cheerful women were about to have their afternoon ruined, but there wasn't much I could do about that.

"Won't take a minute," I said, sliding onto a bright yellow chair, before she could say a word. "Shattered Families. Tell me what you know."

Her friend snorted and said in the crisp way of the transplanted Brit, "Bunch of nutters."

Loreena nodded gently. "I'd have to agree that they are a bit off the wall. They seemed much more interested in payback than in healing. A lot of forgiveness issues."

"Who was involved? Any names?"

"Why?"

"I just need you to trust me on this. It's really important."

"All right. Glass of red, Camilla?"

I shook my head. "Do you think any of them would actually be dangerous?"

"Without a doubt," said Gillian.

"Hard to say," Loreena mused. "Why do you ask?"

"Rollie Thorsten's gruesome murder."

"Oh, boy. That dangerous. Well, there were rumours, but you have to be fair to people. They'd all been through hell, and who are we to say they can't be furious?"

"Let me help you. I've heard of Annalisa Fillmore, France Cardarelle, a cop called Wentzell and a young lawyer named Jamie Kilpatrick. Were they part of your organization? Maybe didn't fit in because of anger issues?"

Loreena leaned forward and refilled her friend's glass, then her own. She shook her head. "Camilla, you know I can't tell you that."

Short of writing "yes" on the grass in red paint, her expression told me what I wanted to know.

"Annalisa's body was found after she apparently torched my client's home." I didn't bother to explain the nature of my relationship to Bunny. "She had an iron-clad alibi for

266

the time of Rollie's death although she hated him with—"

"A white-hot passion," Gillian said, raising her glass.

"Right. I need to know if you think these 'nutters' could band together to plot to kill people they felt had taken their loved ones."

Loreena shook her glossy silver hair. "I really wouldn't like to say anything like that. They've all been through so much."

"I'd bet the farm on it," said the friend. "Two farms."

"I think they provided alibis for each other. I think someone else on the team killed Rollie, and in return Annalisa planned to kill someone for that person, although she failed."

"Well, that makes sense," Gillian agreed.

Loreena pursed her lips and sent her friend a warning glance.

"Anyone else you can think of, Loreena?" I said. "I believe there are five of them, as five people have received, um, anonymous communications from this group."

She didn't meet my eyes. "I can't really tell you that, Camilla. You of all people should understand confidentiality. There's no way I can reveal anything about the people who pass through our group. It would be unconscionable."

I tried to read the expression on her friend's face. She wasn't about to blow the whistle and may not have known enough to, but there was something there. I decided to stall and get a bit of useful information. "Mind if I use your phone?"

Loreena nodded distractedly. Inside the house, I switched my cell to mute and called it from her telephone. Sure enough, Loreena's number showed when I checked. I returned to the backyard and said. "Did I mention there might have been a child in the home that burned? I think the incendiary device was in a stuffed toy, a big green dog. Call me if you think of anyone."

Loreena paled but shook her head again. "I'm sorry, Camilla."

"That's my cellphone number, in case that family being burned out, or the woman who was run down on her bicycle or even Rollie Thorsten being shot in the knees before being dumped from a boat to drown bothers you in any way." I half-expected to hear my name called as I walked away. I tossed my card on the table.

* * *

Next I squealed to a stop in front of Elaine Ekstein's second-floor apartment on Spruce Street, on the crosshairs of what is known as Little Italy and Chinatown. Elaine's battered Pathfinder was parked in the driveway. There was no other vehicle. Mombourquette must have slipped through the trap yet again.

As usual, Elaine's place looked as though something had just exploded. She appeared to be in the middle of a project that involved taking all of her clothing out of every cupboard and drawer and rearranging it somehow. Under normal circumstances, I might have speculated as to how the fastidious Mombourquette could stand visiting her there, but I didn't want to distract myself from the matter at hand. Anyway, Elaine was not pleased by my impromptu visit.

"No, he's not here, and you've got to stop hounding him, Camilla. Give the poor guy a break. He's under a lot of pressure over that Rollie Thorsten case. And now this horrible fire and the dead woman."

"The woman killed in the fire was trying to murder

Bunny and his family as collateral damage. I'm just reminding you of that. So, my calls on that topic are important. And wouldn't you think if he was working a case he'd answer his cellphone at least occasionally?"

"He picks up his calls, Camilla. Just not yours."

"But does he listen to my messages at all? Has he passed the information along?"

She shrugged. "No idea. We never talk shop. Well, except for Thorsten's murder and the fire at Bunny's place. Bunny himself is off-limits. We've agreed to disagree."

"Easy for you. I'm sure he takes every one of your calls."

She didn't bother to suppress her smirk. I didn't suppress anything as I filled her in on what I now believed was going on with Shattered Families. She listened, white-faced without interrupting for once.

I finished up by saying, "Make goddam sure he takes the next call from you. Tell him what I told you. And suggest that he picks up the next call from me. Life and death and all that."

SIXTEEN

*-What do you call 10,000 lawyers
at the bottom of the river?*
A very good start

It was six o'clock when I stepped through the door of my own house, as usual not sure what I'd find. Whatever it was, it sure smelled good. And in spite of my unsettled day, I was hungry.

"Alvin?"

Alvin's beaky nose popped out from the kitchen. "Hi, Camilla. I'm just making a bit of chowder for the party tomorrow. Of course, there's no room in the kitchen, so we'll be holding it in the backyard."

"Chowder? I'm starving. I'd like some of that." Alvin had put bacon in this latest version, the same way my sisters do.

"Help yourself. But it's better the next day anyway. You know that."

I didn't know that, because this was cooking knowledge, and I'd been born without the cooking chromosome, as well as the tall, blonde gene.

"Speaking of girls, where are they? Aren't their events all over? I thought I missed them."

He emerged carrying a dripping wooden spoon and sporting the Cape Breton tartan plastic apron. "They went on that cruise."

"What cruise?" I said as evenly as I could considering I had a bizarre vision of Ray's girls sailing off into the

Caribbean with a crowd of retired accountants.

"That one they sent you the tickets for."

"All right, Alvin. Start from the beginning. I don't know anything about any cruise, not that it makes any difference. Who would be sending me tickets for a cruise? Cruises cost thousands of dollars. It's probably some scam. I can't believe you fell for it, whatever it was."

Alvin gestured with the spoon. "Not that kind of cruise, Camilla. I'm not a fool. The lady phoned and said it was one of those on the Ottawa River, an evening cruise with dinner on the boat for you and a guest. She said that the guests on board would all be lawyers and I know you don't really hang out with many and anyway, you weren't here and the boat was leaving soon. I couldn't imagine that you'd want the tickets."

"I couldn't imagine it either. It's kind of amusing to think of the girls taking my place. But why did I have these tickets?"

"Maybe you won them in a raffle."

I raised an eyebrow. "But I would have had to buy a raffle ticket in that case, Alvin."

"A contest then."

"Earth to Alvin, I don't do contests. You do. Maybe you won the tickets. Okay, another mystery solved. That chowder smells really good actually. Is it ready?"

"They definitely came under your name."

"Okay, step back in time, Alvin. Came how? By mail?"

"No, they were delivered to the door."

"Really? By a courier?"

Alvin sniffed. "I found them in the mailbox. Now I have to check the chowder."

I knew better than to snap "forget the goddam chowder"

and face sulky chowderless silences for a week. I just wanted answers. I followed him into the kitchen, where a large chowder pot was on the stove. The wonderful smell was coming from that. So was a bubbling sound that appeared to be bothering Alvin. He lifted the chowder pot off the burner.

I was not the only audience for Alvin's project. Gussie was already in the room, nose twitching enthusiastically. Mrs. Parnell's cat was sitting on one of the sleek little chairs watching the show. Lester and Pierre were uncharacteristically silent. Perhaps bubbling pots made them nervous.

"Not a moment too soon. I really don't need a lot of interruptions while I'm trying to make a home-cooked meal for two motherless girls."

To my credit, I didn't roll my eyes or utter a sharp remark.

"It's just a bit weird about these cruise tickets, Alvin."

Alvin didn't respond. He was too busy stirring.

"Just explain again how the tickets came to be here." I sat down at the tiny table and waited.

Finally Alvin turned around. "Nothing very dramatic. I was out for a walk, to get this beautiful big stainless pot at the Glebe Emporium, and when I was coming up to the house, I saw something sticking out of the mailbox."

I did my best not to sigh, yawn or say "In our lifetime, please, Alvin." I nodded encouragingly and hoped the chowder didn't start bubbling again and set us back to the beginning.

He turned back to me. "Then the woman called and said there was something for you in the mailbox to express her family's appreciation."

He whipped around and worked that wooden spoon. Gussie's eyes opened wide in case that meant serving time.

I said, "And what was in the mailbox, Alvin?"

"I told you it was a pair of tickets to the cruise. The envelope and the note are still on the front hall console."

I got up and headed back to the hall. A plain letter-sized envelope had been slit open by Alvin. The letter opener lay next to it. My name was typed on it. Plain type, nothing unusual or distinguishing. Naturally, the envelope was empty.

"There's nothing here, Alvin," I called.

"That's because I gave everything to Ashley and Brittany."

"You said there was a note."

"Do I have to do everything around here?" Alvin appeared in full outrage mode. That evaporated when he reached the table and I showed him the empty envelope. Our eyes met.

"Gussie."

Sure enough, a slightly chewed piece of paper had been left on the sofa. What was left of it said, again in plain type, "In repayment for what you did for our family." An indecipherable signature followed. Or Gussie might have drooled that.

"I thought it was kind of nice," Alvin said. "All those years at Justice for Victims working for next to nothing to help people, and how often did either one of us get anything for our efforts?"

I let that slide. "Did you recognize her voice? If she was a client from JFV in the last five years you would have met her. No?"

He thought hard. "No. She didn't sound like anyone I knew. That signature doesn't look familiar to me, either."

"It doesn't even look like a signature. But that's not important, I guess. We'll figure out who it was at some

273

point. Maybe they'll call to see how the cruise went. I think I'll have that chowder now."

Alvin arched his pierced eyebrow. "Are you waiting for me to serve it to you? And there's no need to be snide."

Snide? I hadn't meant to be snide, but I knew better then to get into an argument about snideness. The chowder possibility could dry up.

"Sorry," I said, with an attempt at a sincere smile.

Alvin stared at me with concern. At least, I thought it was concern. He said, "Do you have indigestion? Because if you do, you probably shouldn't eat chowder. It has dairy, and I put bacon in too and that could—"

"I don't have indigestion. Thank you for asking. And I think that dairy and bacon and whatever else is in there will be perfect."

"Ten minutes," Alvin said. "I just have to correct the seasoning."

"Ten minutes?" I glanced at my watch. "Well, whatever else, at least we didn't get any jokes. Wait until I tell you what I think I've figured out, thanks to Mrs. Parnell. If Mombourquette ever returns my calls...Alvin? Why do you have that expression on your face?"

"What?"

"Don't 'what' me. Did we get any jokes?"

"It's not necessary to raise your voice," Alvin sniffed. "Do you know how much I have to do around here with two extra people and all these animals and a big party planned tomorrow? You don't even lift a finger and when you drift in, all you do is criticize." He turned and frantically whipped the chowder with the wooden spoon. Lucky it didn't snap in two. "Maybe you could check the mail."

I have to say, the person who stirs the chowder has the

upper hand in negotiations with the person who hasn't really eaten much all day.

"Sure thing. I'll check the mail then. Although I didn't notice any when I came in. What's the matter with me? It's Sunday. Yesterday was Saturday. Didn't we get the burglar joke on Friday?"

Alvin had trouble making eye contact. "There's always stuff in the mailbox. I put some in the basket on the bookcase behind the sofa."

Don't ask, I told myself, because the answer will merely delay your chowder experience. I had spent five years at Justice for Victims trying to get Alvin to put the mail in the "in" basket, after discarding junk in the recycling bin. To tell the truth, after all this time, he'd been just starting to get better at it. Something about the arrival of Ashley and Brittany and the sale of the house and the notion of a party seemed to have derailed him somehow.

I lifted the basket out from its hiding place and immediately went to get the recycling bin. That took a minute at least. The glossy pizza flyers, the fat package full of coupons and the collection of photocopied sheets advertising local entrepreneurial services all landed in the blue box. The coupons made a nice thud. Next I tossed in the note from my next door neighbour asking me to tell my friends to refrain from blocking her driveway. There were three requests from charities, all containing notebooks or labels especially made for Camilla McPee. Gee, thanks, folks. I put those aside for the shredder.

That left the envelope. My name, spelled correctly, was typed on it. I dashed upstairs and returned with a pair of tweezers. I held it by the corner and opened it.

Camilla MacPhee

I stared at my name. The only words on the page.

I got up and walked to the kitchen, where Alvin was holding a container of sea salt in his hand and frowning at the chowder pot.

"Alvin!"

He jumped. "Lord thundering Jesus, Camilla, do you have to yell?"

"Is that all the mail?"

"Why?"

I kept my temper in check. No point in wasting time. "Because I see my name typed on a piece of paper, and yet, I don't see an envelope with a joke."

"Oh. Oh," he said. "Right. There were some more flyers and stuff sticking out yesterday. The phone rang just as I was about to put it all on the console and I—"

"Just tell me where it might be. Right now. Don't beat around the bush."

He bit his lip. "I think it's in the dining room. On the dining room sideboard. What is it? What's going on? Camilla?"

I made it to the dining room and sifted through that pile of flyers and cheap printed ads that seem to clog the mailbox every day of the week. My heart rate soared at the sight of the plain envelope.

Alvin appeared by my side. "Tell me what's going on."

I lifted the envelope with the tweezers. "You open it with the scissors. Don't smudge anything. It must have been hand-delivered on Saturday.

Alvin managed to open it, and once again I used the tweezers to extract the sheet of paper inside.

He whispered, "What does it say?"

"What do you call ten thousand lawyers at the bottom of the river?"

Alvin said, "Wait, I know that joke."

I grabbed his arm. "Oh my god. The girls are on a boat trip that was meant for me. With a bunch of lawyers. What time does it leave? Where does the boat cruise go? Where do they take off?"

Alvin's voice shook. "I don't remember where or when. I just gave them the tickets and the information and they went. They thought it would be fun. Lord thundering Jesus! Oh no!"

"Do you remember the name of the boat?"

His eyes widened. "Yes! The *Leila Q*. I thought it sounded like a pretty name."

I shouted, "Alvin, you dial 911 and tell them that someone may have tampered with a boat called the *Leila Q* on the Ottawa River. I'll phone too, and I'm calling Mombourquette and Elaine and we're getting in the car as we call. Leave the chowder."

Mombourquette's phone went to message. I left a long, detailed and shaky one. As we jumped into the car, I said, "Alvin, try to reach Mrs. P. and get her to check out Ottawa River cruises. Tell her to call all the companies and find out about the *Leila Q*. Tell her to say that passengers might be in danger and to get that goddam boat back to shore."

* * *

We rocketed out of the garage and up the driveway. I turned right, neatly knocking over my next-door neighbour's wheelbarrow.

"Nice going, Camilla. Maybe you'd better calm down if we want to get there in one piece. We can't save Ashley and Brittany if we're dead."

That would have been sensible advice if Alvin's voice hadn't been higher than a shrieking violin or even if he hadn't been still wearing the Cape Breton tartan apron. Frankly, I didn't care how many wheelbarrows we knocked over. However, I did keep my eyes open for pedestrians as we shot down the Queen Elizabeth driveway and across the Pretoria bridge.

Alvin clung to his own cellphone and the dash with one hand as I turned onto Colonel By Drive on two wheels. He clutched my cellphone with the other. "Violet! She's driving like a maniac. Where did you say the boats depart from, Violet? Hull? Hull, Camilla. Jacques Cartier Park. Then it's supposed to pick up more people at the locks behind the Château Laurier! Floor it, Camilla."

"Tell Mrs. P. to call 911 and tell them that the same people who killed Rollie Thorsten are planning to sink a boat in the Ottawa River. Make sure they understand that this is serious. If the Colonel and the Major have connections, tell them to call in their markers."

As we peeled into the dock area in Jacques Cartier Park in Hull, on the Quebec side of the border, the *Leila Q* had already sailed. People were leaning against the rails, waving gaily. I strained to see Ashley and Brittany, but the boat was too far away.

How would this insane team of murderers kill all the people on a boat? Sink it? Blow it up?

"Back to the car!" We ran along the dock and jumped into the Acura. We raced out of the parking lot, leaving the attendant shaking his fist at us. Didn't matter. We cut in front of a few slow drivers and tore onto the Interprovincial bridge, heading back to Ottawa. Luckily the distance between Quebec and Ontario is greater in the minds of the inhabitants than it is geographically. We were across the bridge and on MacKenzie Avenue in less than three minutes. There's no parking near the boat pick-up. We pulled the Acura into a No Parking area on MacKenzie across from the Château Laurier and ran the rest of the way, up around the Château to the far side of the canal, finally thundering down the stone steps to the locks and the boat pickup area. At the bottom, I bent over, gasping for breath. Alvin was still descending. Didn't matter, because the *Leila Q* had already pulled away.

"Come back," I shouted foolishly. "You're in danger."

People on the path edged away from me. Not that I cared. Alvin didn't help much in his Cape Breton tartan apron.

"Okay, we need to find a boat, Alvin," I said. I looked around for a boat close enough to get into. I kept my eyes on the *Leila Q.*

By this time, Alvin was shimmying in panic. "What can we do? Ashley and Brittany are on that boat!"

"I know that, Alvin. We have to keep calm. Hang on, what are those things bobbing on the water?"

"Where?"

"Out there!" I pointed, then turned to the nearest tourist and said, "I need your binoculars, please."

He goggled at me.

"Now!"

I turned the binoculars toward the boat. "Oh my god!"

"What is it?"

"Life jackets, Alvin. They've thrown off the life jackets. They're drifting away from the boat."

The man who owned the binoculars said, "How deep is it here?"

I had no idea. But the *Leila Q* was steaming away from the life jackets. A low boom echoed across the Ottawa River. The next sound we heard was the passengers on the *Leila Q* screaming.

"What's happening?" Alvin shrieked.

I managed to answer through my aching throat. "I imagine that's some kind of explosion on the bottom of the boat. If our plotters are successful, the boat will take in water and sink. Lots of lawyers on the bottom. That's what they want."

A crowd had gathered, and a buzz went through it. "But everyone will drown!" Alvin shrieked.

"That's what they want. Dead lawyers. Anyone else is just collateral damage. These people are insane," I said, grimly. "Let's hope the 911 calls made a difference. We have to get out there." To our left, two men in a passing motor boat revved the engine. Other people had begun running toward the dock. "I need to get out there," I yelled. "My stepkids are on that boat!" I didn't wait for an okay. I just hopped on board. Alvin was right behind me.

The swirl of sirens sounded in the background. Fire engines parked on the nearest bridge. We could see the fire crews arriving at the dock on the Quebec side. Our boat bounced up and down, its bottom slapping on the waves as we headed toward the sinking *Leila Q*. Others mobilized beside us. The boat went down fast. Dozens of people bobbed and thrashed in the turbulent water.

We were able to reach out and grab for the floating life jackets to toss to the thrashing swimmers. I tossed one to a woman treading water. She seemed reasonably cool, so the four of us worked to haul her thrashing, sputtering neighbour into the boat first. I looked around wildly for

Brittany and Ashley. Ray had trusted me, and now his girls might never come back from their wonderful sporty fundraising week in Ottawa. Had they still been on the boat as it sank?

Alvin shouted. "Look!"

Sure enough Brittany was holding her own, as a panicky man seemed to cling to her. No sign of Ashley, but I reminded myself that Ray had called them his "water rats".

I felt a swell of relief as the first of several Zodiacs with a crew of three firefighters sped toward the bobbing victims. They were joined by more Zodiacs from the Gatineau service. Other emergency personnel had commandeered small boats from both sides and were picking up swimmers and dragging them on board.

As the waters cleared and our boat circled the area, I spotted Ashley, blonde hair darkened by the river water, staying afloat and doing a slow, elegant Australian crawl toward the waiting Zodiac with her arm bent, expertly holding somone's head above water. Of course, leave it to Ray to make sure his girls had lifeguard training.

I took out my cellphone and called P. J. "Here's your payoff. Head down to the locks by Parliament Hill. You'll have the story of your dreams and my nightmares."

SEVENTEEN

So what's wrong with lawyer jokes?
-Lawyers don't think they're funny,
and nobody else realizes they're jokes.

If the amount of time you spend in the cop shop is any indication, it's only marginally better being a witness than being a suspect.

At the end of my long, complex statement, I said, "Leonard here can back me up." I glanced at Mombourquette, who was watching, arms crossed, eyes half-lidded.

"You knew this was going to happen why?" the interrogating officer said. Most likely because of the serious nature of my accusations against Wentzell, Mombourquette had brought in a very senior dude indeed. I had already forgotten his name, if he'd ever given it, but it was obvious from his body language that he was way up the ladder.

"I've already answered that. Twice. I got a joke in my mailbox. And, more importantly, I got what the joke was intended to convey. My, um, friend's daughters went on the cruise in place of me and would have died if I hadn't figured out what that joke meant and passed the information on to our mutual friend, Leonard. But once more, let me tell you the story: Annalisa Fillmore, Jamie Kilpatrick, Kristen Wentzell and France Cardarelle had lost loved ones and blamed the legal system for not taking action, specifically lawyers who help their clients to evade the kind of punishment these people felt they deserved. I guess they also didn't find the existing services to the bereaved sufficiently calming and decided to make a point. So they rigged up a conspiracy: each one of them would contribute a name, someone they felt deserved to die as retribution for a wrong-doing. One was chosen to commit the murder, while the person with the grudge had an unassailable alibi. Each one of them got the satisfaction, if you could call it that, of revenge without much danger of being caught. For instance, Annalisa Fillmore hated Rollie Thorsten, and everyone knew it. So, he was killed while she was in full public view, eliminating her from suspicion. I think I was part of the plan all along. Annalisa knew I shared her loathing for Brugel. They were most likely counting on me to catch on to the joke theme, and they figured I'd work hard to pin the crimes on Brugel, an easy target. I believe the group had solid reasons for a shared hatred for Brugel too. Getting him blamed was an extra motivation for them."

"Who killed Rollie?"

"It had to have been Madame Cardarelle, as Jamie Kilpatrick was being interrogated here by your own Kristen Wentzell at the time. You never got back to me on that, Leonard, but I'm thinking I'm right and it fits perfectly with my theory. These people collaborated beautifully."

The cop and Mombourquette exchanged glances pretty well confirming that.

I kept talking. "So Madame Cardarelle was the only possibility. I imagine that Wentzell would have been able to get her mitts on a weapon that wouldn't be traced."

"So who was Madame Cardarelle's target?"

"Her own husband, the judge. She hated him with a passion, especially since her teenage son died after his father refused to allow him to come home. Judge Cardarelle was killed while she was undergoing surgery. My theory is that Wentzell offered the judge that nut-laced cookie. He might not have respected cops, but he wouldn't have feared her. And if he put up any resistance, she would have had her weapon handy."

I could tell the new guy didn't like this story any more than Mombourquette had. They were both going to hate the next bit. I kept going. "Why Wentzell, you wonder? Well, I'm pretty sure her real target was Anstruther."

Mombourquette jerked. "What?"

"I think if you check that pile of paper I brought in and asked you to read, you'll discover a small item about Anstruther's partner being killed four years ago, shot while they were on a routine patrol in the market. Right outside Red Roxxxy's, in fact. He was a young guy, left behind his grieving fiancée, one Kristen Wentzell. I guess she wasn't even a cop then. But I wonder if there wasn't some talk that if Anstruther had done his job right, his partner wouldn't have been killed. Of course, Wentzell would have a hate-on for Brugel too. As a police officer, she was able to track Bunny's current address. Plus she knew Anstruther had the Brugel connection. And she would have had an unassailable alibi for the night Anstruther was run off the road. On duty in full view of her own partner, I'm thinking."

Again with the looks.

"And Roxanne," Mombourquette said. "Who killed her?"

"I thought for a while it was Wentzell."

Mombourquette shook his head. "Airtight alibi."

"It would have to have been Jamie Kilpatrick then."

"Too bad he drowned when the *Leila Q* sank," the senior

officer said. "We can't really ask him."

"Remind me again, why the burglar was involved?" Mombourquette asked.

He had me there.

"I never told you because I still don't know," I admitted. "But I have to leave something for you guys to investigate. I'm sure you'll work it out."

*　　*　　*

My family managed to stay on top of the Ottawa news even on their Mediterranean cruise. Stan somehow got the *Ottawa Citizen* on his laptop. Don't ask me to explain how that all works. P. J.'s story had quite the impact. They could count themselves lucky that I hadn't given them the blow-by-blow description of my evening at police headquarters and the debriefing about the sinking of the *Leila Q* and the Shattered Families plot. I didn't angle for a sympathy vote by telling them about my shoulder, as it seemed to be mending nicely. Anyway, I didn't want to spend the whole day yakking.

While busily carting dishes and glassware to the backyard, I'd already had awkward telephone conversations with my father and all three brothers-in-law, especially Conn, the recently retired detective. My sister Donalda had given me an earful as I set out the napkins. Now my sister Alexa was squawking. I was holding the phone away from my ear. It's hard to do anything else when there's a full-sister assault.

Before she could launch into more recriminations, I decided on a distraction, "All right, but we're all okay here. In fact, we're just about to have a big party for Ray's girls.

They're upstairs getting dressed and we're rushing around preparing. No, I'm not making the food. Don't be silly. Alvin has done a great job. I think he's used some of your recipes. What? Of course, the place looks all right. More than. That reminds me, put Edwina on."

After the requisite squawks, I said, "Good news. Your Jacki Jewell is a giant pain, but she sold the house. She's picking up the signed offer tonight, in spite of the fact that we're having a party and maybe even because it's not in the least bit convenient. All to say, please, never again set one of your rabid realtors on me. I couldn't stand the woman."

Edwina snapped, "What are you talking about, my Jacki Jewell? Don't try to distract me, missy. How do you get yourself into these situations that—"

"Well, you told her I wanted to—"

"As if I would get mixed up in trying to sell your house. It would have needed to be completely gutted before anyone would take a look at it. And if I did, I certainly wouldn't pick that Jacki Jewell. She's a real flake. There are dozens of terrific real estate agents in Ottawa, why would I—?"

"You didn't send her? No need to snort, Edwina. I guess she fibbed to get the job. That shouldn't be a surprise. Troubling, and entirely in character, in fact. But, never mind, I guess the main thing is, she sold the house. Anyway, I have to go. We have nearly two dozen people on their way to our little backyard shindig any minute. Oh, Mrs. Parnell's arriving now and the girls are all ready to meet the guests."

When the Paratranspo van's door opened, Alvin met Mrs. Parnell with open arms and his Cape Breton tartan apron. He left the Colonel and the Major to look after themselves and took over the operation of getting Mrs. P.

wheeled into the backyard to sit in splendour on the lawn near the table and in front of the Tuscan fresco. It was a beautiful evening, close to the longest day of the year, warm and bright, without the familiar haze of humidity. I was tasked with stacking up cups to serve the chowder. Alvin had a vat of it sitting on a hot plate on a serving table. The aroma was making my mouth water.

I was still stewing about Jacki Jewell's duplicity and Alvin was still blathering, "It's a kitchen party, Violet! But our kitchen is so small we have to move the gang outside. But aside from that it'll be the traditional type."

"Splendid, dear boy. I'm all for tradition, as you know." Gussie nuzzled up to her in greeting. The Colonel and the Major limped behind, jockeying for position.

I have to admit the backyard looked amazing. Even the two-fours of Moosehead and Keith's seemed festive. Alvin had attached lanterns around the perimeter and somehow rigged up a long table in the grass. It was covered with a white tablecloth that draped invitingly and stacks of Cape Breton tartan napkins dotted the surface. As I didn't own any white tablecloths, I was pretty sure that my white sheets had been put to good use. Luckily that's not the kind of thing I get tied in knots over. I didn't like to speculate as to where the two dozen lawn chairs had come from.

Mrs. Parnell was looking very much at home and probably euphoric to be out on the town again. I made sure she had a tumbler of Harvey's Bristol Cream in her hand in record time. "Without your quick work, a lot of innocent people could have died when the *Leila Q* sank, Mrs. P."

She said, "Glad to be of service and wish I could have done more. I suppose this is a bit too late, given that James Kilpatrick is dead, but I found another connection for you."

"What is it?"

"The drunk driver who killed Kilpatrick's grandparents, was a man named Foster Whitby. He's had dozens of drunk driving charges and convictions over the past twentysome years. But the first time he got off from a case that badly injured a young woman, his lawyer was—"

"Roxanne Terrio, before she turned her back on defence and took up real estate law."

"Precisely, Ms MacPhee!"

"If he'd been convicted, perhaps he wouldn't have been on the road to collide with Jamie Kilpatrick's grandparents."

"So it would seem."

"We can only hope the various authorities will be able to confirm that when they interrogate Kristen Wentzell and France Cardarelle. At least the sinking of the *Leila Q* was so serious that they can't ignore my theories any more. Too bad the other information we have about the Shattered Families plot is such a combination of guesswork and circumstance that a good lawyer will have them out in no time. Unless someone confesses. And I'm not too confident of that. We should make sure that Mombourquette knows about this latest twist."

We both turned at the tweedledee of a fiddle. Someone was tuning up. I thought I spotted my grouchy neighbour with her nose pressed to the window. This should be fun, I decided.

I took a minute to leave Mombourquette a telephone message about Kilpatrick and the Whitby/Roxanne Terrio connection and then turned my attention to the party.

"The girls are really excited about the party, Violet. You have to meet them." Alvin trilled. "They've brought some of their friends from the team too. Listen to that. One of them brought a fiddle, and the other one has her guitar. I think we'll have some great music."

Aside from one tuning her fiddle and the one tuning her guitar, the rest of the gaggle of girls in bright skimpy dresses and fancy flipflops were making a fuss over Mrs. Parnell's little cat.

"I imagine they're glad to be alive," Mrs. Parnell said, waving to P. J. who was making a beeline for the bar. "And ready to celebrate that. Are you having a big crowd?"

"You have no idea," I whispered. "It's gotten totally out of hand."

Alvin said, "I'll introduce you. No point in waiting for Camilla to do it."

I heard a screech. Brakes? I dashed to the side fence in time to see Elaine's old Pathfinder come perilously close to my neighbour's glossy Beamer. Mombourquette slithered out of the passenger seat. He looked like he wanted to kiss the ground. I understood. I've been in that passenger seat, although only when I had no choice.

"Why did you invite Mombourquette, anyway, Alvin. What were you thinking? He gave me a lot of grief about this whole thing with the Shattered Families gang. Anyway, he's been such a pain in the—"

Of course, at the sound of Elaine's voice, I snapped my mouth shut.

Alvin put his hands on his tartan hips and said, "Think about it. Leonard is Ray's cousin, isn't he? So in that case, he's practically—"

"Only a second cousin, I believe."

"Whatever. Lord thundering Jesus, if you will let me finish a sentence for once, Camilla, he's related to Ashley and Brittany too."

"What does that make them? Fourth cousins twice removed? Hardly worth keeping on your Christmas card list."

"First, since when do you have a Christmas card list? And second, the relationship is closer than that. You'd better get used to it. If things keep on so lovey-dovey with you and Ray, Leonard Mombourquette could be your relative."

I don't know what got my back up more—lovey-dovey or the prospect of Mombourquette as some kind of kin. Anyway, I didn't know how lovey-dovey things would be once Ray realized that I'd almost gotten his daughters killed.

What a rat's nest this past week had turned into. Elaine rounded the corner and I was glad I had stopped my Mombourquette routine just in time.

"Hi Elaine. Isn't this something?"

Elaine loves a party and she was prepared. "You want traditional Cape Breton foods? Here's my contribution. Nanaimo bars. I bought them myself."

"Traditional Cape Breton foods? But Nanaimo bars aren't—"

"That's cool," Alvin said. "Every Canadian loves Nanaimo bars."

"And deviled eggs, from Leonard."

I suppose there were benefits. Deviled eggs are my drug of choice. When my sisters make them for me, it's always because they want something. Because of the deviled eggs, I often cave in. What the hell did Mombourquette want?

I took both containers from Elaine's hands. "Where's Leonard?"

Elaine stretched and yawned. "Out front. Checking his phone messages. He'll be in soon. I'm really looking forward to meeting these girls, Camilla. What are they like?"

"The girls? They seem kind of magnificent. Although I'm not sure what they're like, Elaine. I haven't gotten close to them." I was saved from that conversational foray by the arrival of Bunny, Tonya, Destiny and dolly. Coco Bentley followed them in. She had brought two bottles of Glen Breton single malt whisky.

She said, "I am so astonished that France Cardarelle has a new little dog, Lulu, of all things. Cute as anything. Were you surprised? Did you invite her here today? She seems quite taken with you and your dog."

I decided against filling Coco in on the details of the Shattered Families' plot while in the middle of our party. I knew most likely France Cardarelle wouldn't have little Lulu for long. It was just a matter of time now before she was arrested and charged with conspiracy and murder. Sad for Lulu. On the other hand, Coco could use some canine company and that would solve a problem. "You know something? I see a little dog in your future, Coco."

As Coco drifted off, I turned to Bunny and his family.

"Tonya," I said, holding up my hand to silence Bunny's latest round of abject apologies. "Bunny said you recognized one of the people in the photos. Who was it?"

"I didn't," Tonya said. "I'd never seen any of them before."

I took a deep breath and went with my latest brain wave. "By any chance, were you talking about the brochure of Jacki Jewell, the realtor that was with the offer to purchase the house? Had you seen her on posters? Something like that?"

"You can hardly miss her picture around town, but I saw her on our street, walking along, right in front of our house. She commented on our unit and even asked me to let her know if I wanted to list it."

"Really."

I slipped back into the house and took a chance on one more call.

"Just deny it if it's not true, Loreena. Was Jacki Jewell one of the members of Ottawa Bereavement Services who left and joined Shattered Families? Maybe after the initial group started?"

Her sharp intake of breath was all I needed. "You know I can't discuss anything to do with—"

I hustled out to the backyard to find Leonard Mombourquette and said, "Good work, Leonard, on getting those resources there in time to save the passengers on the *Leila Q*. I can almost forgive you for ignoring my desperate pleas for help."

Mombourquette said, "Elaine. She's starting. You said I could leave if she did."

"No, no, Leonard. I'm not starting. Just to show you there's no hard feelings, I'm going to give you a chance to make one last arrest. It's a surprise. Hope you've got your gun."

"What gun? You never quit, do you, MacPhee?"

"Not until it's over, I don't. Come with me. Alvin, call 911! Don't stare, just do it. Don't use your cell. Tell them it's an assault in progress and then hang up."

I scampered into the house, followed by Leonard, and waited for the surprise. Jacki Jewell didn't let me down. "Hello," she said. "I know you're in the middle of your party. Your assistant has been very excited planning it. Sorry to butt in, but I brought you some lemon squares. Everyone loves lemon squares. I did up a special large one just for you."

"I bet you did," I said. "Do you want to put them down for a minute?"

"Sure," she said, smiling.

Destiny galloped into the living room, pursuing Gussie, who seemed anxious to get away. She stopped and stared at the lemon squares.

I said, "Tell me, Jacki, did Roxanne ever suspect a thing?"

Jacki's crisp jaw dropped. "I don't know what you're talking about."

"I think you do."

Destiny's eyes stayed on the squares.

I said, "You'd had real estate dealings with her. You were in and out of the Terrio and Fox offices all the time. You would have found out a bit about her habits. Perhaps more than Kristen Wentzell did in their meeting. You could have learned when she was heading out to Gatineau park without exciting the least bit of suspicion. Then, of course, you'd make sure you had an alibi when Jamie Kilpatrick, another cyclist, knocked her off her bike. No one would ever guess Roxanne's connection with the driver who killed Jamie's grandparents. Oh yes, nicely played. Of course, it's just a matter of time until one of the others rolls over on you."

Destiny picked up the large square that was intended for me and licked her lips. Behind her, Gussie licked his lips too. Destiny opened her mouth wide enough to pop in the entire square. Jacki stared. Just in time, I twigged. I snatched the square from Destiny and handed it to Mombourquette. "Better get this analyzed, Leonard. Here's a woman who doesn't mind if a child dies so she can make her point. Do you, Jacki?"

Destiny set up a loud shriek, enough to bring Bunny and Tonya running.

Jacki whispered, "It was for you. I wouldn't have let the child die."

"Very sporting of you. You didn't mind if her father died, though, did you?"

"That's different. He was a thief. A vile thief. He robbed my mother's house. She never got over it, the sense of violation. She died well before her time. People like him do immeasureable harm." She glared at Bunny and curled her lip in contempt. "Some of the victims never recover from the damage." She turned her attention to me. "Do you know that? Do you even care? You certainly had no problem defending him. I remember how easily you made mincemeat out of that inexperienced prosecutor. You earned your living ensuring that criminals like this stayed out of jail. My mother was never the same after that burglary. Her life was shortened. He should have paid and you should have too. Instead he went on to have a wife and a child and lead a charmed life, and you just keep making trouble."

"When you made the deal with Annalisa to burn his house down, he and his child would almost certainly have died. Forget what piddling crimes you think Bunny and I might be guilty of, what kind of monster does that make you? You were willing to become a child killer to act out your revenge fantasies."

Tonya and Bunny stared with horror at the woman who had come so close to ending their lives. I tried not to be bothered by the fact that Jacki would certainly find a lawyer who would bring tears to the eyes of the jury by trotting out the sad case of her mother. And maybe he'd succeed with the crazy defence too.

"Jacki, this is Sergeant Leonard Mombourquette of Major Crimes. Did you know that the sergeant here was a good friend of Roxanne's? He's really looking forward to talking to you at the station."

As she bolted for the front door, the sight of a pair of uniformed officers stopped her. 911. You gotta love it. She turned back to me.

I said, "Don't try to escape through the backyard. There are people here who might take issue with you about your part in the sinking of the *Leila Q.*"

"I wasn't on the boat! Jamie and the others did most of that. My job was to take care of you in case you didn't actually accept the invitations."

"Which I didn't. That almost got my friend's children killed. Their father is a police officer. Don't think he'll be forgetting about that soon. Nor will anyone forget Steve Anstruther," I said. "You took care of him, didn't you? I'm betting that's why you had your vehicle vinyl-wrapped. To hide the damage without actually going to a body shop when the police were investigating Anstruther's so-called accident. It will be easy enough to check for scrapes and dents behind the vinyl. Of course, you planned that ahead of time in order to have your custom vinyl wrap with your photo and name made. Because you like to think of everything, although, in this case, that advance planning will make life a bit more difficult for your defence."

The look on Jacki's face told me these wild speculations hit the mark.

Mombourquette took over. "Sorry, Ms Jewell. I have a bit of bad news for you. It looks like Steve is going to recover. And there's an excellent chance he'll recognize you as the person who forced him off the road. Of course, we'll be able to compare paint from your vehicle to the traces found on his too."

Jacki slumped against the wall as Mombourquette stepped forward. "Even more bad news, lady. Now I get to take care of you. I guess this is your last house party."

He was in the middle of the arrest when I had a horrible thought, "I hope this doesn't wreck the house sale."

*   *   *

As the uniforms, Mombourquette, Jacki Jewell and the lemon squares zoomed off to Elgin Street, I pushed open the back door to return to the party and stopped to watch. Brittany and Ashley were alternately gobbling deviled eggs and regaling Mrs. Parnell with some tale of dragon boat racing, I guess, or maybe their dramatic Sunday afternoon boat ride. No wait. She was regaling them. One of those WW II fighter reenactments.

She paused in the telling to blow a few smoke rings. They add a certain drama to any retelling.

One of the girls threw back her head and laughed long and hard at something Mrs. Parnell said. They sure had amazing teeth. Ray must have spent a fortune at the orthodonist for the two of them. The other one laughed too, reinforcing the point.

Maybe they were turning out all right after all. But they weren't getting all the deviled eggs. Age has its privileges.

The fish chowder was a hit and we all fell on it like wolves. Even Gussie looked impressed at the frenzy. He and the cat got their own small bowls. By the time we were stuffing our faces with oat cakes and blueberry grunt and the surprisingly wonderful date tarts known as Cape Breton Pork Pies, Elaine had ingratiated herself with both the girls and their friends. They all got big giant clinches. When Elaine Ekstein hugs you, you know you've been hugged. P. J. was angling for a wide variety of hugs.

But by far the best part of the evening, better even than Jacki's arrest, was the surprise visitor.

Ashley or maybe Brittany shrieked, "Dad!" They both flung themselves at the grinning man at the door.

I spilled my Moosehead in surprise. I wanted to do a little flinging of myself too, but I wasn't sure how well I'd be received.

*　　*　　*

The food and the guests were gone, the sky was starting to lighten, and Ray and I were sitting alone in a quiet corner, surrounded by party debris, when I finally got to say, "I am so sorry. I almost got your girls killed."

"Lennie explained it to me. No way you could have known. And they didn't get killed. You pulled out all the stops, Camilla. Lennie told me that too. Even so, I guess there's only one thing I can do."

I bit my lip. I knew that Ray had put up with a lot from me. I was going to be lost without him.

He said, "I haven't wanted to talk to you about this until I had everything worked out. This long-distance relationship is really difficult."

I hated my desolate vision of lonely nights without Ray on the end of the phone line. I reached over, and picked up the last soothing Nanaimo bar and shoved it into my mouth in one gulp.

Eventually I was able to swallow and say, "Is it really necessary? I am sorry. I'll try to be more…" I wasn't sure more what.

"I can't change my mind now," he said. "I've put too much into it."

"Into breaking up with me?"

"What are you talking about? I'm not breaking up with you. I've arranged a job with the Ottawa Police Services."

I stared at him.

"Why do you have that look on your face? I know, you think the Ottawa guys are a bunch of bums, but it's a good force and the chief is from New Waterford. Excellent opportunity for me. I've been brushing up on my French with this intensive weekend course. I'm told my Acadian French might not cut it up here."

"I don't understand. You're going to leave Sydney?"

He shrugged. "My girls have left home already. It's too quiet and it's lonely. I miss them."

"I may even miss them a bit myself," I said. To my surprise, that wasn't as big a fib as it might have been.

"They're moving on with their lives. You're here in Ottawa, getting into a lot of trouble without me."

"It wasn't my fault. Things got complicated."

"Life with you is always complicated," Ray said. "Lucky for me, it's worth it. So now you'll just have to put up with me to add to your complications, Camilla. Like now, you have chocolate on your mouth. Let me fix that for you."

Acknowledgements

Every book starts out with major debts to the many people who supported the project, the author and the process. Camilla and I owe so much to Susan McCarthy, who is passionate about the Dragon Boat Festival and who, along with Chris Raines, was generous with time and information. As usual, Janet MacEachen came through to keep Camilla in line. I am grateful to Mary MacKay-Smith, Victoria Maffini, John Merchant and Linda Wiken for insights on the manuscript, and most especially to Lyn Hamilton, who took the time to read and comment on *Law & Disorder* despite her grave illness. Many thanks to Ronnie Keough, Rick Mofina, Stephan Dirnberger, Cody Crosby of Spytech and Lieutenant Brad Grant of Ottawa Fire Services for essential information. If there are any errors, they are mine, of course.

As for the real Beverly Leclair, thank you and your family for supporting REACH, a great cause. Speaking of great causes, the SPCA of Western Quebec's inspired description of their adoptable dogs warms the heart and opens doors.

You may recognize much of Ottawa. But don't tear your hair out looking for previously unknown streets, charitable organizations, restaurants, boat companies, offices or businesses. Sometimes a story requires a little flexibility. It's one of the joys of fiction. And of course, familiar readers will know that Camilla will always make a left turn wherever it suits her, signs notwithstanding.

To the RendezVous Crime gang, Sylvia, Allister and Emma, I appreciate everything you do to make my books come alive. And on the home front, thanks to my husband, Giulio, for ongoing patience and support, and to Daisy and Lily for extra cuddles.

Before she fell into a life of crime, Nova Scotia-born Mary Jane Maffini was a librarian, a public servant and a mystery bookstore owner. *Law & Disorder* is the latest of six books featuring cranky Camilla MacPhee. West Quebec is the setting for the comic Fiona Silk mysteries. The third series features Charlotte Adams, a professional organizer and amateur sleuth in upstate New York.

Mary Jane has been a two-term president of the Crime Writers of Canada, a charter member of the Ladies' Killing Circle, and has served on the board of directors of the Canadian Booksellers Association. She has won two Arthur Ellis awards for Best Short Story. She is a frequent speaker on the writing process, mysteries and Canadian crime writing. Mary Jane lives and plots in Ottawa, along with her long-suffering husband and two princessy dachshunds.

Find out more at www.maryjanemaffini.com

BOOKS BY MARY JANE MAFFINI
The Camilla MacPhee series
*Speak Ill of the Dead, The Icing on the Corpse, Little Boy Blues,
The Devil's in the Details, The Dead Don't Get Out Much, Law & Disorder*

The Fiona Silk series
Lament for a Lounge Lizard, Too Hot to Handle

The Charlotte Adams series
*Organize Your Corpses, The Cluttered Corpse,
Death Loves a Messy Desk*